THE
LAST DRAGON
CHARMER
BOOK 3

REALM BREAKER

ALSO BY LAURIE McKAY:

The Last Dragon Charmer Series
Villain Keeper
Quest Maker

THE
LAST DRAGON
CHARMER
BOOK 3

REALM BREAKER

LAURIE McKAY

HARPER

An Imprint of HarperCollinsPublishers

Library of Congress Control Number: 2016958066
ISBN 978-0-06-230849-8 (trade bdg.)

Typography by Robert Steimle
17 18 19 20 21 CG/LSCH 10 9 8 7 6 5 4 3 2 1
❖

First Edition

To Angie, Valerie, and Leslie,
who bring books to kids of all ages

Contents

THE SUMMER SCRIBE

T he locals called it the summer of red lightning.

Caden, however, knew better. Like all things involving magic and the Greater Realm, the locals had it wrong. It wasn't strangely colored lightning that split the sky. It was banishment spells.

The Greater Realm Council was exiling villains to Asheville, North Carolina. Twelve this summer by Caden's lightning count, and the most recent had been the night before.

The council believed the banished went to the Land of Shadow, a place of punishment, torture, and death. But the council also had it wrong. Asheville was a quaint mountain town full of art and music. The citizens called it the Land of the Sky and proclaimed the city the happiest in the South.

Caden wasn't a local, but he hadn't been banished. He

was an eighth-born Razzonian prince from the Greater Realm's Winterlands, a future Elite Paladin, and a protector of the kingdom. Yet seven months ago, bad magic transported Caden, his noble stallion, Sir Horace, and Brynne, a powerful young sorceress, to Asheville. They'd been stranded in the happy, villain-filled realm since.

To make matters worse, Caden and Brynne had been sentenced to foster care and forced to endure middle school. And the school was where the Greater Realm's banished villains fulfilled their sentences. While the villains' punishment was to teach, Caden's misfortune was to be their student. Even in summer.

It was midday on Thursday in the Ashevillian month of August—the last day of summer session—and Caden marched down the long hall in Primrose Charter School. He'd been summoned to the principal's office. Again.

The classrooms were quiet. Most were dark, too. Caden was one of the few students in attendance. Brynne and his foster siblings, Jane and Tito, didn't have to attend. While Caden's mastery of spoken English was undeniable, his skills didn't extend to the written word, and Rath Dunn—acting school principal, math teacher, and banished Greater Realm villain—had used that to trap him.

There were workers in the hall, men and women in mud-colored jumpsuits, painting the walls bloodred. The week prior, they'd replaced the school's dented pink lockers with sleek gray ones. The once-scuffed tiles shone with fresh wax. If Caden squinted, he could see his princely reflection in the floor.

The changes proved that Rath Dunn had truly usurped control of the school from Ms. Primrose, a powerful being who'd collected the banished, forced them to teach, and who had been principal. The scent of roses, her essence, still lingered. No paint or wax smell could rid the halls of the flowery smell.

At the hall's end, Mr. Creedly, assistant to the principal, sat at a large desk like a smarmy guard. His hair was slicked back, his arms folded across his chest. As Caden approached, Mr. Creedly narrowed his eyes. He uncurled and pointed a too-long finger at the door. "He," Mr. Creedly spat, "wants you to wait."

Not only did Rath Dunn force Caden to take summer classes, summon him daily, and threaten all good people, he now expected Caden to wait? Royalty didn't wait in the hall.

Caden pushed past Mr. Creedly. He placed his palm on the door but hesitated. Truth be told, he didn't want to go into the principal's office. Rath Dunn meant to test him. Not with a math quiz like he'd done in the school year proper. Instead, he meant to determine when and how Caden was cursed.

At the end of last term, Rath Dunn became suspicious when he'd ordered Caden to chop off Brynne's long, beautiful hair and Caden had done so. No future Elite Paladin would be so cruel unless forced. Caden had been compelled to do it. He'd had no choice.

And it was all Brynne's fault.

While her magic was strong, her control wasn't. She'd *accidentally* hexed Caden with compliance for three days each month. During that time he had to do whatever anyone told him to do. While Caden had granted her his royal forgiveness, and she'd forgiven him for slicing off her hair, she hadn't reversed his curse yet.

As he looked at the door, though, his annoyance trickled away. His stomach churned and he tasted bile, bitter and bad on his tongue. What if Rath Dunn figured everything out? He might order Caden to lie, steal, or hurt someone. Without doubt, whatever he commanded would be crueler than cutting Brynne's hair.

Today, however, that wasn't a problem. The curse wasn't active. Today Caden was in control. He centered himself and prepared for the encounter. Each day that Rath Dunn foolishly summoned Caden to his office, there was a chance Caden would learn more about his plot.

For Rath Dunn's treachery extended beyond usurping power at the school. The tyrant schemed to break the barrier between Asheville and the Greater Realm by casting a powerful ritual spell that would be fueled by the destruction of the city. Once the barrier was gone, he could seek revenge on those who banished him.

Already, the tyrant had collected the rare ingredients needed for the spell: tears of an elf, magical locks, blood of the son, and essence of dragon. The magical locks had been Brynne's hair. The very hair Caden had cut and given to Rath Dunn while cursed.

Such complicated ritual magic required proper timing and preparation. As each sunny, sweltering day passed, Caden feared Rath Dunn got closer to his goal. And there were also the recent banishment spells. Those could only mean trouble in the Greater Realm. What was going on in Caden's homeland and how was it connected to Rath Dunn's plot?

Despite the season, Caden wore his enchanted coat. It was a symbol of his people and his family, a gift handed down to him by his father. The imperial Winterbird was embroidered on the back in gold and silver threads. It gave him comfort always; it reminded him to be brave. He held his chin high as he strode through the doorway.

The office looked different from when it had been Ms. Primrose's. Before Rath Dunn took over, the walls were silvery blue. Now they were red. The shelves, once filled with bowls of shiny rocks, beads, and cheap collectibles, were stacked with books—some in neat lines, others in piles. The ones with visible covers showed pictures of delicious-looking foods. There was a large window near the back of the room. A mirror on the wall across from it reflected the sunlight.

There were five people inside.

The first was Rath Dunn. He stood behind the desk. His bald scalp shone in the window's light. One of his eyes was brown, the other blue. A scar split his face from his blue eye to his mouth. He wore a red linen shirt and red slacks that made his torso blend weirdly into the wall. Truth be told, he looked like one of the feared floating heads of the Springlands Mist Swamps.

Despite their reputation, Caden found the floating heads to be friendly and quite polite. Rath Dunn was to be feared much more than the floating heads. His current wolfish smirk meant nothing good for Caden.

The second was Ms. Primrose, once principal, current vice principal and placement counselor. She wore a flowery dress. Her blue-and-silvery hair was pulled into a tight bun; her mouth was set in a scowl. She looked like an old school marm and the scent of roses was strong. Her smell and appearance were misleading, though.

She was one of the eight legendary Elderkind of the Greater Realm, and one of four Elderdragons. Caden suspected she was either the more kindly Silver Elderdragon or the more vicious Blue. He'd seen scales of both shades on her arm: the silver when happy and sated, the blue when angry and not. Caden had yet to find out how she came to be in Asheville and collect trinkets, villains, and students; and currently he was in no position to ask her.

The other three people stood together, two restraining the third. Mr. Faunt, the sixth-grade math teacher who had fingertips like razors, stood on the left side of the detained man. Stout and strong Mrs. Grady, the evil eighth-grade math teacher, stood on the right.

The man between them was soot covered, but his eyes were bright. A long gray braid fell over his shoulder. The end was scorched and black. No doubt it was he who had arrived on the lightning the night before. Was he being detained because he was so dangerous? He didn't look it, but looks could deceive.

Rath Dunn slammed a book to his desktop. Caden and the others snapped their attention to him. With a flamboyant bow, he stalked around the desk, pausing at the mirror to check his tie. "Well, if you didn't wait outside, I assume you're *not* following orders today?"

And there it was. The reason he'd summoned Caden. To test Caden's compliance.

This Thursday the moon wasn't half-full. Caden's will was his own. Rath Dunn, however, didn't know that. Caden's plan was to confuse him. He kept his shoulders square and breathing even. He needed his wits to be as sharp as a griffin's tooth.

"I wasn't ordered to wait," Caden said. "It was suggested. And I declined."

"Did you now?" Rath Dunn said. "It's just as well. The fun can start sooner, can't it?" He motioned to the soot-covered man. With clear amusement, he said, "I think he recognizes me."

When Caden turned, the soot-covered man's eyes

widened. "Your Highness?" he said in the Greater Realm's Common Tongue.

Rath Dunn chuckled. "It seems he recognizes you as well. I suspected as much." As if that was a cue, Mr. Faunt and Mrs. Grady laughed, too. Caden, however, found nothing amusing about the trio of sinister, snickering math teachers. Nor did Ms. Primrose, it seemed. She checked her watch with an impatient huff.

The soot-covered man stared at Caden. "Your Highness," the man said. "You're alive."

Although scratchy and frightened, that voice was familiar. Suddenly, Caden felt he knew him, too. If he imagined the man without the soot, his pointed nose and crooked eyebrows were familiar. An image of the Northern Tower popped into Caden's mind, of the spiraling stacks in the Winter Castle library, of the scribes hurrying about. This man was one of them. Caden had spoken to him before. After all, Caden spoke to everyone.

"Scribe Trevor?" Caden said.

Scribe Trevor kept the library quiet; he was strict with the lower scribes. He'd even told Caden that Sir Horace *shouldn't* be allowed in the stacks. Setting that aside, he didn't seem the type to be banished, the type to turn traitor.

Then again, Caden's faith in people had failed him before. Rath Dunn's accomplice in the other realm was none other than Caden's second-born brother, Maden. Caden still found that hard to believe even though Caden had learned firsthand that Maden was a traitor.

As it was doubtful Scribe Trevor understood any English, Caden kept to the Common Tongue. "How did you come to be here?"

Scribe Trevor started to answer, but Rath Dunn interrupted. "You're not here to ask questions," Rath Dunn said. "You're here to listen."

"I don't listen to tyrants," Caden said.

"Tyrant?" He raised his brows and motioned to himself. "*Moi?*"

Caden could speak French; he'd heard French spoken by a tourist. "*Oui. Vous.*"

Rath Dunn chuckled. "It's a cute trick," he said. "The language thing. Won't save you, though. Won't save anyone."

Despite the sweltering heat outside, the room became cold. Ms. Primrose let out a sharp sigh. She glanced at her watch again. "Can we get to it," she said, though she spoke in English. "I have other business today, Mr. Rathis. Snap. Snap."

Mr. Faunt and Mrs. Grady held Scribe Trevor in place. The scribe's gaze darted from Caden to Rath Dunn and back again. "Your Highness," he said in the Common Tongue. His voice shook slightly. "You must leave."

It seemed that Scribe Trevor was more concerned for Caden's welfare than his own. Whether he was guilty or not, his concern seemed genuine. However, Caden doubted

Rath Dunn would let either of them leave yet.

"*We* must leave," Caden said.

"Leave? I don't think so. Where's the fun in that?" Rath Dunn said. "I know. Why don't you dance for us today?"

That was a question. Not an order. That was Rath Dunn's routine. First he asked. Next he would order. Caden raised a brow. "I must decline." He stepped toward Scribe Trevor and the math teachers who held him. "My countryman and I have much to discuss."

"I haven't excused you yet, boy. I am not finished with him either." Rath Dunn leaned closer. "Now, dance for me, prince."

That was an order. The first one was always something meant to embarrass Caden. Like dancing. Or singing. Caden hesitated. He needed to get Scribe Trevor out of the office as soon as possible. There were math teachers and an impatient Elderdragon in the room. Still. If misdirection was Caden's goal, it was best he complied.

Caden caught Scribe Trevor's gaze. "We'll go soon," he said. He tried to sound confident and reassuring, but his stomach twisted. He raised his chin. "First, I'll dance."

In the Greater Realm, most dances were done with partners. Trevor didn't seem like the dancing type, and Caden wasn't asking Rath Dunn or either of his math minions to be his partner. He forced his most charming smile and offered his hand to Ms. Primrose.

She looked down at it with obvious displeasure. "I don't dance," she said. Then she waggled her finger at him.

"Don't think I've forgiven you." She narrowed her eyes toward Rath Dunn. "Either of you."

She was mad at Rath Dunn for stealing her school and Caden for not stopping him. It wasn't Caden's fault. If she was to blame someone other than Rath Dunn, she should blame herself. But Caden had found her anger only increased when he pointed that out, and it seemed Caden would dance alone.

His great father, King Axel, once said, "The only one who can take away your dignity is yourself." As such, and with great dignity, Caden moved: left foot, right foot, right foot, left hand up, right hand down. Twist. Both hands up. Twist. Swirl.

Caden's father also once said, "Never shame the king or kingdom." Well, if Caden danced with confidence, that wouldn't apply. He pivoted. Left foot. Right foot. Twist. Hands down.

"Stop," Rath Dunn said.

At the end of a dance, it was customary to bow. Caden slid to a stop and did so.

Ms. Primrose wore the expression of one who'd witnessed a slime slug birth. "Oh my," she said. "I'm embarrassed for you, dear."

Caden cut his gaze to Scribe Trevor. It seemed from Scribe Trevor's tight frown and wide eyes that Caden's fancy footwork only frightened him further. Best they get out of this dragon-and-despot-occupied office soon. If Rath Dunn's pattern continued, he would order Caden to do something more troublesome next.

As such, Caden wasn't surprised when Rath Dunn motioned to Scribe Trevor. Whatever Rath Dunn ordered, however, Caden wouldn't have to follow it. Not today. Caden felt his brow furrow. He held Rath Dunn's gaze.

"Now we decide," Rath Dunn said, and leaned against the front of the desk, "whether *Scribe Trevor*, banished traitor of Razzon, teaches with us . . . or doesn't."

Scribe Trevor glanced at the door. No doubt he thought of running. But he was locked in place by Mr. Faunt and Mrs. Grady and glanced at Caden as if he wouldn't leave without him. Like the Elite Paladins, like his brothers and guards, those in the castle often protected Caden.

"I'll let you choose, prince," Rath Dunn said. "Shall he teach, or shall he not teach?"

First a question. He answered with certainty. "He should teach." Ms. Primrose devoured the banished who weren't made teachers. Caden turned to Scribe Trevor. "Jasan is also here." Jasan was Caden's seventh-born brother. "He was wrongly banished; he is innocent and teaches the gym class here." The next thing Caden said, he wasn't sure of. But he went with his instinct. "Like you, his sentence was a mistake."

Scribe Trevor's lip trembled. "Thank you, Prince Caden," he said, though Caden hadn't actually done anything for which to be thanked.

"Touching," Rath Dunn said, and leaned forward.

Ms. Primrose complained about the time, about the need to polish a bead. Caden couldn't stop the glare he sent her way. "Don't give me that kind of look," she said. "I've things to do, you know. This," she said with a flap of her hand, "is mostly your fault."

That was completely unfair. But Caden couldn't argue with a dragon while a tyrant tested him and threatened a castle scribe. Caden turned his attention to said tyrant. It was also a prince's duty to protect his people. "Let him teach," he said.

"Now, now," Rath Dunn said. "Don't be so hasty." That was an order. "Think about your choice." As was that. "Choose that he *not* teach. That he die. Choose it now." Those were orders, too, and he growled them low, like a threat.

Caden, however, wasn't bound by orders yet. He squared his shoulders. "No," he said.

Rath Dunn leaned back. He raised his brows. "No?"

And since both Caden and Rath Dunn knew this was a test, Caden said, "That order, I don't have to follow." He nodded to Scribe Trevor. "I won't harm a noble Razzonian library scribe. You can't order me to harm others." At least, not until the half-moon filled the Ashevillian sky. Caden kept the last part to himself.

Rath Dunn's surprise wore off quickly. "It's something *I* can do, though," he said, and his voice came out low and mean. "Harm others."

With as much calm and respect as he could muster, he looked to Ms. Primrose. "Let Scribe Trevor teach." Although she was mad, it seemed smart to remain polite until he found words to regain her better graces. "That is my choice, ma'am."

"Dear," Ms. Primrose said in a tone that suggested he was slow and pitiable, "that's for the principal to decide. Not me." She shook her head and added pointedly, "Not you."

Rath Dunn looked almost giddy. He gestured to Scribe Trevor. "We already have enough Razzonian pests under contract."

Caden felt his eyes widen. If Scribe Trevor wasn't put under contract, Ms. Primrose would devour him. "Wait!"

Rath Dunn was the only one who could save him.

"Wait!" Caden said. He needed to think of something quickly. "I'll trade you information if—"

"I don't need any information from you."

What could tempt Rath Dunn? What could Caden tell him that he didn't know? "I'll tell you about my curse."

That gave Rath Dunn pause. He peered at Caden. And for a moment, he did look tempted. "That would rob me of the joy of discovery." He motioned to Scribe Trevor and spoke to Ms. Primrose. "For you."

She wouldn't really eat Scribe Trevor, would she?

Ms. Primrose tugged on the waist of her dress and sniffed irritably. "When I ran the school," she said, "I was careful not to overindulge." She turned to Rath Dunn with a cold glare. "If I eat too much, I lose my compassion."

That seemed to excite Rath Dunn. "But you still follow our contract?"

Ms. Primrose had contracts with all the banished villains. If they didn't follow her rules, if they failed to follow the laws of the land or failed to teach their classes, she terminated them. Literally. Rath Dunn had used the contract to his advantage, to gain control, and now he ran the school.

His question about whether she followed her contract sounded more like a statement, like something he already knew but was triple-checking. "If I didn't follow it," Ms. Primrose said, "I'd have eaten you last spring. And I'd have taken time to savor my meal."

Then she set her gaze on Trevor. The room grew cold. Her eyes took on a reptilian sheen. Her pupils became pinpricks, then elongated into slits. Her nails became sharp and long. Caden felt like he was in the presence of something massive.

Oh no.

Mr. Faunt and Mrs. Grady let go of Scribe Trevor and scurried to the back of the room. Scribe Trevor lunged for Caden. He turned his head from front to side to back, from Rath Dunn to Ms. Primrose to the evil math minions by the shelves, as he tried to focus on the danger. He put his arm around Caden's shoulders. It felt strange and awkward and protective. "Your Highness, you need to get away from here."

That wasn't accurate. "*We* need to get away." Caden pulled him toward the door. "We'll get away together, then home together. Run!" Scribe Trevor didn't budge. "That's a royal decree."

Scribe Trevor's eyes were bright. He strained to move, but he seemed to be glued to the tiled floor. "I can't move. You run, Your Highness!"

"I'm not the one about to be eaten!"

That seemed to panic Scribe Trevor. He thrashed, but his feet remained in place. Caden felt dragon's breath on his neck. He sensed sharp teeth.

"There's nothing you can do, prince," Rath Dunn said. "He teaches or he becomes dragon chow. That's how it works." He laughed loud and hearty. "It's hilarious."

"No, it's not," Caden snapped. He pulled with all his strength. "We have to go. We'll stop the villains. Together. You, me, Jasan, Brynne . . ."

Whap. Caden flew back. He hit the oak door with a loud *thunk.* Mrs. Grady and Mr. Faunt stood against the bookshelves. In the middle of the room, Scribe Trevor looked toward the ceiling. His mouth was agape. His face pale. A jaw with sharp teeth and a blue tongue hovered above him.

Caden scurried to his feet. "Trevor!"

Trevor snapped his gaze to Caden. "Something's amiss in Razzon," he screamed. "I found runes, near the river, for ritual contact on Archer's day. They blamed me, but it wasn't—"

Freezing wind rushed against Caden. He put his hand to his face to protect it. There was a sound like a jaw snapping shut. Caden felt his breath leave him. That sound didn't mean anything. It didn't mean anything.

Caden lowered his hand. He started to run to Scribe Trevor, to try to move him, or save him, or something. But all that was in front of Caden was a pair of boots. Maybe Scribe Trevor had been pushed out of them.

Caden looked behind him, to the right, to the left. Ms. Primrose still stood beside the desk, licking her lips. Rath Dunn still leaned on it. Mr. Faunt and Mrs. Grady huddled near the shelves. Scribe Trevor was nowhere.

"Where is he?" Caden said, and his voice cracked.

Rath Dunn wore a wide smile. His eyes creased at the sides. "Even you, son of Axel, can't be that slow." He pushed off the desk and kicked at one of the boots. It fell over heavily. Rath Dunn looked up at Ms. Primrose. "You left some."

"I don't eat feet," she said. "How crass do you think I am?"

Rath Dunn crinkled up his nose. "I guess I'll have to have Creedly clean this up."

Caden looked at the boots, then at Rath Dunn, then at Ms. Primrose. She brought a small handkerchief out from her sleeve and dabbed the side of her mouth.

"What did you do?" Caden said.

"I gobbled him up, dear."

What? Caden stared at her.

"Close your mouth. You'll catch flies."

"How could you do that?"

She looked insulted. "It's in my nature, dear. Those banished who don't serve the school and those who stop serving the school, I eat. You know the rules. You know what I am." She pulled at her dress. The fabric looked snug. "Normally, I would take time to savor my food, but I made it quick. That's a favor I didn't owe you or your scribe."

Rath Dunn's eyes were wide, his smile gleeful. Truly, he seemed to enjoy carnage. "My marvelous Ms. Primrose, I hope you enjoyed your meal."

Caden looked to where Scribe Trevor had stood. How could this have happened? He stepped back. He didn't want to be in the office anymore. He didn't want to try to charm dragons and outwit despots. He wanted his father to show up and fix this. His hands felt cold, his legs weak.

Twelve people had been banished this summer. Scribe Trevor was the most recent. He'd been devoured. Who were the other eleven? Had they been eaten, too? Was that why Ms. Primrose looked chubby—Rath Dunn was feeding her the banished? Did he *want* her to lose her compassion? Perhaps she was easier to control without it.

Ms. Primrose released a dainty burp. "Oh my," she said. "Excuse me."

But there was no excuse. Innocent lives should mean

more than her rules; justice should mean more than any contract. Caden felt his heart pound. He needed to get away. He could stand it no longer. He turned, threw open the door, and ran.

"Get back to class, boy!" Rath Dunn yelled after him.

2

OF HORSES AND DRAGONS

Caden didn't go back to class. He bolted down the long hall. The red paint made it seem narrower, more suffocating. Ms. Primrose had eaten Trevor. In one bite like he was a Winterlands juiceberry.

And Rath Dunn had been amused.

All his life, Caden had wanted to slay a dragon. But it wasn't until this very moment that he understood how dangerous dragons were.

Caden sped up, turned right, and charged toward the school's exit. When he flung open the door, the humid heat of the Ashevillian summer washed over him. He hesitated there, between the cold, red-painted school halls and the dizzying lush green of the outdoors.

If he left, he'd be truant, guilty of skipping school. Ms. Primrose once threatened to eat Caden for that. The warning felt more real now than it had before. But it shouldn't. In exchange for Caden finding out who had caused accidents at the school last spring, she'd agreed not to eat Caden, his classmates, or his brother Jasan. If only Caden had thought to extend that pact to his people, to scribes like Trevor.

Ms. Primrose couldn't eat Caden, so what could she do? Give him detention? Future Elite Paladins like Caden weren't thwarted by detention and, for all Caden cared, the school dragon and math despot-turned-principal could burn in the eternal flames of the Autumnlands Firefields. Caden wasn't staying in school; he wasn't following their rules. He dashed into the sun. He needed his horse and the wind and a fast ride up a steep slope.

Sir Horace resided at the horse prison—the locals called it a "rescue"—during the day. Most nights he escaped from his stable. There were reports of him on the news sometimes. Townspeople would send in pictures of Sir Horace stealing apples from an orchard or running playfully with mares from a neighboring farm. No doubt foals would soon be born all around Asheville that possessed Sir Horace's majesty despite the plain-brown hair of the regional horses.

Caden made his way to the rescue and crouched near the edge of the trees. His brow itched with sweat, a feeling he was still not used to. The Winterlands Mountains were never hot; they were never green. They were cold and icy and *tall* like mountains should be.

Sir Horace was larger than the other horses. His mane shone white in the summer sun. His hair, the color of dim-lit frost, was as magnificent now as it was in the winter. He stood in a shady spot near the stables, his noble tongue hanging from the side of his mouth, drool plopping like ice beetle dung onto the grass beneath him.

Sir Horace was Caden's battle partner and friend. He came when needed. When Caden whistled, Sir Horace immediately perked up his ears. Then he let loose a mighty whinny, cantered for the fence, and soared over it.

Caden stood from his hiding spot as Sir Horace approached. He grabbed Sir Horace's mane and pulled himself onto his steed's back. Then he and Sir Horace flew through the forest. Not even the hot summer haze could slow them down.

Later, when the sun was low and the intense afternoon heat had shifted to the steaminess of evening, Caden sat on a moss-covered log while Sir Horace drank from a stream.

In his pocket, Caden's phone buzzed. He ignored it and rested his chin on his hands. The forest was green all around him; insects chirped and water trickled. His racing thoughts slowed and unmuddled as evening eased over the mountains.

Caden realized his upper right arm ached, and he slid off his coat to see why. Enchanted with warmth and pro-tection, his coat wasn't magicked to keep him cool. His

Ashevillian short-sleeved T-shirt—the blue one with printed snowflakes—was wet from his sweat, the right sleeve brown and sticky with blood from the reopened slash on his arm.

The wound had been made months ago by the blood dagger, an evil and enchanted blade brandished by Rath Dunn. Any wound the weapon made would reopen in its presence and never truly heal. Caden's bloody sleeve meant Rath Dunn had his blade in the office today.

Caden stared at his arm, surprised. He'd been so pre-occupied by all the curse testing and scribe eating that he hadn't noticed. Or had the wound become such a normal part of him, he didn't register it anymore?

He held his coat in his hands and traced the only imperfection in the wool: the rip the blood dagger had made when it first cut him. The events of the afternoon ran through his mind once more. Rath Dunn had ordered Ms. Primrose to eat Scribe Trevor and she'd done it. "She is a dragon, Sir Horace," Caden said.

Sir Horace turned back, water dripping from his nose, and snorted.

"Yes, I knew she was a dragon already, but I don't think I understood what that meant until now."

Of course, Ms. Primrose wasn't any dragon. Normal dragons were side effects of bad magic. They spawned from the hate and envy connected to it. Those were the kind of dragons common in the Greater Realm, the kind Caden had been sent to slay. Ms. Primrose was different, unique.

She wasn't a proper old lady who sometimes turned into a dragon. She was the reverse—a powerful Elderdragon that often choose to look human, one with no remorse for eating someone. He knew that, and he'd still misunderstood

"She is a dragon," Caden said again, and clenched his fists. "And Elite Paladins slay dragons." Why had he wanted to charm her? Why had he felt sorry for her when she lost her school? No more. "If she and I are to be enemies, so be it."

Sir Horace didn't answer. Instead, he turned to dunk his muzzle back into the creek. He drank while his tail swayed back and forth. Ashevillian fireflies flickered in shadows between trees.

Caden's phone buzzed again. Truth be told, a future Elite Paladin could only ignore communication for so long. He pulled the device from his pocket: *Eighteen missed calls. Twenty-eight missed messages.*

Suddenly, thoughts of dragons vanished as a new worry flitted across Caden's mind.

He'd left school early. He hadn't told Rosa he wouldn't be there when she came to pick him up. He hadn't called her or anyone to tell them he'd needed time alone. It was highly possible Caden was in trouble with his foster mother. Matter of point, Caden was often in trouble with Rosa. Was that what it was like to have a mother?

Caden had never known his mother, the second queen.

No one spoke of her, not the king, not the servants, not the guards. The only sign the second queen had ever even existed was that Caden himself existed.

It wasn't like that with the first queen, with his brothers' mother. Her cleverness, beauty, and kindness were celebrated. The Southern Tower stood like a monument to her. All Caden's brothers—even treacherous Maden and surly Jasan—spoke of her with love, with reverence.

Caden stared at the missed calls from Rosa. He'd been gone only an afternoon, and Rosa had called him so many times? If she thought Caden was dead like those in his homeland did, she'd mourn. She might even cry.

Was the second queen somewhere in the Greater Realm mourning his death? As far as Caden knew, she'd never tried to contact him. Not once in thirteen turns. Maybe she pretended Caden never existed just as Caden's father, brothers, and kingdom did her? But why? As he frowned at the phone, it buzzed with another call. From Brynne. This time he answered.

"Caden?" Brynne said in a hushed voice.

This was his phone; obviously it was him. He shook away thoughts of mothers and poor dead scribes as best he could, but his voice sounded strained when he spoke. "What is it, sorceress?"

He heard her let out an annoyed huff. "What do you mean 'what is it'? Where are you? Are you okay?" She paused and lowered her voice. "Hold on a minute."

There was noise and sounds of movement. Then Caden heard Rosa speak to Brynne. "You've no idea where he might be?" she said. "Brynne, if you know, you need to tell me."

"I really don't," Brynne said. And she didn't. Caden hadn't had a chance to tell her. Yet to Caden's ears, even muffled over the phone, Brynne sounded guilty. If Caden were Rosa, he wouldn't believe her.

"If you know anything, young lady," Rosa said, and her tone sounded like forced calm and underlying worry, "you need to tell me."

Then came the chime of a doorbell. More movement. A moment passed before Brynne spoke again. "You need to come back, prince. Everyone is worried. Rosa went to pick you up, and you weren't there."

"You were worried?"

"A little," she said. "And Rosa and Officer Levine are very worried." Officer Levine was the policeman who had found Caden and Brynne when they'd first been transported to Asheville and had brought them to Rosa. Brynne continued. "Prince Jasan was here earlier, and he was furious."

Caden wasn't sure what to think about his brother going to Rosa's house. "Jasan was there?"

"He argued with Rosa."

Now Caden was just confused. "He doesn't speak the local language well enough for that."

When Brynne next spoke, she seemed giddy. "He let me spell him to speak it."

Elite Paladins, especially ones as noble and brave as Jasan, didn't rely on magic. That's why Caden worked to learn to read and write the local language. He wouldn't rely on tricks. Hard work was the only solution. Caden felt a brush of annoyance. "Jasan wouldn't allow you to spell him."

"Well, he did." Brynne sounded offended. "He's not stubborn like you." She started speaking more quickly. "I hear Rosa coming. Hurry back," she whispered. "And best you use that gift of yours to explain why you left or you will be forever grounded, prince."

Then she hung up and Caden sat in twilight's quiet on his mossy log.

His gift of speech? While it gave him the ability to speak any language he heard, it supposedly had a deeper aspect. It also gave him the ability to charm people, to convince them to do what he wished. Had that part of his gift ever worked, though? People sometimes did what Caden asked; but people sometimes did what Brynne and Tito and vile Rath Dunn asked as well, and none of them was gifted with speech.

As such, he wasn't sure what he could say to calm Rosa.

Sir Horace trotted over and nuzzled Caden with his wet nose.

"It seems like I'm in great trouble, Sir Horace," Caden

said, but truly he felt too tired to care. His arm ached; his heart ached. His stomach turned like it was full of nothing but bile, and his foster mother, the only mother he had, once more would be disappointed in him. He patted Sir Horace, then stood and swung up onto his back. "I suppose you will be in trouble with your stable as well."

Sir Horace lifted his magnificent head. His nostrils flared, and his ears turned as he listened to birds chirping. Like the proud Galvanian snow stallion he was, Sir Horace showed no remorse.

"Let us ride before night falls," Caden said.

Near to Rosa's house, they parted ways. Caden praised Sir Horace for being his impressive horse self, then ordered him to return to the rescue. They would both have to face the consequences of their actions. After Sir Horace's hoofbeats faded, Caden snuck through the trees and to the edge of Rosa's yard.

Rosa's house was careworn and three stories high. She was a metal artist. Her larger works—flowers with sharp, copper petals; a bench formed from iron chains—were scattered among the yard's swaying green grasses. Her latest work, a horse made from twisted aluminum, steel pipes, and other found objects, stood tall and proud near the drive. The metals glinted in the last rays of the sun and made a *clink, clink* sound as the wind blew.

Officer Levine stood on the porch. His car sat in the driveway and he wore his uniform. His bushy hair looked damp in the humidity. Rosa stood beside him. Her hair was pulled back and frizzed. Despite her bright-green pants and vibrant purple top, she seemed somber, serious, and tense.

Brynne was right. Both Rosa and Officer Levine seemed weary. Caden had caused them to worry. No doubt he was in the greatest of foster mother trouble. He squared his shoulders and stepped into the yard near the bench.

3
PUNISHMENT SPRINGS

osa saw him in an instant. Suddenly, all the heaviness in her expression, in her stance seemed to fall away, and she rushed to him. "Where have you been?" she said, but she sounded relieved. Before he could answer, she grabbed him into a tight hug.

Officer Levine peered at him, seeming thoughtful. He reached out and squeezed Caden's shoulder. "I'll give his brother a call and let him know he's back," he said.

"Go ahead," Rosa said. There was an edge to her voice. Caden was too drained to think much on it. Then she leaned back; her eyes were wide with suspicion. "Where have you been, Caden?"

That was actually easy to answer. "In the woods."

Her muscles tensed; her brow tightened. "In the woods?"

It was a question, but it sounded like a trap. Truly, Caden should probably keep silent at this point. "I needed time to think," he said. "With Sir Horace."

She peered at him as if she could see into his mind. Were all mothers like that, or did Rosa have mind powers? "Hiding in the woods with your horse and telling no one is not acceptable behavior in this house. Do you understand?"

"Not really."

Rosa's brow twitched. Her mouth turned to a tight line. "Let's get out of this heat. We're going to talk about why you did this, why you won't do it again, and then we're going to talk about your punishment."

Caden raised his chin. He was far from his home. His people were in danger, and he'd been unable to save his scribe. "What can you take from me that hasn't already been lost?"

Rosa didn't hesitate. "Your phone," she said. "Your computer privileges. You can stay inside and study while the others go downtown to play."

"We don't play downtown. We scout for information."

"For the next two weeks, you're confined to your room."

As an eighth-born prince, Caden only had to follow commands from his father. Well, during his curse time he had to follow orders from everyone, but only then. Not now. Caden pulled away. "I can escape my room any time I want."

It was possible Rosa was going to explode. For a

moment, she stared at him as her cheeks turned redder and redder. "Then for the next two weeks, you'll just stay with me."

It seemed this bad day wasn't yet over. "You aren't my mother," he said.

"But I am your guardian."

Then she made Caden sit on the green interrogation couch. Officer Levine stood beside her with his arms crossed and his brows furrowed as she scolded Caden. "Do you understand how worried I was?" she said. "Tell me why you didn't come home and didn't answer your phone."

A spring in the couch cushion poked at Caden's thigh. Even the punishment couch was being difficult. He shifted but held Rosa's gaze. "When I tell you things, you doubt my royal sanity."

"Tell me anyway."

He squared his shoulders. "I watched a man I knew be eaten by a dragon I trusted." His chin quivered. "And Rath Dunn laughed."

Rosa looked as unbelieving as Caden expected. "Caden . . ."

He knew she'd doubt him. She always did. One thing about the second queen, wherever she was, she'd believe him about dragons and villains and Rath Dunn. He felt fresh anger heat his cheeks. "That's what happened. I don't care if you—" He clamped his mouth shut. It was important that he always be honest. Even when angry. Every muscle in his body felt strained. "You should believe me," he gritted out.

Officer Levine sat on the coffee table in front of him. "I believe you," he said.

Rosa turned and narrowed her eyes. When she spoke, her tone was as tight as a guard wire. "I'm not sure that's helpful, Harold."

"Maybe we should just hear Caden out?" Officer Levine said. "Most of his tales have had some truth in them, haven't they?"

Some truth? "All my tales are true."

Officer Levine leaned in and whispered, "Just work with me here, son."

Rosa let out a slow exhale and sat beside Caden. She reached out as if to take his hand. When he jerked away, she redirected and put her arm around his shoulders. Immediately, she went still. "You're shaking, Caden."

Caden glared at her. "I'm fine."

Rosa pulled him closer. For a moment, they sat together in silence. Then she let out a long, slow exhale. Her voice was firm and gentle when she spoke. "What is it you need from me?"

What did Caden need? He needed Scribe Trevor not to be eaten, Rath Dunn not to be principal. He needed his sixth-born brother, Chadwin, alive; and he needed Jasan cleared of his murder. He wanted to know why the second queen left. Rosa couldn't give him any of those things.

Caden crossed his arms. "I need you not to punish me." He knew he sounded angry and challenging, but he felt that way, so he cared not. "I need my phone and my computer privileges. I need not to be *grounded*."

Officer Levine looked from Caden to Rosa. He seemed unsure of what to think, unsure of how Rosa would respond.

She'd asked, though. So Caden had told her. If she truly wished to make him feel better, she could. It probably wasn't fair that Caden was mad at her. Truth be told, he wasn't sure why the brunt of his emotions seemed directed at his foster mother, but they were, and he wasn't one for hiding such things. He held her gaze. She studied him for a long moment as if weighing his words with care.

"Okay," Rosa said.

Okay? Was she agreeing to his terms? Caden blinked at her. "I won't be punished?"

Rosa nodded. "Not today."

This was unexpected, and Caden was unsure how to react. Then he decided the best course of action was to make further demands. "I also need to go to my room."

Rosa moved her arm from around his shoulders. "If that's what you need."

It was getting difficult to stay mad at her when she was being so accommodating. He felt his brows crease. Sometimes, he didn't understand Rosa at all. Then he thought of another even better demand. "I need you to believe me," Caden said.

On that Rosa hesitated. In a careful tone she said, "I believe that you believe."

"That's not good enough."

"I'm sorry," Rosa said.

"I believe you, son," Officer Levine said. "If you need to go upstairs, why don't you go rest and let me and Rosa talk."

Rosa turned to Officer Levine with an expression that could wither flowers. After all, in this household, Rosa was in charge. With a raise of brow, Officer Levine seemed to realize he'd pulled rank. He cleared his throat. "If, of course, that's all right with Rosa."

She turned back to Caden. "Call me if you need anything else."

Caden was tired and deflated, and the springs in the punishment couch were pinching him again. "As you wish." He stood up and trudged to the stairs. As he neared the second floor, he heard Officer Levine say, "I think you did the right thing, not punishing him."

"He was trembling," Rosa said. "If he says he needs not to be punished, that's something I can give him right now."

Caden hovered near the landing and listened.

"According to him, he witnessed a man killed at the school," Officer Levine said. "This is serious. We need to find out exactly what happened today."

"Harold," Rosa said, and she sounded completely

drained. "I hope you don't believe his stories."

"I've seen some strange things lately, and I think he witnessed something bad today." Rosa must have glowered, because Officer Levine added, "I'm saying we should keep an open mind, that's all."

4
ARCHER'S DAY

Caden trekked upstairs to the attic bath-closet. No, he would not call it a bathroom. It didn't deserve that title; it was too small. As he hung up his coat on the back of the door, he noticed a soot smudge near the shoulder. That was where Scribe Trevor had placed his hand. He stared for a moment, then quickly brushed it off. He didn't want to see it.

Once clean and dressed in his nightclothes, he went to the attic room he shared with Tito. They utilized a line of black tape to divide the room into Caden's well-kept, clean side and Tito's cluttered, books-and-clothes-strewn side.

Some of their classmates teased Tito about his crooked smile and asymmetrical face. Rosa said Tito's appearance was striking. In Caden's royal opinion, it was a fitting description.

As soon as Caden entered the attic, however, he felt exposed. Not only was Tito there, sitting cross-legged on his bed, Brynne and Jane were also in the room. They sat on Caden's bed, crumpling his orange-and-pink quilt. Beside the open attic window stood Caden's seventh-born brother, Jasan. By far, Caden was most surprised by him.

All four stared at Caden.

Brynne spoke first. Her hair was short and dark and had only begun to grow out. Her silvery eyes made her look like the sorceress she was. In her black pajamas, she also seemed a bit wicked. "You look terrible, prince."

Caden looked nothing but royal and fine. Still. "It's been a terrible day."

"We were worried about you," Jane said. "Are you okay?"

Though Jane was born in Asheville, she was half elf and an enchantress of metals. She often let her shoulder-length hair cover her ears. Sometimes Caden wondered if she was self-conscious about their pointed tips.

"I'm as good as I can be."

Tito raised his brows, his mouth dipped into his lop-sided frown. "Well, that's great. You kinda freaked us all out today."

Caden's attention, though, wandered from his foster brother to his blood brother. Jasan wore Ashevillian clothes instead of his Elite Paladin uniform: a light-blue button-down shirt over a white T-shirt and gray slacks. It seemed he approved of running shoes, because he wore those as well.

His jaw was clenched. As were his fists. His hair and eyes were a golden color that shone in lamplight like ember fire. With quick steps, he stomped to Caden. "You should have contacted me." He spoke in English so it seemed Brynne's spell remained active. "You'd better explain."

First Rosa was mad, now Jasan. Caden bristled. "To be fair," he said, "I didn't contact anyone, and I was fine."

"This isn't the first time you've disappeared," Jasan said.

Surely, Jasan couldn't be mad at him for getting stranded in Asheville. Caden hadn't wanted to be snared by a spell. Unless Jasan meant the time Caden had gotten lost in the catacombs. But he'd entered them to save his cat. Come to think of it, he'd also been missing once after falling into a crater wasp nest.

None of these was intentional. "I never intend to get lost."

"Today you could have called, and *not* been lost."

Rosa had said something similar, although she'd said it nicer. Caden felt too spent to try to find an excuse. "I didn't think about it."

It seemed to take the depths of Jasan's inner strength not to hit something. Or someone. Likely, it was Caden he wanted to wallop. When he raised his hand, however, he didn't strike out. He put it under Caden's chin and examined him closely.

Silver paper clips wound around Jasan's wrist. Jane had imbued the clips with magic, and Caden saw her craning her neck to get a better glimpse of her work. They were enchanted to bind things together. Without them, Jasan's hand would fall off. It had been lopped off by Rath Dunn and his blood dagger, so it was imperative that the paper clips do their job and bond Jasan's hand to his arm. If they failed, Jasan would bleed out, and bleed out fast. Looking at them made Caden's gut twist.

Jasan's scowl deepened, and he likely noticed Caden's dismay. "Tell me what happened."

It was a story Caden no longer wanted to tell. But his friends, his brother, needed to know. Rath Dunn had fed a man to Ms. Primrose. He rarely did anything solely for his sick amusement. Rath Dunn always acted with purpose, and his actions surely could be connected to the four-part spell. The scene in the office had also left Caden wondering just how much control the despicable despot had over Ms. Primrose. Caden began to fear it was more than he'd first realized, more than simply usurping her as principal.

"It was Scribe Trevor," Caden said. "He'd been banished." As Caden summarized the events of the morning, Jasan's face fell into shadow, and Tito took notes in his green binder.

As Caden came to the end of his tale, Tito looked up

from his work with high concern. "So she ate the poor guy?" he said.

"Not his feet," Caden said.

Brynne crinkled her nose. "Eww."

Jasan started to pace back and forth. The attic floor creaked with each angry step. "I don't like that Rath Dunn used you as a witness to such treachery," Jasan growled. "I should find him and end him. I'll cut him off at his boots."

That would likely end badly for Jasan. Rath Dunn had many allies and much protection. As Rosa did earlier, he looked like he might explode. "No, Jasan," Caden said. "He's protected by villainous teachers and an Elderdragon."

Jasan never liked being told not to kill someone. He narrowed his eyes but then closed them and appeared to be counting silently to ten. It seemed to take great inner strength not to detonate, and it was best to let Jasan be while he de-escalated.

Caden turned to the others. Maybe what Scribe Trevor said would help them. "Before Trevor was eaten, he said that he'd found runes for ritual contact indicating a connection on Archer's day."

Brynne wrinkled her brow.

Jane broke the silence. "Caden," she said, and brushed her hair behind her ear, "what's Archer's day?"

"It's the middle day in the fifth moon," Caden said.

"In the Greater Realm, Archer's day wouldn't yet have passed, but it should be soon," Brynne said. She blinked and looked upward as if numbers and facts flashed in front of her. "Well, there are three hundred and seventy days in a Greater Realm turn," she said. "There are only three hundred and sixty-five in a year here. Is that right, Sir Tito?"

Tito looked up from his notebook. "Yeah. Usually."

Usually? "What does that mean?" Caden said.

"Some years have three hundred and sixty-six days," Tito said. "Not this one, though."

"I see," Caden said.

"We should be able to convert days here to days there." Brynne moved so she sat next to Tito.

They discussed hours and inter-realm calendar conversions while Caden and Jane waited. Jasan kept counting. It seemed ten numbers weren't enough to quell his temper. After a moment, Tito and Brynne seemed to come to a conclusion.

"September twenty-second," Tito said. "Thirty days from now."

"That day on this realm's calendar correlates to Archer's day on ours," Brynne said.

Jasan was listening now. His eyes were open again, and he seemed deep in thought.

Tito tapped his pen against his green notebook. "You said planet and moons all were important in magic, right? September twenty-second is the fall equinox." Tito looked at Caden, then at Jasan, and seemed to decide that they didn't understand. Which Caden didn't. So bravo to Sir Tito. "During the equinox," Tito said, "night and day are the same length. Happens twice a year."

Not only did the seasons change in Asheville, so did the amount of light each day. "Every day has equal night and day in the Greater Realm," Caden said.

"Sounds boring," Tito said.

Caden ignored that comment. Tito was simply defensive of his strange realm's celestial fallacies. "Your seasons and days don't make sense. That's all."

Tito sighed, set his notebook down, then reached over and grabbed one of his books. He opened it to a page with a picture of a slanted sphere. "It's because the world is tilted on its axis, bro. See?"

"Ah," Caden said. The seasons and day lengths were strange in Asheville because the planet wasn't placed correctly. "Indeed," he said. "I see."

"Yeah," Tito mumbled. "I'm not sure you do." He reached for his green notebook again, but it was gone, lost to the much quicker hands of Jasan. Jasan held it up toward the light and squinted at the pages.

"Hey! That's mine," Tito said.

Jasan ignored his outrage. "What are all these notes about?"

Tito reached out as if he wanted to grab his notebook back. "It's all the information we've learned about the spell so far."

"As well as some theories about how it will work," Brynne added.

Those two had done *some* work during the summer when they weren't eating ice cream. They sent him texts with pictures of large cones while Caden was in school and they were supposed to be investigating the spell. Caden had forgotten about that but decided to let it go. Rosa had pardoned Caden; Caden would pardon the ice cream.

Jasan started to pace back and forth again, and the floorboards groaned like wounded banshees. "Make me a copy, in a language I can read when I'm not magicked." He tapped the notebook. "This might be useful."

"Might?" Tito said. "Dude, that's got everything we know in it. I even summarized the teacher contract."

Jasan cocked his head and studied Tito. Under the intense scrutiny, Tito sank back onto the headboard. One thing Tito didn't like was rapt attention. "Then well done, Tito."

"Sir Tito," Caden corrected. When no one acknowledged Caden, he felt the need to explain. "I knighted him."

Jasan raised a brow. "You knighted him?"

"With a broom," Tito said. "I wouldn't worry too much about it."

"My sword was taken." Caden crossed his arms. "And at the time, I was the highest-ranking Razzonian royal in Asheville." Then, like he'd fallen in a snow blow, Caden realized that he'd forgotten something, and it was something important. Jane—noble ally, enchantress, and Elite Paladin-in-training—hadn't been knighted. Wasn't she as deserving as Tito?

Caden stood tall and kept his voice firm. "Jasan, you must knight Jane. You're the highest-ranking Razzonian royal in Asheville now. It's your duty."

Jasan seemed less than receptive. He gestured to Jane. "You want me to knight your little friend?"

"Caden," Jane said, sounding uncomfortable, "I don't need to be knighted."

"But you deserve to be knighted," Caden said.

Sometimes Brynne was indeed a good ally, for she said, "I agree." Then she added, "That is, if you want to be knighted, Jane."

Who wouldn't want to be knighted? Well, Brynne, but she was a sorceress of questionable morals. Certainly, Jane wanted to be knighted. She trained with Caden and Tito. How could she not? Jasan, however, looked bothered; he looked like he needed to be convinced.

Caden turned to his brother. "I want you to knight the enchantress who has mastered fighting forms four and five, who has bravely stood against evil, and who enchanted the paper clips around your wrist."

Jasan sighed.

The sparring broom had been burned in battle, but Caden grabbed the sparring mop from the attic's corner and held it out to his brother. Jasan didn't reach for it.

"She saved your life, Jasan," Caden said.

With an irritated snort, Jasan said, "As you wish, then," but he didn't take the mop. Instead, he reached behind his back. He pulled a small, short sword from beneath the buttoned shirt—one that had seemingly been strapped to his back. The hilt was ruby-encrusted; the blade was sleek and sharp. It was a Razzonian sword. Before Caden had a chance to ask where Jasan found it or examine it closely, Jasan pointed it at Jane. "Kneel, Jane Chan."

Jane's cheeks went a bit rosy when Jasan said her name. She knelt. Then she stared at the floor as if embarrassed.

Jasan flicked the sword from her left shoulder to her right. His movements were so fast, they were hard to follow. "With what remains of the honor of the Razzonian royal family," Jasan said, "I dub you Lady Jane, protector of Asheville and the Greater Realm."

Her eyes became misty.

Truly, Caden should've done this earlier. Jane deserved the honor, and it seemed she appreciated it, too, no matter what she said.

"Thank you, Mr. Prince," she said.

Jasan brought the sword to his side and Caden examined it further. As he looked, he realized the sword was very familiar. It was the same one the police had taken from Caden when he'd first arrived in Asheville. Why did Jasan have it? Had Officer Levine given it to him when he refused to return it to Caden? Caden wanted to complain.

But it was best not to argue with Jasan right now. Jasan's foul mood had only begun to lift.

"Serve your people well, Lady Jane," Jasan said.

Tito reached out to give her a hand up. "I didn't kneel," he said. He sounded proud of that. "I refused."

Jasan slid his gaze from Jane to Tito. And if Caden wasn't mistaken, somewhere in Jasan's irritated expression there was a bit of mischief. With a cool smile, he pointed the sword at Tito. Then he pointed at the ground. "A proper knighting isn't done by a child with a broom."

Caden should have been offended by that. He wasn't a child. And he should've demanded Jasan give that sword to him. But Jasan had knighted Jane and seemed happy for a moment. Caden couldn't help but grin. Still, he should say something. Staying silent for so long was never a good thing. He grinned at Tito. "I agree that a proper knighting should be with sword and steel. When possible."

"Nah, no thanks," Tito said. "It's okay, really."

Jasan was enjoying himself now. He loomed over Tito. "It isn't 'okay.'"

Jane's smile was sweet, but her eyes glinted. "I think you should be knighted with a sword, Tito."

When it came to Tito, Jane's power of persuasion was even greater than Caden's. Tito looked like a cornered firefox. "Fine," he said. "Whatever."

The spectacle of Jasan re-knighting Tito was so

distracting, Caden didn't notice the footfalls on the attic stairs until he heard the third step creak. The door opened a moment later. That's how Rosa found Jasan in the attic, sword in hand, and Tito on his knees with Jasan's blade at his collar.

THE RED ASSEMBLY

Rosa looked from Jasan to Tito to the sword near Tito's neck. She stepped into the room cautiously, slowly, and when she spoke, her voice was elvish forged steel. "What's going on here?"

Frantically, Tito jumped to his feet. "It's not what it looks like!" He motioned to Jasan, who looked surly. "He was, um, Mr. Prince was knighting me?" Tito said.

"And me," Jane said.

"Lady Jane is correct," Caden said. "You should be proud, Rosa."

Rosa reached over and pulled Tito behind her. She didn't seem proud; nor did she seem happy to see Jasan. Matter of point, there was fury in her voice when she spoke. "How did you get in here?" She glanced back at Tito. "Who let you back inside?"

Tito raised up his palms. "No one, I swear." He pointed to the open window. "He climbed in the freaking window. Scared the crap out of me, too."

That seemed to anger Rosa more. "You came into my house without permission, brought a weapon, and scared my child?"

Jasan fastened the sword back under his shirt. When he spoke, his tone was cold. "I came to speak to Caden."

Truly, Caden didn't know what to think. Brynne had said Jasan and Rosa had argued, but Caden hadn't expected them to act like this. Why were two of his dearest people arguing?

"I didn't give you permission to talk to Caden," Rosa said. "Nor the others."

"I'll talk to Caden when I like," Jasan said. "He's my brother."

"I'm waiting on the DNA test to confirm that," Rosa said.

Jasan scowled at her. He stood tall and sure. "It will."

Rosa showed no fear. "Caden is in my care. I'll do what I believe is best for him."

What was happening? Jasan and Rosa were both good people, both soldiers even. They should be friendly. Caden felt his mouth fall open.

"Maybe *my* brother should be in *my* care, as you misplaced him today."

That seemed to hit Rosa like a punch, but she didn't

back down. "Leave my house now, or I'm calling the police."

There was little chance that Jasan feared the police. Still, Jasan stepped back toward the window and nodded to Caden. "We'll talk later." With a slight smirk, he put his hand on the frame, then jumped out, no doubt sliding down the side of the house to the ground.

Rosa widened her eyes. She, Jane, and Tito all rushed to the window.

"He's gifted in speed and a skilled Elite Paladin," Caden said. "Exiting from this height is no problem for him."

Rosa stared out a moment longer. Apparently convinced Jasan was not dead in the yard among her copper flowers, she ushered Jane and Tito away, and shut and locked the window. "Oh good grief!" she said. Her cheek twitched, and she was quiet for a moment. "He isn't allowed here without permission. Do you understand?"

"Not really," Caden said. "My brother is a noble person."

Rosa peered at him. "Don't let him inside without permission." Her gaze shifted to Brynne, then Tito, then Jane. "Do I make myself clear?" The three of them nodded. "Caden?"

Caden considered. "You do."

"Good." Then she turned to Brynne and Jane. "Girls, go to bed."

The girls hurried from the room, but when Rosa wasn't looking, Brynne held up her phone. She'd text them later.

Once the girls were gone, Rosa focused on Caden and Tito. "You two go to bed, too." She took a deep breath. "And, Caden?"

"Yes, Rosa?"

She rubbed at her temple and spoke firmly. "Promise me you won't jump out the window."

With fate's favor, Caden's curse recurred the week between summer school and normal school. He had four weeks until it would hit him again.

He had no desire to go back to the school, though. He wanted to refuse to go; he wanted to stay home, but he couldn't. Rosa seemed unsettled as well. No matter what happened, she always sent Caden back. She always sent Brynne, Tito, and Jane back, too.

He suspected it had to do with the matriculation paperwork. Just as the villains signed contracts to work at the school, parents and guardians signed forms to enroll the students. At the Primrose Charter School, the paperwork had power.

However, just because he had to go didn't mean he had to stay. The last day of the summer session, he'd skipped most of the day, after all. What did Tito call that type of thing? Oh yes. A loophole. And Caden had discovered it. He would use it if needed.

Caden wore his magnificent horse T-shirt and his enchanted coat for the first day of eighth grade. The school looked like a fortress set into the mountain. Bright-red roses were planted around the walls, but instead of beauty and life, they made Caden think of spilled blood.

The front hall was crowded. Caden saw many familiar faces. Some he liked: Olivia from science class, Tamera and Phoebe from math; some he didn't: Derek and his friends Jake and Tyrone. When they saw Caden, they pointed at his coat and snickered.

"Bro," Tito said. "Did you really have to wear the coat?"

"Yes, I have to wear it. It honors my people and my father," Caden said. "It's a challenge to evil and to Rath Dunn. It's a symbol of Razzon."

"It looks nice, Caden," Jane said.

That was also true. "I know," Caden said.

They followed the crowd toward the rebuilt auditorium for Rath Dunn's ironically named welcome assembly. Like Rath Dunn's office, the walls inside were red. The stage was outfitted with slick-looking Ashevillian technology. None of the chairs creaked, and the cushioned seatbacks reclined. The acoustics of the new building were like that of an elvish concert hall. Rich velvet curtains hid the stage.

Tito pulled them toward seats near the back. It wasn't where royalty belonged, but Tito seemed content, Jane and Brynne looked comfortable, and Caden felt generous. Jasan tapped his shoulder a moment later.

His teacher name tag and bright-yellow physical education whistle hung around his neck. "Move over," he said.

He spoke in Royal Razzon, not English, which meant he hadn't let Brynne spell him. Once Caden and the others had shifted one seat over, Jasan sat down beside them. Soon almost every seat in the auditorium was filled.

Onstage, Mr. Creedly stood in front of the curtains, hair slicked back, limbs curled to his body like a strange human bug. He hissed into a microphone. "Quiet," he spat. "He wishes to speak."

Then the curtains parted, and Rath Dunn stood center stage. "Thanks, Creedly, for the fine introduction." His suit was red, his tie black. Most teachers, like Jasan, sat in the audience to control the students. Six, however, stood onstage, three flanking each side of Rath Dunn.

On Rath Dunn's left stood Mr. Bellows, the English teacher. With gray, sallow skin and sunken eyes, he was a necromancer, a reanimator of dead things. The other two Caden didn't know, but neither looked human. Rath Dunn introduced them as the new drawing teacher, Ms. Levers, and the new music teacher, Mr. Wist.

Caden was fairly certain the music teacher was a Springlands banshee. He had a large mouth, likely full of teeth, and a thick throat and body. Banshees had poisonous bites. Their screams paralyzed both man and beast.

The art teacher was a blood wraith. Her eyes shone red when the auditorium lights caught them. Her movements seemed practiced; her skin looked tough and stretched thick over her frame. Wraiths tended to be ruthless in battle.

Were these two among the twelve banished during the summer? Maybe Ms. Primrose had only devoured ten? Caden thought of Scribe Trevor. Or maybe Rath Dunn only gave her the innocent to gobble up.

"I know Ms. Levers and Mr. Wist will declare war for their arts," Rath Dunn said.

On Rath Dunn's right stood stout Mrs. Grady and thin Mr. Faunt. Truly, the math department was particularly wicked. Mr. McDonald, Caden's literacy teacher, also stood with them. He was ghost pale, and his bright-white hair was the color of a surrender flag. From Caden's interactions with him, he suspected Mr. McDonald's only real crime was cowardice.

Caden noticed Ms. Jackson, the lunch witch, was also on the stage, behind and to the left. She reclined in a wooden chair like a cruel queen. Her chef's uniform was black. Around her upper arm she wore two red bands—vows of vengeance for her lost brother and sister. In her right hand, she held the Aging Ladle of Justice. Enchanted by Jane, it was stuck to her permanently and drained Ms. Jackson's ill-attained youth. Her hair was streaked with gray, and her brown skin had lost some of its glow, but she remained beautiful. No doubt, she also remained powerful.

Jasan whispered to Caden, "Manglor and I continue to follow Rath Dunn and Ms. Jackson."

Manglor was a reformed villain, the noble school janitor and the father of Caden's literacy class friend Ward. Caden spotted Manglor on the other side of the room. He towered above everyone else even sitting down, and his dark-brown skin and long, braided hair made him stand out even more. He was as big as Caden's second-born brother, Maden, who himself was as big as a small frost giant. The students behind him had to stand to see over his head.

"They have yet to do anything we can act against. But Archer's day is still some time to come." Jasan clutched the armrest between them as if to make it suffer. Around the edge of his right sleeve, near where the enchanted chain of paper clips kept Jasan's hand attached to his body, Caden saw the cuff stained pink.

"Your wrist has bled."

"Don't worry about it," Jasan said. "I'm taking Ashevillian supplements."

But Caden would worry. Since getting wounded, Jasan had often been pale. He'd seemed more tired than usual. Caden felt his brow crease and his expression drop.

Jasan let out a long breath. "There are even blood transfusions the locals can do."

Had Jasan been so sick he needed Ashevillian blood? He'd lost a lot when his hand was cut off, even if Caden had reattached it with the clips. "Have you had to have transfusions?"

"I'm taking care of it, Caden," Jasan said, as if that was the end of it. He leaned to the side so he could also speak to Brynne and the others. "I want you all to gather information from the students. Find out if they've seen anything useful. Note any strange behavior from your teachers."

Tito and Jane didn't speak Royal Razzon. They exchanged a confused look, so Caden translated for them.

"We can do that," Jane said.

Jasan seemed to have understood her answer. He had, after all, started to learn the local tongue. "Good." Then he nodded to the stage, to Mr. McDonald. "Keep an eye on McDonald. Follow him when you can. Sometimes cowards and lackeys know more than expected."

Mr. McDonald was the least dangerous person in the school. Likely the only reason he was onstage was because Rath Dunn found his terror amusing. "And many times they don't," Caden said, and scrutinized his brother. "That sounds dull and tedious and made to keep us busy."

Jasan didn't deny it. "That's right," he said. "But dull, tedious work can uncover information." He held Caden's gaze. "And as the seventh-born son, I outrank you." Perhaps Jasan did know Caden quite well, because he added, "If you want to be an Elite Paladin, and want me to consider you one, I expect you to follow my orders."

Caden should have been annoyed, but he wasn't. He felt a bright smile flash across his face. Jasan often gave those training to become Elite Paladins boring assignments. It was his way of testing them. "Everything Mr. McDonald knows," Caden said, "I will find out for you."

Jasan looked like he was having second thoughts about

assigning Caden any mission. "Stay out of trouble. Contact me if Rath Dunn summons you again. I've had words with him about that already." He surveyed the audience and frowned. "And keep away from Ms. Primrose."

At the mention of the Elderdragon, Caden scanned the audience, too. The sixth-grade gifted teacher, Mr. Limon, a man with long hair and a prominent brow, noticed him and scowled. As did Mr. Frye, the lanky sixth-grade English instructor. The school nurse, a large, sturdy woman, didn't look too friendly either. Now that Caden thought about it, there were many teachers, and all were villains.

Then he saw Mrs. Belle, the science teacher. She tapped her bloodred nails against the armrest of her chair and smiled warmly at him. Mrs. Belle had always treated him nicely.

Ms. Primrose was noticeably absent, and he hadn't seen her since the incident in the office. No matter, he didn't want to talk to her anymore anyway. "I'll do my best to avoid her."

"You'd better," Jasan said. He motioned to the front. "Now, tell me what the tyrant is blabbering about."

Onstage, Rath Dunn threw his arms out as if to embrace the audience. "This will be a new year, a new age. A new start for those of us willing to work for a common goal. Ms. Primrose is still with us and hungry to fulfill her duties assisting me. And I promise as principal"—when he said this, he looked out at the audience, his gaze finally landing on Caden and Jasan—"I'll work to see that all of you and your families finally get what you deserve."

Then Rath Dunn's speech shifted to the amazing cafeteria food he and Ms. Jackson intended to create to further innovate the lunch program. "Let's all try to survive the upcoming autumn," he boomed into the microphone. With a grand flail of his arms, he added, "Now get to class! Anyone who is late or who skips will live to regret it." He laughed. "Or maybe not, who knows?"

THE DRAGON IN THE HALL

s Caden had been promoted from seventh to eighth grade, he had a new locker. No longer was he bound to unlucky locker twelve-four. His new assigned locker was the less unlucky thirteen-thirteen, and it was clean. He mentioned his improved fortune to Brynne, Tito, and Jane.

Tito leaned against locker thirteen-twelve. "Keep telling yourself that."

Caden noticed Derek and his friends had stopped in the middle of the hall. They surveyed the red walls and shiny tiles with uneasy expressions. Now that Caden considered it, many of his schoolmates looked nervous. Some shuddered. The school had a cruel energy. Everyone seemed to feel it.

While Caden arranged his books, notebooks, and Ashevillian writing tools, Jane traced a finger on the edge of Caden's sleek new locker. She seemed thoughtful, too thoughtful. "I could enchant this," she said.

Caden froze, his reading book halfway between locker and hall. The locker was metal, and Jane enchanted metal. "I wouldn't want you to do that," Caden said.

"But it could be enchanted to always be clean and to hold more stuff," Jane said.

Caden pulled out his book. Truth be told, a locker of cleanliness and holding was tempting. But only a little. Enchanting drained her of life force. He motioned to three cylindrical jars in the back. "I have three varieties of cleaning wipes. This locker is fine. But thank you, Lady Jane."

"Jane," Brynne said. "You shouldn't waste your life force on something like that. Enchant something small, like our plan." She produced a copper coin from her pocket. "Something that will only require a minute influx of life force. Like a penny."

Tito knocked his fist on innocent locker thirteen-twelve. A dent formed in the smooth surface. "How about this?" he said. "Don't enchant anything."

"I was just thinking about it," Jane said, and smiled at him. It was an easy smile, but Caden started to think that expression might mean she was unhappy. "It's my decision, not yours." Then she took Brynne's coin, turned on her heel, and marched off toward her English class.

"I'll talk to her," Brynne said. She gestured to the red

hall and sleek lockers. "The school doesn't feel safe. Be careful in your class, prince."

Despite improving his reading and writing over the summer, Caden remained in Mr. McDonald's special reading class. Brynne walked after Jane, but Tito lingered. He shifted his stance like he was uncomfortable.

"What is it, Sir Tito?" Caden said.

"Dude, is there any way to convince Jane not to enchant things?"

Future Elite Paladins were always honest. "Enchanters enchant," Caden said. "She is what she is. You must accept her as such. At least Brynne has convinced her to use some moderation."

Tito leaned on locker thirteen-twelve. "I just worry about her." Then he glanced around the near-empty hall. The late bell would ring any moment. "Crap. I better get to class."

As Tito turned to go, though, a large shadow spread across the tiles and blocked his path. There was the *tip-tap* of someone approaching. The scent of roses drifted into the air. The other remaining students hurried out of sight until only Caden and Tito remained.

Ms. Primrose came around the corner a moment later. Her gnarled hand was clenched in a fist. Cold surrounded her, and if not for his coat, Caden would have shivered. She narrowed her ice-blue eyes at them. Jasan had told him to avoid Ms. Primrose not thirty minutes earlier. Now Caden and Tito stood in the empty hall, and an Elderdragon blocked their path.

Caden felt the blood drain from his face. He didn't move. Her blue shadow was immense. It spread over the walls and made them appear a deep purple. As she approached, her pale eyes barely passed for human.

"Uh, hi," Tito said. "Good morning, Ms. Primrose."

"It's hardly a good morning, Tito," Ms. Primrose said. "Everything at school is wrong." Then she pursed her lips and looked to Caden as if she expected a greeting.

Caden, however, wasn't ready to wish her a pleasant day. She'd eaten his scribe. How could she have done that? He raised his chin and said nothing. His anger battled with his fear. And Ms. Primrose couldn't devour Caden or Tito. It was against their pact. Why should he be nice?

When he didn't speak, the hall became colder, darker.

Tito nudged Caden with his elbow. When Caden still kept silent, Tito said, "Yeah, we were just about to go to our classes." As he finished the last word, the late bell rang. "Oh, oops? Maybe we could get late passes. . . ."

Ms. Primrose didn't seem to be listening to Tito. *Tip. Tap. Tip. Tap.* She moved until she stood not a floor-tile length from Caden. She'd gained more weight since he'd seen her in August. "It's rude, dear, not to greet your elders." Although if she meant the Elderkind or simply those older than Caden, he didn't know.

She was correct, however. Not speaking was rude. And

Caden was an eighth-born prince. He was never rude. "Good morning, Ms. Primrose." It was possible, however, to be both polite and not nice. "You're looking quite portly."

For a moment, there was silence. She looked shocked. Tito looked shocked. Then Tito said, "I think he means healthy, ma'am."

Caden suspected she was self-conscious about her now snug-fitting clothes. In fact, he mentioned her weight to bother her. "That's not what I meant," Caden said.

"I know it's not," Ms. Primrose said. She leaned close, and Caden felt chilled. "Is this how you princes behave these days?" Her small pupils elongated to slits. "I may not be able to eat you, but don't think I can't punish you. Don't give me cause to get creative, dear."

As his intention was to anger her, it seemed his gift of speech had worked quite well today.

"Well, um, we should get to class," Tito said again.

Caden wasn't ready to get to class. He was mad at Ms. Primrose. He'd expected better of her than to eat poor Trevor. And then he told her so. Blue scales seemed to cover her face, though Caden also saw a silver scale near her ear.

"Dude, stop it," Tito said. He glanced at Caden, then at Ms. Primrose. "Um. I mean, it wasn't like you wanted to eat Caden's scribe, was it?"

"Don't you think I'd rather choose my own dinner?" she snapped. "It's humiliating being controlled by an inept principal. Look what he's done to my beautiful school. Everything is red."

Did she care at all about the consequences of not having a choice? Or was she simply unhappy to be force-fed? Caden didn't know.

But he did know what it was like not to be in control of his actions. Every month when his curse recurred, it was horrible. It was an unintentional order that had compelled Caden to chop off Brynne's hair. He hadn't wanted to do it; he'd tried to resist, but he hadn't been able to stop himself, and he still felt responsible.

A question tickled his tongue. "If it had been your choice," Caden said, "would you have let him live?"

When she turned to Caden, her mouth seemed stretched and distorted, her tongue blue, her teeth sharp. "If I had a choice right now, I'd eat *you*." Though she stood in front of him, Caden felt cold breath above him. He dared not look up lest he see an Elderdragon's jaw. He felt his courage waiver and fear grip hold. She continued, "And I would take time to savor my food. First an arm. Then a leg. I'd enjoy my dinner."

Tito stared, eyes wide, mouth agape.

Caden felt his body start to tremble. If ever there was a right time to say the right thing, it was now. The only thing Caden could think to say, however, was to agree with her. "Well," Caden said, and swallowed, "royal meat is the tastiest."

She blinked at him. "It certainly is," she said, but the feeling of a gaping jaw above him receded. The chill lessened. "I won't tolerate this again. I expect you to behave respectfully." A small yellow pad appeared in her left hand, a pen in her right. She scribbled something, tore off a sheet, then gave it to Tito. "Your late pass, Tito." She cut her gaze to Caden. "You don't get one."

As she tip-tapped away, Tito spun on Caden. "Bro," he whispered, "were you trying to tick her off?"

Caden looked down. He cleared his throat. "Only at first," he said.

"Well, how about only never from now on."

That seemed a good idea, but Caden still felt conflicted. "But she ate Scribe Trevor."

Tito took a deep breath and nodded sympathetically. "Yeah, I know. But, well, it sounds like she didn't have a choice," he said. "And we *don't* want her mad at us, remember?"

Tito was right, of course.

If she could have chosen, would she have chosen differently? Would the school have a new librarian now? During the three days of the half-moon, Caden had no choices. It was a terrible, helpless, terrifying experience, much more so than he let on to his friends. Maybe Ms. Primrose felt the same.

Like Tito had done a moment ago, Caden also took a deep breath. He still felt shaky. The encounter with Ms.

Primrose had been a disaster. He'd learned nothing and possibly made her more of an enemy.

If Caden's father, King Axel, ever found out about it, his brow would crease in disappointment; he'd sigh under his breath. If Jasan knew, he'd be infuriated. Jasan had finally trusted Caden with a mission; Caden didn't want to make Jasan rethink it.

"Sir Tito?"

Tito was staring at the late pass crinkled in his closed fist. He looked up. "Yeah?"

"May I ask that you don't tell Jasan about what just happened?"

Tito crooked a smile at him. "Usually, Jasan and I don't even speak the same language. But I'll tell you what, your recklessness," he said. "Promise me you won't purposely tick off any more Elderdragons, and I'll never tell a soul."

Caden placed his hand on Tito's shoulder. "Dear friend," he said, "it is indeed a promise."

7

THE PARK AT DAWN

For the next three weeks, Caden went to school. Rath Dunn stopped him in the halls many times, to order him about, to check his compliance. Sometimes Ms. Jackson came out from the cafeteria line during lunch and sniffed him like she might be able to smell the curse. Luckily, the half-moon didn't rise during that time.

As for Caden, he investigated Mr. McDonald—asked him questions, asked others about him. The day before Archer's day—Thursday, September 21, by the Ashevillian calendar—his persistence paid off. As Caden sat at his computer, his classmate Ward on his left, his classmate Tonya to his right, Mr. McDonald announced, "If I'm late tomorrow, start your lessons without me."

Never had a teacher been late for a class while Caden was enrolled. He swiveled around to face Mr. McDonald. "Why would you be late?"

"I just might. Now, mind your own business."

He was wrong, though. "You're my teacher; it is my business."

"Don't start with me today," Mr. McDonald said.

Tonya swiveled around, too. The overhead lights reflected in her glasses as she chewed on a strand of her blond hair. Neither she nor Ward was in the class to learn the written word. Tonya was there to work on her stuttering. Caden wasn't sure why Ward was in the class unless it was because he rarely spoke. But they knew of the evil at the school and helped gather information when possible. Indeed, Tonya was a good and smart ally, for she said, "But why would you be late, Mr. McDonald?"

Mr. McDonald threw up his hands. "I'm running errands! Important errands. Now be quiet and get to work. Both of you."

After Mr. McDonald slinked back to his desk in the corner, Ward leaned toward Caden. He'd been small before the summer. Over the too-hot months, however, he'd stretched and grown tall. Though his hair was cropped short, it was now easy to see he was Manglor's son. He whispered, "Pa once had to be late, back when Ms. Primrose was principal. He had to get her permission first."

"Rath Dunn is now the principal," Caden mused. "It's his permission that's needed."

That evening, the last of the Ashevillian summer, Caden sat on the porch steps with Brynne. The sky was orange and pink, the mountains dark-blue mounds beneath it. The air was cool and smelled of dirt and grass. It felt like change was coming.

Tito and Jane practiced fighting stance seven on the lawn. They moved fast. Jane's strikes with the sparring mop had deadly intent. Tito's slashes with sparring stick number eight looked strong and sure. Caden felt pride swell inside. He'd taught them well.

"We need to track Mr. McDonald before dawn," he told Brynne. "We need to find out what his early-morning errands are."

Click. Clack. Tito and Jane connected with powerful volleys.

"That early?" Brynne said. "Ugh."

"It's important."

As Jane's mop clashed with Tito's stick, the sparring stick snapped in two. He stepped back and frowned at the splintered end. "I guess we'll find another one, huh?" Tito wiped sweat from his brow. "Number nine, right?"

As he was distracted, Jane took the initiative and used the sparring mop to sweep him off his feet and knock him onto his back. "I win," she said.

"When you don't play fair," Tito said, but he grinned and let her help him up.

"Villains won't fight fair," Jane said.

"You should know that by now, Sir Tito," Caden called over.

Tito threw half of sparring stick number eight at Caden's royal face, but Caden caught it. Then Jane skipped over and sat beside Caden and Brynne on the steps. They watched Tito clean the sparring area. It was the loser's duty to do so.

As he finished, Tito checked to make sure Rosa was nowhere nearby. Then he pulled out his cell phone and showed a map. "Jane and I found Mr. McDonald's address. He rents a room above a consignment store."

"You have done great work finding his home," Caden said.

"We just googled it," said Jane.

Brynne and Caden snuck out of Rosa's house hours before dawn. Truly, Caden didn't think Rosa would excuse punishment a second time if she discovered he was gone, and he was grateful Jane and Tito volunteered to stay, to cover for them if needed and to collect data Brynne texted back.

The mountain was dark. Brynne pulled out her cell phone to light their way. Once beyond the tall grasses of the side yard, Caden whistled for Sir Horace. His horse couldn't be stabled when the night called to him. While they waited, Brynne stretched like a wind cat. "One day," she said, "I want a car. Then we can travel by auto and not smelly horse."

Caden was aghast. Simply aghast. "There is no better way to travel than on Sir Horace."

Like the name was an incantation, there came a pounding of hooves on the ground. A thunderous snort echoed in the mountains. Sir Horace stuck his head around a large maple tree a moment later.

"I want a pickup," Brynne said. "Like Rosa's, only with a better sound system and Bluetooth." She turned over her phone and showed him a picture of a shiny silver pickup. "I've already chosen it."

A pickup couldn't nuzzle Caden's neck like Sir Horace. A pickup wouldn't stand beside Caden proudly or charge ice dragons. A pickup couldn't gallop up a rocky mountainside with a Galvanian stallion's speed and agility. Cars needed roads. No sleek silver pickup could match Sir Horace's frost-colored hair and magnificent mane.

"Sir Horace need not compete with soulless silver pickups," Caden said. "I don't understand you at all, sorceress." He reached up and covered Sir Horace's ears. "Don't listen to her, friend."

With a look a disdain for Brynne and her pickup, Caden pulled himself up onto Sir Horace's back. Brynne switched her phone so it showed a map, then hopped on behind him. Surprisingly, Sir Horace didn't complain about his second rider even after she'd insulted him by saying she'd prefer a truck. Then they were away, galloping toward the apartment over the consignment shop like a white flash in the predawn night.

Caden, Brynne, and Sir Horace peeked from around

the shadowy corner of a brick building. A lone streetlight cast a yellow glow near a door beside the shop. It wasn't long before the door swung open and cut into the light. Mr. McDonald exited; he carried large rolls of papers—maps, Caden suspected—under his arm and steaming coffee in his left hand.

"Text Tito and Jane. Let them know we have found the objective, and he seems to be carrying maps." All details were important, even ones that didn't seem to be. "And coffee."

"I already have. You know," Brynne said, "if you let me spell you, you could just text them yourself. With more than emojis."

He turned to her. "Future Elite Paladins don't rely on magic."

She smiled slyly, and he knew what she was about to say. "Prince Jasan lets me magic him to read and write some days, and he's a *current* Elite Paladin."

"I don't know why he lets you do that."

"Because he's not so fussy."

"Or he's being rebellious."

"Or practical," Brynne said. "You should let me magic you."

Once, Brynne had cursed Caden with a fluffy white tail. Another time, she'd turned his skin the color of desert amethysts. Worst of all, after arriving in Asheville, she was the one who had cursed him with compliance for the three days at each half-moon. That last spell she'd yet to find a way to break.

"You've put enough spells on me."

If she felt any guilt, she hid it. "I'll fix that curse, prince."

"So you've said. But so you haven't done."

Brynne twisted her hands together and looked away.

Mr. McDonald piled his papers into the back of a rusty sedan, then slid into the front seat. The engine started with a coughing sound. Caden reached for Sir Horace; so did Brynne. "He's moving. Let's go."

They followed him to French Broad River Park. The river looked gray in the half-light of predawn. Paved paths wove around picnic tables and along the shore. Most of the trees remained summer green, but a few had leaves of yellow and red. The air was cool. Summer had finally surrendered to the chill of the Ashevillian autumn.

At Caden's command, Sir Horace waited nearby in the woods. It would be hard to hide him without tree cover. Sir Horace would come if called, and he would wait if not. Then Caden and Brynne hid near the edge of the park. There was a road bridge there that stretched low and long across the water. Its cement pilings gave them cover, and they watched. There were two villains by the bank now.

The first, of course, was Mr. McDonald. His hair looked paper white in dawn's light. His shoulders were slumped; his maps crumpled under his arm. Like Caden and Brynne, he'd been waiting awhile.

The second figure had just arrived. It was Ms. Jackson, the lunch witch. The moment she pulled her organic food van into the parking lot, the mission became more meaningful. More dangerous. More worthy of a future Elite Paladin. As always, she dressed in black with red bands tied around her arm. She grasped the cursed ladle in her right hand. In her left, she held a large witchy pot that looked a lot like the cafeteria spaghetti pot.

A car rumbled across the bridge. Loose dirt showered down. Caden glared up and brushed it from his shoulder. This Ashevillian bridge was utilitarian at best and was nothing like the bridges in his homeland, in the Greater Realm's Winterlands. There—in Razzon—the bridges were monuments.

The most impressive, the Bridge of the Divide, stretched from one mountaintop to the next. The suspensions were carved to look like the wings of the imperial Winterbird. The expanse was painted in golds, silvers, and deep royal blue. It was higher than the clouds, and at full speed it took Sir Horace half a day to cross.

Lately, even small bridges reminded Caden that he was stranded in a strange land far from home. And hiding under bridges was completely undignified. Caden wasn't a barter troll. He crossed his arms and whispered that to Brynne.

She wore a sleek black jacket, jeans, and delicate-looking boots. Her silvery eyes were a brighter version of the gray sky. "Of course you're no troll," Brynne whispered back. "If you were a barter troll, prince . . ." More dirt spilled down. "You'd be useful and force those cars to pay tolls. We could make spending money."

This was his ally. A sorceress who would be happy with barter troll–type extortion. Caden motioned toward the bank. "At which point, the villains would catch us."

"Better to fight a witch and a coward than die of boredom under a bridge," she said, but she fidgeted like she couldn't relax.

"Jasan said to observe and report," Caden said.

"Jasan also said to let him and Manglor follow Ms. Jackson, not us," Brynne said.

Ms. Jackson was no minion. She was high-level, powerful, and hard to track. Brynne motioned to the black-clad figure by the bank. "Yet here we are, and there Ms. Jackson is."

"She wasn't the one we followed here, so we've done as we were told. And we need to know what they are plotting."

"Agreed," Brynne said. "They're waiting here for a reason." She leaned her cheek against the column. "I've a bad feeling about this, prince."

It was never a good sign when a spellcaster had a bad feeling.

Overhead, another car bumped over the bridge. Its headlights flashed across the mountainside, park, and river, then the car pulled around the park gate. It looked as if it were drenched in blood. A red Audi. The man inside was dressed in a matching crimson sweater. He pulled the car onto the grass and stopped.

Rath Dunn stepped out. He stretched as if to honor daybreak. Then he closed the door, petted the top of his Audi like it was a cherished pet, and walked toward the shore where Ms. Jackson and Mr. McDonald were waiting. Now Mr. McDonald clutched the large witchy pot.

Just as Caden and Brynne had been spying on Mr. McDonald, Jasan had been watching Rath Dunn. Yet Rath Dunn was here at the park. Jasan wasn't.

In the quietest voice possible, Caden said, "Call Jasan."

Brynne crouched down. She coddled her phone to her and tapped on it. It glowed a dim blue as she raised it to her ear. "He's not answering," Brynne said. Then she switched to the Common Tongue and left Jasan a whispered message.

Why wasn't Jasan answering? What if Rath Dunn had harmed him or killed him? Jasan was strong, but Caden knew even strong people could be lost. He felt fear surge through him.

Brynne scooted closer to Caden. She held her phone near her chest. It glowed with a new call. She cupped it with her hand to hide the light. "It's Jasan," she said quietly, and Caden felt weak with relief. She tilted her head. "He's on his way." Brynne shrugged, then scrunched her face into a frown. "He says to stay hidden. It's an order."

Caden was just grateful Jasan was alive. "Very well."

From the bank, Caden heard Ms. Jackson and Rath Dunn laugh. She carved symbols into the mud with her cursed ladle. Though she was evil, Caden admired her ability to adapt the cursed item to her benefit.

Rath Dunn stood near the water. His beard looked neatly trimmed, his bald head as if he'd waxed it. His sweater seemed too red for the gray of dawn. He clamped his hand on Mr. McDonald's shoulder and grinned.

Mr. McDonald was as stiff as a locking battle chain, and his face turned as white as his hair. He stumbled away from Rath Dunn, filled Ms. Jackson's witchy spaghetti pot with river water, then sat it on the bank.

Caden looked at Brynne as she watched the villains. The wind blew her short hair back in soft black waves. She narrowed her silvery eyes. "The grass is turning black," she said.

Caden realized he was staring. And not at the villains. At Brynne. He felt his cheeks heat and quickly turned. A tree near the shore turned from healthy brown to hollow black. The green leaves on its branches scattered like ashes. The smell of rot filled the air. Ritual magic drained life and caused destruction.

In the quietest of voices, Brynne said, "The communication spell?"

Communication spells seemed fueled by the death of

plant life. If they were about to witness one, the tiring night of following Mr. McDonald was about to become worthwhile. He and Brynne would witness any contact made with the other realm.

Caden tugged his coat tighter. Usually, it brought him comfort, but not even the enchanted wool could ebb the cold dread he felt. His second-born brother, Maden, allied with the villains. Likely, Maden was on the other end of this communication spell.

"Caden?" Brynne whispered, and nodded toward the bank.

This was no time to remember when Maden used to hoist Caden on his shoulders, nor of Maden showing Caden tricks for fighting enemies with greater physical strength. This was a chance to learn the enemy's plan— even if Maden was part of it. Caden squared his shoulders and fumbled in his pocket for his sparkly cell phone. He needed to record these events. He'd prove to Jasan that he was capable.

The villains turned toward the water. Their voices were soft and indistinct. Caden couldn't make out what they said. "We need to be closer," he whispered to Brynne.

Brynne pulled a purple hair band from her pocket and used it to pull her hair away from her face. She set her jaw. "Agreed."

They crept from the relative safety of the bridge, then scrambled to the area behind the public restrooms and peeked out. Caden could see the villains more clearly. And Rath Dunn carried his blood dagger. Caden was near enough to it for his arm to ache. The villains' voices, however, remained muffled. They needed to be closer.

On the bank, the witchy spaghetti pot glowed red. It looked as hot as a Razzonian forge. Red was the color of fire dragons and angry spells; it was the color of magic fueled by hate.

Caden pointed to a picnic table. It wasn't the best cover, but none of the villains knew that Caden and Brynne watched them. Rath Dunn, Ms. Jackson, and Mr. McDonald had no reason to peek under a picnic table. Brynne nodded. Caden grabbed her hand and they dashed for it.

Caden hopped between the bench and top so that he was beneath it. Brynne slid in beside him. He tapped the icon on his phone to record the voices.

Mr. McDonald stared at the ground while Ms. Jackson crouched beside the pot. Rath Dunn leaned over it. He spoke in the Greater Realm's Common Tongue. "Today just after sunrise. Then three days after at dusk," he said. "Don't mess it up."

Next Caden heard a voice that was not Rath Dunn's, nor Ms. Jackson's, nor Mr. McDonald's. It was a faraway voice, and it rippled from the spaghetti pot like it was coming from a cell phone. "Everything will be ready on this side." Maden. His voice sounded colder than Caden remembered. "Don't *you* mess it up, villain."

Maden didn't seem to like Rath Dunn, but that changed nothing.

"I don't mess up," Rath Dunn growled. Then he kicked the red-hot pot into the river. It sizzled and steamed as it fell beneath the waters. The conversation was over.

"That was my best pot," Ms. Jackson said.

"I allowed myself to be immersed in the moment." Rath Dunn feigned contrition. "And now your pot is immersed in the river." He chuckled as if amused with himself. "Soon I shall have a new one fashioned for you. Gilded with the armor of dead Razzonian royalty."

His words seemed to do little to appease Ms. Jackson. "Don't try to bribe me," she said.

"Of course, of course," Rath Dunn said. "My apologies."

Mr. McDonald acted more frightened than ever. His gaze darted from Rath Dunn to Ms. Jackson. He stepped away, but as quick as a snow snake's strike, Rath Dunn pulled Mr. McDonald back.

"We need you here. Remember?" Rath Dunn said.

"What for? I've done my part," Mr. McDonald said. "I mapped each location as it matches up with its counterpart." His voice shook. "I helped make the runes!"

"You're an important part of this undertaking, Mr. McDonald. You're needed."

Brynne pinched Caden's elbow.

It was no time for Brynne to pinch him. They were under an Ashevillian picnic table and in the presence of

Ms. Jackson, the lunch witch and ritual magic master; Rath Dunn, the bringer of the Blood War; and Mr. McDonald, the cowardly reading teacher. Two of these three people wanted to make Caden a corpse. Caden and Brynne needed to be as silent as a prowling wind cat. Caden stifled an *"Ow"* and turned to glare at her.

She pointed to the sky and the rising sun. Soft golden rays stretched across the gray morning.

"So?" he mouthed.

She leaned close. She smelled of the damp earth and the morning breeze. In the quietest voice possible, she said, "Today, just after sunrise."

The villains had contacted Maden, but they weren't leaving. They'd no reason to stay around unless they planned to do more. Caden peeked between the bench and tabletop. Ms. Jackson pulled a vial from her pocket, one with glowing green liquid.

It was one Caden had seen once before while hiding beneath a desk. Much like bridges and picnic tables, desks weren't dignified places to hide under. But such was fate's disfavor that Caden found himself crouched under Ashevillian structures.

That vial was one of four that Rath Dunn had collected. Each contained an ingredient—the tears of an elf, magical locks, blood of a son, and dragon's essence—and each was an ingredient for a four-part spell. If completed, it would blast a pathway back to the Greater Realm. The amount of life drained by a powerful barrier-breaking spell would be far greater than the autumn grass and the park trees. No doubt it would drain plant, animal, and human life. The consequence of such a spell would be the destruction of the city and its people.

Rath Dunn dragged Mr. McDonald to the edge of the water. Mr. McDonald's eyes darted from side to side. Then they widened and locked under the picnic table, on Caden and Brynne beneath it.

Caden heard Brynne suck in a breath.

Mr. McDonald was a proven coward. He'd left Caden and his classmates to killer bees last year. Like all teachers in the middle school, he was a villain banished from the Greater Realm. But he had once claimed innocence. Hoping Mr. McDonald had some spark of nobility in his cowardly body, Caden held Mr. McDonald's gaze. He made the message clear: don't tell Rath Dunn and Ms. Jackson we're here. Maybe Mr. McDonald would keep them secret. Maybe.

The picnic table started putting off heat. Lines etched into the wood began to glow. Runes. Around the park, symbols appeared everywhere—carved into the paved path, painted on the public restrooms, twisting around lampposts and trees.

It seemed Ms. Jackson had been busy. The sigils carved on the trees and painted on the paths and buildings must have taken meticulous work, and since Caden doubted Jasan or Manglor knew about these runes, Ms. Jackson had been sneaky enough to carve and paint them when no one spied on her. Truly, she was a witch—tricky, smart, and powerful. She stood beside the river and cackled with glee. The vial glowed green.

Oh no. Today wasn't just a day of communication. They'd stumbled across something even more important than that. She had the vial. That meant something more, something worse. Today was the day Rath Dunn and Ms. Jackson meant to cast the first part of the spell. Caden glanced toward the road, then toward the forest. Where was Jasan?

Not here, but they couldn't let the spell begin. "We have to stop her," Caden said.

"I know," Brynne said.

Time was short. Without the vial, she couldn't cast the spell. They scooted from their hiding spot. "I'll distract Rath Dunn," Caden said. "You get the vial."

Brynne dashed for Ms. Jackson, Caden toward Rath Dunn. Before either was even halfway, Ms. Jackson's voice rose over the sounds of morning. "Rain fall, river rage, let the tears of elf begin the break, and join distant river and lake." She dumped the vial.

The winds roared. The river's waters started to foam. Rapids rammed the bank. Waves sprayed across the bridge.

Brynne's purple hair band flew off and tumbled away with flying leaves. She skidded to a stop. Caden did the same.

Was the first part of the spell complete? To make things worse, Caden and Brynne were exposed now. Their enemies would see them if they so much as glanced their way. Caden detoured to Brynne and gripped her hand. Best they run and hide, and do so fast.

Brynne resisted. She creased her brow. "Ritual magic requires sacrifice, and she hasn't sacrificed anything for the four-part spell, Caden. The plants were used for the communication spell, not this."

They stood in the howling, unnatural wind and turned back toward the villains.

Rath Dunn grabbed Mr. McDonald by the neck and dragged him toward the angry river. Mr. McDonald fought against him, but he was too slow and too unpracticed to have any effect.

"Help!" Mr. McDonald screamed. "Help me!"

Rath Dunn followed Mr. McDonald's line of sight to Caden and Brynne. When he saw them, he smiled. Brynne stepped closer to Caden. "Without a sacrifice, the spell won't work," she said.

That was when Rath Dunn, still smiling, tossed Mr. McDonald into the river.

Mr. McDonald screamed. All Caden could see was his white hair bobbing in the raging waters as the rapids swept him in the direction of the bridge.

"Save him!" Brynne yelled.

If Caden could catch him, he could reach for him and

pull him to safety. He darted diagonally in the direction of the bank and the bridge. A true Elite Paladin never refused a call of aid. Not even from a cowardly villain.

There was a flash of heat and light. Pyrokinesis magic—a type of sorcery that gave the caster mind power over fire. It was one of Brynne's more powerful spells, and one of her least controlled.

Caden glanced back. Brynne stood on one side of a massive wall of fire. Rath Dunn and Ms. Jackson stood on the other. A bench in the flames melted. The fire grew on the raging winds. Only at the river, where the water extinguished it, did it cease. Rath Dunn dashed in that direction.

Mr. McDonald's head was now underwater, but he reached his hand up above it. His fingers scrambled for branches and rocks. Brynne yelled. Ms. Jackson cackled. On the wind, Caden heard a mighty whinny. No doubt Sir Horace ran toward the sounds of battle.

Caden grabbed for Mr. McDonald's hand. His fingers were slick with water and mud and it took all Caden's strength to keep from being swept into the river along with his teacher. Caden pulled, and Mr. McDonald's head popped above the water.

The current raged. It felt like Caden would be swept into it.

Mr. McDonald sucked in a breath. "Don't let go! Don't let go!"

The muscles in Caden's arms burned. "I won't!" he

said, but neither he nor Mr. McDonald were a match for the river's fury. Mr. McDonald's hand began to slip. A massive wave washed over him. After the wave passed, Caden's hand was empty. Mr. McDonald was nowhere in sight. The river had swept him away.

Someone grabbed on to Caden's coat.

From near the firewall, Brynne screamed, "Caden!" She sounded too far away to be the one holding his coat. If not Brynne, who was behind him?

Rath Dunn snarled into his ear. "You can't save anyone. Haven't you learned that yet," he said. "Not the scribe, not McDonald, not your family, not yourself." Then he shoved Caden off the bank.

Caden dunked into the cold, raging river. He felt a twig rush by his cheek and scrape him. Water pushed up his nose and into his mouth. Now it was he who struggled in the rapids, and there was no one to save him.

TO SWIM OR TO SINK

Caden battled to keep his head above water. The waves smacked against his face. He swam with all his might, but the current was too strong, and his muscles quivered as he fought the rapids. The current tugged him down. He couldn't breathe; he couldn't break the surface.

Strong hands gripped at Caden's shoulders. Suddenly, he was thrown out of the river and onto the bank. His coat was wet, his jeans were soaked, his boots were heavy and filled with water. Caden turned on his side and coughed and coughed and coughed.

When he finally looked up, he saw Jasan looming over him. His golden hair was backlit by Brynne's firewall, and strands blew in the strong wind. From the chest down, his hoodie and pants were wet, evidence of how far into the raging river he'd ventured.

The short sword with the ruby-encrusted hilt was stuck in the bank as if Jasan had thrust it into the earth. Brynne fell to her knees beside Caden. She was out of breath. "Are you okay?"

Caden tried to say he was fine. Mainly, though, he lay on the bank and gasped for breath. After a moment, he pushed to sit up, and Brynne put her arms around him to help.

With a boom of thunder, it started to rain—strange, salty-tasting drops that stung the scratch on Caden's cheek. Suddenly, Caden remembered. Rath Dunn and Ms. Jackson were still there—Rath Dunn near enough that he'd shoved Caden into the river, Ms. Jackson on the other side of the flames. He scanned the area.

The flame wall smoked and extinguished in the downpour. Ms. Jackson walked back and forth behind the fading fire, inspecting it as if impressed. Rath Dunn stood a few strides away. Jasan snatched up the ruby-encrusted sword—the one he should return to Caden—and blocked the red-suited tyrant from coming nearer to them. With his clothes sticking to his body and the sword grasped lightly in his left hand, Jasan looked tall and lean and dangerous. His stance was loose, his focus intense.

Rath Dunn stepped back. He looked hesitant. With a dramatic bow, he said, "Another day, then." A moment later, he and Ms. Jackson got into their vehicles—he his bloodred Audi, she a local organic produce truck—and drove away.

Caden didn't see Mr. McDonald anywhere.

A cold chill ran down Caden's spine, one unrelated to the cold autumn air against his wet skin. Deep in his being, he knew Mr. McDonald was lost to the river. Another life Caden had failed to save.

Sir Horace trotted to Caden's side. His warm breath flared from his nostrils and staved off the cold. He always understood when Caden was troubled. He nudged Caden's cheek and stomped the ground. Caden wrapped an arm around Sir Horace's neck and pulled himself to a standing position. "I'm all right, friend."

They took shelter under the small canopy by the public restrooms. Jasan stood with his eyes closed. He took slow breaths as if he needed to calm himself. Brynne and Caden stood beside him. Sir Horace leaned his head out of the rain.

Caden scratched Sir Horace's neck and peered at his brother. Certainly, Jasan was fast; he was gifted with speed and quick of mind and body. But Jasan hadn't been in sight when Caden was tossed into the river. How had he reached him so quickly? Was Jasan's gift that strong?

Sir Horace, ever faithful, crowded between Brynne and Caden. With a flip of his nose, Sir Horace pushed her away.

Brynne shoved Sir Horace back. "Watch it!" she said.

Caden snorted.

Jasan opened his eyes. His face was pale, and his wrist bled slightly at the paper clips. "This isn't time for laughter. The spell has started," he said. "And I told you to stay hidden." His angry gaze flashed to Brynne. "Both of you."

Brynne fought with Sir Horace for better shelter. "We did." Her voice weakened. "For a little while."

Jasan narrowed his eyes.

"We moved closer during the communication spell," Caden explained. "We needed to hear what was said." Though his coat was wet, it was drying quickly, and his cell phone remained dry in his enchanted coat's pocket. He pulled it out and played the audio for Jasan.

Jasan's face turned to stone.

"After that"—Caden smoothed Sir Horace's mane— "Ms. Jackson started the first part of the spell. We had to try to rescue Mr. McDonald. We had to stop them if we could."

"No, you didn't."

That was nonsense. Of course they did. "It was our duty. We had to try. I almost saved Mr. McDonald and thwarted them. And it was bad luck that Rath Dunn snuck around Brynne's flame wall at the river's edge. If he hadn't, I wouldn't have ended up in the water."

Brynne turned toward the smoldering remains of her firewall. She seemed disappointed that only embers were left. "I have to find a way to burn water," she said.

She needed to find a way to control her magic, not increase its power. Caden shot her a concerned look. When he turned back, Jasan was looking at Brynne with a similar expression.

Jasan stabbed the sword into the bathhouse and growled. That was not a respectful way to treat Caden's favorite sword. Caden forgot he needed to appease Jasan. "Don't mistreat my sword."

"It's my sword now."

"It's mine." And really. Didn't Caden need it more? "You should give it back to me." He turned to Brynne. She knew how badly Caden needed his sword. Teachers kept attacking him. Matter of point, he'd just been thrown in a river by one. "Tell him."

"We all need our weapons," Brynne said, which Caden found unhelpful.

This wasn't acceptable at all. It was Caden's sword, the one he'd been trying to get back since he'd arrived in Asheville. He glowered at Jasan. "Why did the police give it to you anyway? Only a parent or guardian can claim it." And since Caden was feeling a bit irritated and cold, he added, "Not a banished brother."

"Banished adult brother," Jasan mumbled, and reached out into the torrential rain. "Officer Levine returned it to me."

Sir Horace busied himself by sneezing into Brynne's hair.

Jasan pulled his hand back from the downpour. "I am your guardian here."

"No, Rosa is," Caden said. This much of Ashevillian law Caden understood.

"For now. But I'll be your permanent guardian soon. Manglor the Conqueror helped me with the tedious paperwork. Once it's done, you'll live with me."

No one had consulted Caden on this turn of events. Did Rosa want Caden to live with Jasan? It didn't sound like it, and she didn't act like it, but Caden caused her much trouble. Was this why Jasan and Rosa didn't get along? And who wouldn't want Caden's charming, royal self in their home? "What about Rosa?"

"She won't have a choice in the matter." For a brief moment, Jasan looked uncomfortable. Sir Horace seemed to sense it and leaned over to lick Jasan's face, but Jasan ducked away. "We're family. You're my obligation."

"Obligation? That's not a flattering description."

Brynne suddenly looped elbows with Caden and pulled him toward her. "What about me?" she said. "Where will I live? Caden and I have to stay together. We're partners."

"That is true," Caden said. "We've vowed to be allies until we get home."

Jasan almost looked amused at that, but the expression soon passed. "Brynne, you'll stay where you are; Caden, you'll move in with me." He scanned the sky and river. The downpour had turned to a drizzle, although the river continued to rage. "You *partners* should return before Rosa realizes you're gone. Sir Horace will get you home safely."

"Of course he will," Caden said. "Sir Horace is *my* horse."

Soon after, Caden and Brynne galloped east toward Rosa's house and the rising sun. It was the first day of the Ashevillian autumn—the equinox—and Rath Dunn moved against them. The four-part spell had begun.

OF PRINCES AND PEASANTS

"So, you almost drowned, huh?" Tito said as Caden summarized the morning's events.

"Almost," Caden said, and changed into dry clothing. The attic room's floor creaked as he moved about. No one needed to know how much seeing Mr. McDonald go under, then going under himself, had rattled Caden. He kept his voice confident. "It's not the first time I've fallen into a river." He'd fallen in quite a few Greater Realm waters, though none had raged quite like the French Broad had at dawn. "It happens."

"Not to normal people," Tito said. There was the glint of amusement in Tito's eyes. But then he frowned, and his face went lopsided. "Do you think Mr. McDonald washed up somewhere?"

Brynne said they had needed a sacrifice to complete

the spell. Rath Dunn had pushed Mr. McDonald into the river. And it was only after Caden had lost his grasp on Mr. McDonald's hand that the strange, salty rain had fallen.

Caden lowered his voice. "I doubt he survived."

"Oh," Tito said. They stayed silent for a moment. After all, Mr. McDonald had been a coward, but that didn't mean he had deserved to be tossed into an angry river. "You okay?"

Caden nodded. "Though I'd be better if I could actually save someone."

In the kitchen, Rosa was seated at the table. There was a sheet of paper in front of her. Officer Levine stood near the counter with a steaming cup of coffee. "Morning," he said when Caden and Tito walked into the room.

Brynne and Jane hadn't come down yet.

Rosa inhaled deeply. Her mouth was set in a firm line. Like Officer Levine, she had a steaming cup of coffee in front of her. She fiddled with the cup handle but didn't sip the coffee. "Tito," she said, "we need to speak to Caden alone for a minute."

Had she realized Caden had snuck away and almost drowned? No, if that were the case, she'd also want to speak to Brynne. He felt his brow furrow.

She tapped the paper. "The DNA tests came back yesterday."

Tito started to step toward the living room, but Caden reached out to stop him. "I've no secrets from Tito," Caden said. Rosa opened her mouth, likely to object. Before she could, Caden added, "I'd like him to stay."

Officer Levine and Rosa glanced at each other. Like they'd communicated with a telepathy spell, they seemed to come to an unspoken decision. "If that's what you want," Rosa said. She motioned him and Tito to sit.

"You and Jasan share twenty-five percent of your genetic markers," Officer Levine said. "That's consistent with siblings who share one parent, or with uncles and nephews."

It seemed the Ashevillian test didn't consider Caden and Jasan full brothers. "We have different mothers," Caden said. Though Caden knew more about his brothers' mother, the first queen, than he did the second queen. No one talked about Caden's mother. Caden looked first at Rosa, then at Officer Levine. Maybe the test uncovered something. "Does this DNA test know anything about my mother? What she looked like? Who she was?"

Officer Levine and Rosa were quiet for a moment. Then Officer Levine shook his head. "Sorry, son, we just tested to see if you and Jasan were related. That's all."

Caden didn't fully understand. "But it knows Jasan is my brother," he said. "It must know something."

Rosa reached across the table to take his hand. "I'm sorry, Caden. We don't know anything about your mother."

Caden felt the disappointment fall across his face. Rosa, Officer Levine, and their DNA test might not know about the second queen, but there was someone in Asheville who did. Jasan. The king had forbade anyone to speak about Caden's mother, but Jasan wasn't so set on their father's commands anymore. Jasan might tell him.

It wasn't like Caden cared that much anyway. He was only wondering about his mother because the police had used DNA to confirm his relationship to Jasan, and because Rosa kept, well, mothering him. He straightened his posture. This wasn't about the second queen, though; this was about where he would live. "Does this mean I'll be sent to live with Jasan?"

"I want you stay with us." Rosa squeezed his hand. "Your brother thinks you should stay with him. The law tries to keep families together when possible."

What did that mean? That wasn't a yes or a no.

Officer Levine seemed pensive. "Jasan knows more about where you come from than us." He held Caden's gaze. Officer Levine knew Caden was from another world; he knew Jasan was also. "It might be the best thing for you."

Rosa seemed skeptical. She moved her coffee cup toward her but didn't sip from it. "Whatever happens," Rosa said, "you're always welcome here. All my children are."

It sounded like she already thought Caden would be moving in with Jasan. "Do I have a choice in where I live?"

Neither Rosa nor Officer Levine answered. Caden wouldn't be cursed again until the middle of next week.

Despite the fact that he wasn't under the spell of compliance yet, it seemed his opinion on the matter bore little weight.

Tito hadn't said much. He slumped in his chair with his eyes on the table and his arms crossed. Caden was the one caught between Rosa and Jasan. It wasn't Tito who should be upset. Tito wasn't the one with a straw vote on where he was to live.

Officer Levine washed his cup in the sink. "I'll stop by later. I'm on patrol this morning." He pushed on the door to the living room, but there was a bump. And an *ow*. He opened it more slowly to find Brynne and Jane on the other side.

Jane looked contrite. Brynne gestured toward the cereal boxes on the counter. "We were coming down for breakfast," she said. Like many things Brynne said, it was true but incomplete. They likely had been coming down for breakfast; they had just been eavesdropping, too.

Officer Levine shook his head and stepped around them to get out. Caden heard the front door open and close a moment later.

Rosa stared Jane and Brynne down. "Privacy needs to be respected, ladies," she said.

Caden didn't mind that they'd listened. It would spare him the chore of answering questions later. "It's all right," he said, and inhaled deeply. Maybe he still had river water in his system, because he started coughing. When Rosa rubbed his back to soothe him, he wondered why his mother had never been there to do the same.

Like most days, they had to go to school. After Rosa dropped them off and pulled away, Brynne looped her elbow with Caden's. "I don't want you to go live with Prince Jasan," she said.

Jane fell into step beside them. The grass had begun to brown, and it was slick under her feet. "It must be difficult being caught between two people who want you."

Tito snorted. "Yeah, poor Caden," he said. "Rosa *and* his brother want him."

Jane rubbed at her eyes and turned to Tito. "Rosa wants you, too, Tito."

Tito kicked at a patch of grass. "Whatever, it's not like she's going to adopt me." The school bells chimed; the morning classes would soon start. Tito walked faster. "C'mon. I don't want to be late."

As they went inside, Caden matched his pace. "As always," Caden said, "you are welcome in my home whether I dwell with my brother, in the woods, or in the Greater Realm."

"Yeah," Tito said, and he sounded a bit sad. "Thanks, bro."

As Brynne and Jane walked behind them, Caden heard Brynne ask Jane, "Are your eyes all right?"

"Just itchy," Jane said.

* * *

Since Mr. McDonald typically supervised Caden's morning class, Caden didn't know what to expect as he entered. He collected his nerves.

Tonya and Ward were already seated. Any other morning, Mr. McDonald would have been sulking in the corner desk, his head behind a large book. Caden walked back to the corner. "Mr. McDonald is gone," he said.

Neither Tonya nor Ward seemed surprised. "We know," Tonya said.

They did? Caden turned back. "How?"

Ward peered at him. Sometimes it took Ward a moment to find his words. Finally, he said, "Your brother told my pa this morning."

"And Ward told me," Tonya said.

There had never been more than a few people in the room, but without Mr. McDonald, it felt emptier. "What happens to our class when our teacher is swept into an angry river?"

Tonya blinked at him from behind her glasses. "We get a substitute."

Just as she said that, the classroom doorknob turned. Ward sucked in a breath. Tonya watched in fear. The door creaked open, and cold air entered the room.

Someone was coming.

10

THE MAN IN THE GOLDEN VEST

large figure appeared in the doorway. The light back-lit his muscular frame. He ducked as he entered so as not to hit his head on the door frame. Caden's heart stopped. The man was big like Maden, Caden's second-born brother and Rath Dunn's ally. Was Maden here now? Was that part of the plan? Part of the spell? What would Caden do and say? What would Maden do to him?

When the man stepped into the room, however, Caden saw he wasn't Maden. He was Ward's father, Manglor the Conqueror, the school janitor. He was the only person Caden knew who was as large and commanding as his second-born brother.

Caden released a breath he hadn't realize he'd held. But whether he was relieved or disappointed, he didn't know. Had it been Maden, maybe Caden could convince him to stop whatever he was doing.

Manglor wasn't dressed in his janitor's uniform. Instead, he wore an ivory-colored suit that looked expensive next to his brown skin and a golden vest. His braids were pulled back. He wheeled in a case filled with books behind him. When Manglor closed the door, it looked like it took great care for him not to crush the knob. "I'm your new teacher."

"You are?" Caden said.

Manglor gazed at him for a long moment. "I am."

Although this was a good turn of events, Caden didn't understand. "Why would Rath Dunn agree to let you teach? You're enemies."

"I volunteered. I'm qualified and available," Manglor said. "Mr. Rathis had no grounds to object." He looked first at Caden, then at Ward, then at Tonya. "Know at least in this class, and in your brother's gym class, you will be safe."

When Caden first met Manglor, he'd known immediately he was from the Summerlands and that he was a banished villain. The school was full of villains. It wasn't that surprising.

Two things had surprised Caden, though. One, Manglor seemed repentant. Two, he claimed to be a liar. People from the Greater Realm didn't lie. Even those evil and treacherous like Rath Dunn told the truth. But Manglor had claimed he was different.

Caden looked up at him—in his suit and vest, he could pass for a well-dressed giant. "You've said you don't always speak the truth," he said.

As Ward was Manglor's son, he turned and glared at Caden.

Tonya said, "He's not a liar, Caden."

"He once told me he was."

"But if he was a liar," Tonya said, "that wouldn't be t-true."

Tonya made a confusing case. Caden felt his brow crease. "But if he told the truth to me, the truth is, he's a liar."

Manglor motioned for them to quiet. His gaze settled on Ward. "About your safety," he said, "I am sincere."

That, Caden did believe, and Jasan considered Manglor an ally, one loyal enough to inform of the morning's events.

Suddenly, the school intercom beeped. "Mr. Rathis," Mr. Creedly hissed, "has an announcement."

Caden and the others looked at the speaker.

Rath Dunn's voice came on a moment later. "Dear students and faculty," he said. "It's my solemn job to inform you of the loss of one of our teachers. Mr. McDonald is gone, dead, lost to the river. But don't let his death be in vain. Let us continue his work, our work." He rattled on in a dramatic fashion. "Let's get through this together. Those not with us will surely suffer alone."

Just as he finished, someone knocked on the classroom

door. Then Ms. Jackson glided around the room like a beautiful, aging wraith. "I've come to pay my condolences," she said.

"Noted," Manglor said. "Now leave."

Ms. Jackson didn't seem intimidated. She sashayed toward Mr. McDonald's corner. "I've also come to collect his personal items."

"That doesn't seem like your duty," Caden said.

"He has no one else. I do it as a last favor to my lost colleague," Ms. Jackson said. "Isn't it best that his belongings be useful to someone else? Hmm." She picked up one of Mr. McDonald's books. "Dead man's tome." She cackled. "Always a good find."

The way she said it, it sounded like a spell ingredient. Caden felt his face heat. He clenched his fist. Mr. McDonald wasn't a full day gone. Even a coward like him deserved some respect.

Manglor seemed to agree. "You should leave, witch."

Why was she here, anyway? It seemed unlikely it was only to get Mr. McDonald's book. She strolled back over and stopped in front of Manglor. "Careful, Summerlands Conqueror," she said. Her gaze shifted from Manglor to Ward. "Get involved and you'll risk losing something more precious to you than your life or your old kingdom."

One thing Caden would never do was threaten Manglor. Even more foolish was to threaten his son. And Manglor had already chosen to be involved. Everyone in the room knew it. He stared down at Ms. Jackson like he wanted to crush her.

Ms. Jackson backed away, but she seemed unafraid. She paused bedside Caden. With flared nostrils, she sniffed the air. "I smell magic on you."

When Rath Dunn had first suspected Caden was cursed, she'd sniffed Caden and said something similar. He held her gaze. "My coat is enchanted."

Ward and Tonya watched. Manglor glowered at Ms. Jackson and stepped toward them.

Quickly, she leaned down and whispered in his ear. "No," she said. "The scent is stronger at certain times of the month. Soon, I think, it will be at its most pungent."

Had she figured out the timing of Caden's curse? From how he smelled? Caden sniffed. Surely he smelled like nothing but royalty and the lilac bath soaps Rosa bought.

Manglor stood over them. "Leave the boy alone," he said. "Or deal with me."

She stepped toward the door. "Local lamb-and-turnip puree today for lunch," she said, and she glided out the door. After she'd disappeared from view, her shrill cackle echoed in the halls.

In his mind, Caden counted the days until he was cursed again. The last time was the week between summer session and regular school. That had been the very end of August. A little over three weeks had passed since. The next cycle would be Wednesday of next week.

Had Ms. Jackson figured out the timing of his curse? If so, would she tell Rath Dunn? Caden hoped not, but she and Rath Dunn were allies. Then again, if she didn't tell Rath Dunn, what would she do with the information? She blamed Caden for her siblings' deaths. It made sense that she would want revenge.

"What was that about?" Manglor asked.

Brynne, Tito, and Jane knew of Caden's curse. Ms. Primrose knew, too. Caden also had told Jasan. Beyond them, only Rath Dunn and Ms. Jackson suspected anything. Manglor didn't know, nor did Tonya or Ward; and Caden's forced compliance for three days of the moon cycle was one aspect of his life he didn't want to share.

"Nothing I wish to discuss," Caden said.

Caden learned more that morning in his literacy class than he had all last year. Manglor was a much better teacher than poor, dead, cowardly Mr. McDonald. Yet Mr. McDonald had been Caden's teacher for a while. Coward or not, Mr. McDonald had yelled for help, and Caden hadn't been able to save him. Caden hadn't been able to save Scribe Trevor either. A cold, empty feeling settled in his stomach.

He pushed those thoughts from his mind and wrote an entire English paragraph about Sir Horace jumping a gate. He was so impressed with it that for a fleeting moment, his worried stomach settled, and he showed the paragraph to Tonya.

"That's good," she said.

"It is," Caden agreed. "I'm going to take it and show Rosa."

Tonya smiled. Ward and Manglor seemed not to care. Caden explained. "It's rare I do something that makes her happy."

Maybe if Caden pleased Rosa more, he would be allowed to stay with her. Then again, Jasan was Caden's brother. Would it be better for everyone if Caden lived with his brother? His gut twisted again, and he cursed it. He shouldn't be worried about living arrangements when dark spells were amuck.

As he switched from his literacy class to physical education class, Caden replayed the events of the morning. Maden had mentioned that all would be completed on his side. He said to be ready at dusk in three days. What was happening in the Greater Realm? How did what was happening there and what was happening here connect?

Caden didn't know.

He felt a cold realization overtake him. There was someone at the school who could answer all his questions. The Elderdragon. She was one of the Elderkind. She knew all there was to know about spells and magic. Her knowledge far outshined Brynne's, and Brynne's magic sense was impressive. Last time he'd spoken to Ms. Primrose, however, she'd threatened him. But she would know. He was certain.

Caden hurried to the gymnasium. He needed to talk to Jasan before class started. A few strides before the entrance, he came face-to-face with Mr. Bellows, the sallow-skinned English teacher. He was the necromancer who'd stood on Rath Dunn's right during the assembly.

"Caden," Mr. Bellows said. "Too bad about McDonald. I heard you were there."

Mr. McDonald had also stood beside Rath Dunn at the assembly. Now he was drowned. Caden raised a brow. "You should be cautious," Caden said, "lest you be sacrificed next."

Mrs. Belle, the science teacher, rushed by them on her way to class. "See you soon, Caden," she said, and smiled. Of all Caden's teachers, she was the nicest to him. Caden suspected that she and Mr. Creedly were allied against Rath Dunn.

After she'd hurried past, Mr. Bellows turned in her direction. "I'm not too worried. There's plenty of useless prattle to feed that fire."

Most of Caden's eighth-grade class was already in the gymnasium and lined up. He saw Olivia and Tamera. Derek, Tyrone, and Jake stood in the back. Brynne was in the front. He didn't see Tito or Jane.

Jasan stood under the basketball hoop. A portable

whiteboard with intricate and precise drawings of exercises was positioned beside him. Since he was teaching with drawings, Brynne's magic had worn off. His English was limited to what he'd learned.

One of the girls, Kali, raised her hand. Jasan pointed at her.

She read the whiteboard with a troubled expression. "Mr. Prince, is that what we're doing today?"

Jasan seemed to understand. "Yes." The resulting groans and disheartened pleas from the class seemed to please him.

Caden wasn't sure why his classmates didn't like Jasan's lessons. They were challenging even for Caden and always provided a thorough workout fit for an Elite Paladin-in-training. He didn't want to miss it, but needed to speak to Ms. Primrose. And as a teacher, Jasan could send him to her office.

"Hey." Tito walked up beside him. Jane wasn't with him.

"Where's Jane?" Caden said.

"Rosa had to come get her. Something's wrong with her eyes."

Suddenly, a basketball zoomed between them. It hit the door frame—*thunk*—and fell to the wooden floor with a sad hiss. Tito glanced at the ball, then Caden, then across the gym to Jasan.

"Jasan doesn't like it when people don't fall in line,"

Caden said. "He makes no exceptions for friends or brothers."

"Yeah," Tito said. "I got that. Let's join everyone."

"I have to talk to Jasan," Caden said. He took a deep breath. "I need him to send me to Ms. Primrose."

Tito shook his head. "Why? She hates you now, remember?"

"We had a disagreement." Caden regarded Tito carefully. "She can help. And of all of us, I'm best at dealing with her."

"I'm not sure that's still the case," Tito said. "She seems really mad at you, bro."

Another basketball. This one grazed Caden's cheek. *Thunk*. It plopped to the floor and flattened. "He's going to hit us with the next basketball," Caden said.

While Tito got in line, Caden went to Jasan, who regarded Caden coolly. "Join the others," Jasan said.

Caden stood firm. "I want to talk to Ms. Primrose. She could help us stop them. It's to her benefit." He squared his shoulders. "I can convince her."

Jasan considered him. "I don't think she cares, Caden."

How could she not? "She does. This is her school. Her treasure."

"It's Rath Dunn's school." Jasan pushed his hand though his hair. "Once taken, some things can never be returned the same."

Was Jasan still talking about Ms. Primrose, or was he

talking about himself and how his reputation and birthright had been tarnished? Caden concentrated. "But they can be returned."

Jasan pushed the whiteboard to the front of the gym.

Caden kept talking. "She will know how to stop the spell. We just have to convince her to tell us. And she won't eat me because of our pact." He spoke quickly. Jasan always responded better to words spoken fast. "This is something I can do. She's an Elderdragon. Her help might make the difference."

If Jasan had known about Caden and Tito's encounter with her, he'd never have agreed. But only Caden and Tito knew of that. Jasan peered at him. "You'll be careful?"

"I will."

Jasan grabbed a pink notepad and scribbled something on it. "Don't make our situation worse," he said quietly. Then louder and in thickly accented English, he added, "Report to . . . the . . ." Jasan seemed to have to think hard to bring out the words. "Vice principal's office." He signaled to Brynne, who had left the line to gather the basketballs Jasan had thrown. "You. Also."

Brynne twisted her mouth into a pretty frown. "Me? Why?" She dropped the balls and rested her hands on her hips. Truly, she looked hurt. "I've never gotten sent to the office before."

Jasan either didn't care or didn't understand. He gave her the pink note and switched to Royal Razzon. "After you speak with Ms. Primrose," he said, "return here immediately." He looked at Brynne and added in a lower voice, "Don't do anything foolish."

"We will act with courage and intelligence."

"And not be foolish like you were this morning," Jasan said.

11

THE DRAGON TONGUE

As Caden and Brynne walked down the hall, she turned on him. "Why did you want to visit Ms. Primrose's office?" It was cold enough that he saw her breath fog as she spoke. Her silvery eyes sparkled in the strange blue light. "She ate your scribe. I thought you decided you and she were enemies."

That was all true, but with Caden's curse set to recur once again, he'd begun to wonder if Ms. Primrose was also a victim. "Rath Dunn forced her to eat Scribe Trevor. Had she been in control, she might have chosen differently." Besides, was it fair for Caden to judge her for acting like an Elderdragon when she was one? "We can't expect thunder cattle not to charge."

Brynne stared at him, mouth agape. "She's not one of your pets, Caden. She's not Sir Horace."

"Sir Horace isn't a pet." But that wasn't the point. This wasn't about noble Sir Horace; this was about dragony Ms. Primrose. "We can't expect her to act human. She's not. But she'll know about the spell. She probably even knows how to stop it. We just have to convince her to help us."

"How?" Brynne said.

Caden crossed his arms. "By speaking to her like she's a dragon, not an old lady."

"Do you know how to do that?"

Caden shifted. "I hope so."

"I hope so, too, prince." Then her silvery eyes twinkled. "You know what occurs to me?" She didn't give Caden time to answer. Instead, she started pulling items out of her sleeve: a piece of red candy, her magical hairpin/lock pick, a woolen Springlands concentration square, a pearl button, and a smooth purple quartz stone. "Dragons like treasures." Everything but the button and the stone she magicked away somehow. "I think we should bribe her, prince. With something shiny."

Ms. Primrose's new office was a small room near the east side of the school. Unlike the principal's office, there was no window. If there had been, it would no doubt have been covered in ice. The room was as cold as a Winterlands night.

The walls were blue, and it was probably the only room left in the school that hadn't been painted red. The wooden desk was small. Half the room was filled with tall, neat stacks of boxes. They towered like the downtown skyline of Asheville at twilight.

Ms. Primrose stood beside her desk. Her arms were crossed. "Why are you here, dears?" Her tone was frosty. "You belong in class."

Brynne was wide-eyed and shivering. She held out their note. "From Prince Jasan." She opened her palm and held out the stone. "And from me." She fidgeted. "I thought you might like it."

Ms. Primrose took the note first. She let it hang from her fingers as if it were goblin snot. "It says you're here to propose an alliance." Ms. Primrose flapped the note in the air. "What have you done for me that I'd want an alliance? This is no reason to come and bother me."

Brynne bit at her lower lip. "I didn't want to come bother you," she said.

Caden turned to Brynne and glared. Then he returned his attention to Ms. Primrose. If there was one thing Caden had learned from his and Tito's earlier encounter, it was to remain sincere and flattering when speaking. He cleared his throat. "You are smart beyond measure." Instead of seeming pleased, her expression turned from frost to ice. Caden plodded on. "We request your advice, ma'am. We wish to help the school, and the city. We wish to help you." For a moment, he thought he saw a crack in her icy expression. He continued. "But first, we need to stop the villains."

The moment passed.

Caden continued. "Rath Dunn and the others have begun the spell that will rip the city apart. We believe the second part is to be cast on Monday. We need to know how to stop them. And we need to contact our families in the Greater Realm to warn them. It seems dark deeds are happening there also."

Ms. Primrose narrowed her strange pale eyes and took the stone from Brynne. She sniffed it. With a gnarled hand and nails like claws, she crushed it into a fine powder. "The time when you could gain my favor with flattering words and pretty stones has passed."

Her stare looked like it could have turned them to grave dust. Her skin looked like it was made of blue scales; her eyes turned reptilian. She smacked her lips.

"The more I eat, the more I grow accustomed to this . . . portly . . . figure." It seemed she was still angry about that. "And the more I must feed."

And she looked plumper still. Caden hadn't seen any banishment lightning lately. But, now that he thought about it, the teachers' lunch table seemed to have fewer members. Was Rath Dunn feeding her teachers? If he found reason to fire them from their jobs, he could do so.

Blue scales seemed to cover Ms. Primrose's face. The silver one he'd seen near her ear was now as blue as the rest.

"With a pathway to your world open, there would be many I could devour. Those without contracts, agreements. Those not protected by ancient order and local birth."

"The spell would likely destroy the school and the city," Caden said.

"The locals gave my school to Mr. Rathis. They stole it from me. Why should I help those who steal my treasures?"

Caden couldn't stay quiet. "Rath Dunn stole it."

"They allowed it." She stepped closer. "You allowed it." Her gaze strayed from Caden to Brynne and back again like they were the finest of Autumnlands harvest dinners. "If the city falls, I could feast. I've been good for so long. I've had enough with moderation."

Brynne's eyes were saucers. Shakily, she produced the button. She offered it to Ms. Primrose as she had the stone before it. "Maybe you'd prefer a button," Brynne said in a small voice. "It would match your dress."

It did seem smarter to talk about Ms. Primrose's collections and not all the people she believed she'd get to eat if the barrier between worlds fell.

Brynne kept her arm outstretched.

Ms. Primrose didn't take the button. She huffed and gestured to the side of the room. Some of the scales on her arm were still silver. "What use is a button to me? My collections are in boxes." She spat out the next word. *"Boxes."*

If he wished to charm her, wished to use his gift of speech, he needed to consider what was important to her as a dragon. A question tickled Caden's tongue. It felt strange, but it felt right. He spoke as respectfully as he could. "Why not display them somewhere like before?"

She huffed and puffed. "I'm not crass enough to go put them hither and yonder. They belong in my stolen office, the one with a window that lets in sunlight and moonlight."

Caden understood. This school was no longer hers. She was in a strange place and forced to do others' will. "They belong in your home," he said.

Ms. Primrose arched a thin brow. "In my lair."

"Of course."

When she was angry and when she'd eaten Trevor, she'd seemed Blue Dragon. But other times she seemed like the Silver Elderdragon—less vicious, an educator, a collector of things small and shiny. Occasional silver scales still shimmered among the blue. Caden felt more and more certain she was both Blue and Silver Elderdragon, and he suspected the Silver part of her was the part that loved her treasures most.

"Your beads and baubles should be seen." He shifted his gaze to the pearly button. "Your buttons, too."

More scales flashed silver. "And my rocks." She glanced down at the powder from the crushed stone and seemed regretful. Then she waved, and the powder fluttered away. "But they're not. My office taken, my school overrun, and I'm stuck in this windowless closet." She glowered at Caden. "I blame the city. I blame you."

How could he respond without angering her? He couldn't. But he realized that maybe her anger could be contained. What she needed was someone to be blunt.

Blunt but polite and sincere. He raised his chin. "You should blame yourself, too," he said.

"Pardon me?" She spoke in the same tone she'd used before she'd threatened to eat him limb by limb. But then Caden had been trying to anger her. Now he attempted to connect with her.

Ms. Primrose needed someone to share her burden. "That is to say, we all share fault. And we should work together to fix our problems."

The room was so quiet for a moment, Caden heard a locker open and close in the hall. Brynne seemed to be holding her breath. Caden waited.

Ms. Primrose said nothing for far too long. Finally, she spoke. "What problem of mine can you two fix? My problems have only increased since I admitted you here." Then something like curiosity flooded into her cold anger. "But I suppose it is in your nature to talk, and in mine to listen to you. So speak, but I suggest you speak well."

Brynne's idea was to bribe Ms. Primrose. What if Caden used his gift of speech to offer her something she wanted? To bribe her? Then the offer would only be more tempting. He needed to offer something she wanted, though.

Caden gestured to the boxed trinkets. "I offer you a space where you can display your treasures. A place where you can appreciate and polish them. That is the first problem we'll fix."

"I don't impose on other's lairs," Ms. Primrose said.

"That's not within my nature."

"Of course you don't," Caden said. "Your manners are impeccable." A little flattery never hurt. But best he think of something fast. "It will be no imposition."

Ms. Primrose cocked her head. "You're offering me a shelf somewhere?" Truth be told, she didn't sound impressed. "I don't need a shelf."

Maybe Caden had miscalculated.

Ms. Primrose set her hand on top of one stack of boxes. "A shelf is far too small, dear."

Then Caden had an idea. He knew of a place he could offer. And if she accepted, it would help him in many ways. "Jasan's town house," Caden said. "The lighting is good. The evening sun shines in. The moonlight, too."

And Ms. Primrose couldn't devour Jasan. She was pactfully prevented. Not only that, if Caden needed to charm her, if Brynne needed to bribe her, if they needed to ask her for help, they'd be able to find her beyond school hours. They could try to gain her favor when she was surrounded by her treasures and not as close to Rath Dunn's power as principal. Also, Jasan wouldn't trust Caden to live with the dragon, and he'd let Caden stay with Rosa and his friends.

This might be one of Caden's most brilliant ideas. He bowed to the Elderdragon. "On behalf of the Razzonian royal family, I offer you use of his house as your own. My brother's home is your home. It's a gift. It will belong to you as much as him. You and your treasures are invited."

Ms. Primrose ran her hand across the boxes. "I do miss seeing them gleam," she said, and raised a brow. "But that's not how you invite a dragon to share your home." The air became heavy. There was pressure against his temple. Brynne latched on to Caden as if she needed his support to stay standing.

Caden had felt this type of power before. Ms. Primrose was about to speak in a language of power, in a forgotten tongue. Agreements made in that could not be broken. It was such an agreement that kept Ms. Primrose from eating Caden and Jasan.

Her next words were lyrical and terrible. "Say it so I know you mean it."

Brynne set her head on his shoulder, and he could feel the grimace on her face. She started to shake. The forgotten tongue affected most people like that. Not Caden, though. His gift of speech offered him some protection. The words hurt, but he could stand them. He could even speak them.

"Our home is your home," he said, the words sharp like bee stings in his mouth. "I invite you to share the town house."

"For how long?" Ms. Primrose said, and the words felt like a dagger to his eye.

"For as long as you desire," Caden said.

After another agonizing moment, Ms. Primrose said, "I accept." The words were powerful. The pressure in the room became almost unbearable as the agreement was completed. Then the air felt normal again.

Brynne remained hunched against Caden. He rubbed his temple and returned to English. "That seemed a bit extreme for an invitation," he said.

The forgotten language always pleased Ms. Primrose. The room was less chilly. Her eyes seemed almost human again. The room less blue. "Did it?" Ms. Primrose said.

Caden suspected she simply liked talking in the head-splitting languages. "Somewhat." Or was she testing his gift? It seemed to amuse her enough. There was something more he needed to say. He forced his most apologetic smile. "Also, please forgive me for my behavior in the hall," he said. "I was out of sorts that day." He took a deep breath. "So, in the spirit of our new pact, will you tell me how to stop Rath Dunn's spell? Please."

She walked behind her desk and sat down. "A four-part spell that requires four ingredients and four sacrifices. You stop it by stopping it."

"I see," Caden said.

"No more questions from you today," she said.

And although he wanted to ask more, he kept his mouth closed.

It took Brynne a moment longer to recover from the effects of the forgotten tongue. Once she did, she lifted her head and blinked at Caden slowly. He could almost see her mind putting together what had happened.

Brynne glanced at Ms. Primrose. He guessed Brynne

also noticed the change in her appearance. When Brynne took a deep breath, he was certain. He was also certain she was about to do something brazen.

Before Caden could stop Brynne, she said, "How does Rath Dunn's spell connect to the Greater Realm?"

Caden expected Ms. Primrose to shush Brynne as well. Instead, Ms. Primrose cocked her head. "Is that what you really want to know?"

What did it matter *how* the spell connected to the Greater Realm? They just needed to know how to *stop* it. Brynne didn't change her answer, however. "Yes, that's what I want to know."

Ms. Primrose peered at her. Whatever Silver attributes had appeared seemed to be fading again. "I'll tell you what, dear. If you give me the button, I'll answer one question. After all, you also came to bargain with me. I'll either tell you how the spell is connected or I'll tell you how to break dear Caden's curse. The choice is yours."

12
THE SORCERESS'S CHOICE

What? Caden was taken aback. Ms. Primrose would tell them how to break his curse? Caden's life might depend on that information. Rath Dunn knew about his curse. He and Ms. Jackson worked together to figure out the timing. This was the best thing that had happened in months, and offered in exchange for a trinket.

Brynne appeared equally shocked. She opened her mouth, but instead of immediately choosing "how to break Caden's curse," she closed it and seemed to hesitate. "Are they equivalent?" she said.

"No," Ms. Primrose said.

So Ms. Primrose admitted one answer was worth more than the other. Although, Caden realized, she hadn't said which she deemed more valuable. The more valuable information was how to break his curse, right? Knowing details about the spell didn't matter, only stopping it. Suddenly, though, he wasn't so sure. Maybe that was why Brynne had hesitated? She wondered the same thing.

Brynne shook her head like she didn't know what she'd been thinking. "It doesn't matter. Of course I want to know how to break—"

Although impolite, Caden interrupted. He turned to Ms. Primrose. "May Brynne and I confer first?"

Ms. Primrose's not-horrible mood seemed to be fleeting and fading fast. She spoke to Brynne. "Brynne, you have ten seconds to decide or I retract the offer."

Caden and Brynne huddled together.

"What are you doing?" Brynne snapped.

"Why did you hesitate?"

"Nine seconds," Ms. Primrose said.

"It's weird she'd ask me to choose between those. I've been asking her how to break your curse for months," Brynne said. "Why would she make an offer like that?"

"I don't know," Caden said. "Because you asked about the spell?"

Brynne frowned. "Perhaps."

"Six seconds," Ms. Primrose said.

"It doesn't matter," Brynne said. "It's my fault you're cursed. You're my ally. I'll choose you, Caden. The villains are going to figure it out. And next Wednesday you'll again be cursed."

But Brynne was being tested. Ms. Primrose liked to

do that to people. Brynne had sensed breaking Caden's curse wasn't the best choice, but she was going to choose it anyway.

"No," Caden said. "You're right. It is strange."

"Three seconds," Ms. Primrose said.

Brynne looked torn.

Caden's curse would recur on Wednesday of next week. A mere five days away. That was his problem to suffer. It was Brynne's problem to fix. Protecting the innocent, protecting the Greater Realm, that was their responsibility. If Ms. Primrose offered information on the spell and how it connected to their homeland, that was what Brynne had to choose.

Caden held Brynne's gaze. "I know you will break my curse with or without help. Don't let guilt guide you. It's a test. Choose whichever you think you should to pass. You are good at passing tests."

"I suppose I am," Brynne said.

"One second," Ms. Primrose said.

Brynne reached out and squeezed Caden's hand. Then she turned to Ms. Primrose. "Tell me how the spell Ms. Jackson casts connects the realms."

Ms. Primrose peered at her. "If that is your choice, so be it," she said, but Caden couldn't tell if she thought the choice a good one. Then her tone became more instructive, more like a teacher. "The ritual cast here must find the ritual cast there. Two spells to join to one. Two four-part spells for one goal."

"Oh," Brynne said after a moment. "Could you be more specific?"

The room was growing colder again. Ms. Primrose narrowed her eyes. "No."

Brynne looked from Ms. Primrose to Caden. He could see Brynne itched with more questions. They needed details. How exactly did the spell in this realm connect to the one in the Greater Realm? Were sacrifices needed there as well? But they'd asked all they should for today. Truth be told, they'd likely asked one thing too many.

"We should return to class now," he said.

"Bless your hearts," Ms. Primrose said, "you'd better."

They scurried from the small room into the empty hall. Brynne had been pale after the Forgotten Language of Power, but rosiness returned to her cheeks. She seemed pensive as they walked back to the gymnasium.

"You needn't feel bad," Caden said.

"What makes you think I feel bad?" Brynne said.

At the least, she felt conflicted. Caden felt conflicted. "It was the right decision. I'm certain."

"I agree, prince," she said. "But I don't know how what she said will help."

"We will figure it out."

Brynne arched a brow. "You mean *I* will."

"And if *we* keep pleasing her, she might help us more."

Brynne smiled at him. "I think you're right."

"I often am," Caden said.

"Sometimes," Brynne said. "Now you must tell Prince Jasan you gave away his house."

"I didn't give away his house," Caden said. "I offered that he share it. That's different."

They walked a length farther. Then Brynne turned to him, her face bright even in the blue light. "I don't think Prince Jasan will want you at his town house if she is there. He might deem it unsafe, and you won't have to go live with him."

Caden had also considered that. "I am also clever," he said.

Brynne rolled her eyes. "And ever so modest? I assume you think that as well."

When they returned to the gymnasium, the students were assembled in three lines of seven and practiced hand-to-hand formation four. They worked far enough apart so they wouldn't injure each other with untrained strikes and kicks. Tito was front middle. Derek was in the back. Jasan stalked through the ranks correcting form. His brow was furrowed, his mouth a tight line.

When Jasan noticed Caden and Brynne, some of the tension eased from his face. So, he'd been concerned. That seemed unlike his brother, and Caden felt strangely guilty about plotting to stay at Rosa's house. Truly, this day was one of mixed emotions.

Jasan grunted at them to join the ranks. Brynne found a space near Tito. Caden, however, waited under the basketball hoop. He wanted to share what he and Brynne had learned. Also, it was best he let Jasan know his house was now not only his.

The students showed various levels of skill. Tyrone, Derek's friend, spun and ducked. His side kick was slow, but his form was nice. Olivia, the girl with freckles and red hair, was bent over, exhausted. Brynne, of course, did great as soon as she joined. That was no real surprise. While she might not be a trained Elite Paladin, she was trained to fight. Tito also showed skill.

As for Derek, he completed a forward strike, but it was so slow and poorly formed, it looked like he was waving. As Caden was always polite, he waved back.

When Derek noticed, his cheeks glowed red like a fire-stone.

Jasan shot Caden a glower as he fixed Derek's strike. He instructed Tito in a more advanced technique. Brynne, he ignored, which made her scrunch up her face. Then Jasan walked up to Caden. "Report," he said in Royal Razzon, "then join the line with the others."

Quickly, Caden explained about Ms. Primrose and the house. "Are you impressed?"

Jasan seemed as surly as ever. "You gave her my house?"

Caden wouldn't give away his brother's things. "No, I told her you'd share it with her."

"Why?" Jasan said, and frowned.

"To regain her favor," Caden said.

"And what favor of hers did you gain?"

Appeasing a fickle Elderdragon like Ms. Primrose was not an immediate process. "It takes patience to charm a dragon," he said. "And it's not like she didn't tell us anything useful. We know now there is a similar spell being cast in the Greater Realm. We know each spell requires the other."

"It would have been better if you asked how to contact home," Jasan said.

Jasan was never satisfied. Caden crossed his arms. "We were each allowed only one question. That will be my first question next time."

With a huff, Jasan ran his fingers through his hair. "It doesn't sound as if you were cautious."

"You're the one who needs to be cautious," Caden said. "You now share a house with a dragon."

Jasan didn't seemed amused.

13

THE GREEN BINDER

When Rosa picked them up from school, Jane was in Caden's front passenger seat. Dark glasses covered her eyes. "Jane gets the front today," Rosa said. "In the back, Caden."

Jane shrugged as if she were sorry, but when Rosa wasn't looking, she stuck her tongue out. Tito and Brynne were already seated and buckled in the back. Caden motioned for Tito to move over.

"Nah, bro," Tito said. "Last one in gets the middle."

"I don't want the middle."

Rosa turned back from the driver's seat. "Caden." His name sounded like a warning.

"Look, prince," Brynne said, and waved to the middle. "Your throne awaits."

Tito flattened himself back as if to make room for Caden

to pass. "It's a place of honor," he said. "You can tell from the special little seat belt."

Caden squashed Tito's foot as he climbed over him, and Tito responded by pushing him toward the foot well. Fast as a Summerlands firefox, Caden grabbed Tito's arms. If Caden was to be on the floor, so should Tito. They struggled, and Tito's seat belt pulled taut.

"Boys!" Rosa scowled back at them. "Enough."

Truly, Tito didn't like to annoy Rosa. Immediately, he let go, and Caden fell, his back against the gritty floor mats.

Caden wasn't as worried. Truth be told, he was a bit annoyed with Rosa. She'd given Jane his seat; she said she wanted Caden to live with her yet still planned to send him to Jasan's. Although, since Caden had invited Ms. Primrose to use Jasan's house as her lair, he doubted that change in living arrangements would happen.

Caden wondered if he could make Rosa angrier. It would be good practice for his gift of speech. There were times when it was useful to make someone mad, and Rosa was a good person to practice on because her anger came from a place of caring. Besides, it was her fault he was on the gritty floor mats. "If I were seated in the front," he said, "there would be no struggle."

Rosa's cheek twitched.

Brynne nudged Caden's ear with her boot. "Rosa, would you like me to kick him in the head?"

Best Caden get his royal head away from Brynne's foot. He scrambled up.

"No one is to kick anyone in the head ever," Rosa said. And she definitely sounded angrier than before. "Do you understand?"

"Yes," Brynne said, though she sounded more disappointed than contrite. Caden glared at her as he squeezed into the middle seat. Then he buckled his special little seat belt.

In front, he saw Rosa take a deep breath. She looked over at Jane and placed her fingers under Jane's chin. "Eyes any better?"

"They're still dry and itchy," Jane said.

Rosa furrowed her brow. "Any worse?"

"Maybe a little."

In Jane speak, that meant a lot.

Rosa stared at Jane a little longer. Then she looked roadward and turned the key. The engine revved and vibrated with power. As Rosa pulled the pickup onto the road, Tito leaned across the seat. When he finally spoke, he gestured to Jane and whispered, "In the freaky first part of the spell you saw this morning, they used one of the ingredients, right?"

Brynne blinked and her face seemed to blossom with understanding.

Caden shivered with cold realization. Each of the four spell ingredients had been stolen from someone of unique status—Rath Dunn had gathered Jane's tears (tear of elf), Brynne's hair (magical locks), Jasan's blood (blood of son), and Ms. Primrose's perfume (essence of dragon).

"Tear of elf," Caden said. "The green vial."

"Jane's tears, right? Could that be what's wrong with her eyes?"

The ingredient used that morning was tears of elf, the ingredient stolen from Jane. Now her eyes were dry. Mr. McDonald was dead. Only part one of the spell was complete. What would happen when the other ingredients were used? Better they not find out.

By evening, Jane's eyes were redder and more irritated. She seemed in good enough spirits, but her sight was clearly affected. After dinner, Caden gathered with Brynne, Tito, and Jane in the girls' room.

The walls were painted sunny yellow. There was a large window. In the daytime, it overlooked the colorful mountainside, but night was arriving sooner now that summer had ended. The view out the window was only of shadows and sky.

Small metal objects were strewn about the floor and nightstand—tiny objects Jane had collected to enchant. On the bed, there was a large pile of Brynne's clothes. Caden itched to fold them.

Brynne sat on the floor and stretched like a cat. "Don't move that," she said.

"I'll put them in your hamper."

"I don't want them in the hamper."

"But that's where they belong." He held Brynne's gaze. She didn't blink, didn't falter, and Caden drew back his hand.

After a moment, Jane took in a deep breath and addressed them all. "So you think my eye problems are a side effect of the spell?"

Brynne reached up to twirl a strand of her short black hair. "Exchange is a principal of magic. I use my physical and mental energy to fuel my sorcery; I exchange it for the magic. Just like you use your life force to make your enchantments, and Ms. Jackson uses the life forces of others to power her ritual spells."

Tito looked concerned. "You think something similar is happening with Jane's tears?"

"When the four-part spell devoured the contents of the green vial, it's possible it affected Jane's eyes—also like an exchange." Brynne turned to Jane. "Your tears were sacrificed to magic so you can't make new ones. It could be coincidence, but it seems unlikely since the morning your tears are used, your eyes dry out and your vision blurs."

Obviously, Brynne was troubled. First for Jane, who seemed to have lost her tears. Second for herself. Brynne's hair, her "magical locks," was also a spell ingredient. If Jane was no longer able to make tears, what did that mean for Brynne's hair?

Brynne prized her hair. She'd been upset when it was cut short and was thrilled as it started to grow back. If her hair was to stop growing, she'd be devastated. And as Caden was the one who had cut her long hair short, he might feel her fury. She'd placed the compliance curse on him when she was mildly annoyed. Who knew what she'd do if her hair stopped growing altogether?

Jane squinted toward Brynne. "If we stop the spell, will my eyes get better?"

Brynne took a long time to answer her. "I don't know. I hope so."

"Then we'll have to stop it," Tito said. He held up his binder and a large sheet of paper. "It's a map of the city."

"I see," Caden said.

"We can plot location facts about the four-part spell," Brynne said. "Mr. McDonald had maps that helped Rath Dunn and Ms. Jackson. We should have the same."

As a future Elite Paladin, Caden had studied the local terrain and the layout of the city. It was important to know the lands in which he traveled. The red mark was in a low area near a stream of blue. "This is beside the river? By the park?"

"Yeah," Tito said.

Caden traced a gray line that crossed the blue. "This is the bridge?"

"Yeah," Tito said.

Brynne hopped off the floor and considered the map.

"It's where the first part of the spell was cast."

Jane seemed grateful to have something to discuss other than her failing eyes. She traced her finger over the red mark, tapped the sheet. "And there are three more locations."

"And three more ingredients," Brynne said.

"And three more sacrifices to prevent," Caden said.

"According to Maden, the next part of the spell will be cast in three days at dusk. That's Monday."

Knowing which day and what time the next part of the spell was only part of what they needed to know. If they wanted to stop it, they also needed to know where it would be cast.

Brynne must have been thinking similar thoughts. "We need to figure out where," she said.

"You're the sorceress," Caden said. "Shouldn't you be able to figure that out?"

"I don't do that kind of magic, Caden," Brynne said, but she peered at the map. "It will be cast in the city limits, though. The first part was, and the magic that binds and banishes the villains seems connected to Asheville proper. A spell to break down barriers would be, too. The first part of the spell happened at dawn, the second part will happen at dusk. The second location will be different from the first, too." She grabbed a marker. "We can likely exclude the area around the river. The park was on the western side of town so maybe somewhere east, north, or south next?"

"Great," Tito said. "That just leaves everywhere else."

Brynne began to get huffy. "At least I'm trying."

"I feel like it will be toward the north of town," Jane said, and placed her palm over the map. "That area feels funny."

Tito frowned, and his face went crooked. "You got any facts to back that up?"

Even if Jane was correct about the north part of town, which was a big "if," that wasn't specific enough. They needed the exact location. Then they could stop the spell. Caden could save someone. "We don't have enough information," he said.

Something more bothered him: about Mr. McDonald, the river, the sacrifice. Something didn't make sense. "Why would Rath Dunn sacrifice an ally, even one as cowardly as Mr. McDonald? It seems like Mr. McDonald mapped out locations for the spell. Why kill him when he could sacrifice anyone?" Caden said. "The city is full of potential victims who aren't nearly as useful."

The others were quiet. Caden looked to the window, to the dark. In the distance, he thought he saw something zoom through the air. When he blinked, it was gone. Perhaps his eyes were deceiving him. Shadows often seemed to dance on the small mountains.

"Well," Tito said, and Caden turned back to him. "According to the employee contract, the teachers have to respect the local laws while in the city. That's why when they kidnapped Jane they kept her outside the city limits. They found the loophole."

"The park is in the city limits, and killing people is against the law," Jane said.

"If Rath Dunn were so bound," Caden said, "he shouldn't have been able to kill anyone in the city limits, Mr. McDonald included. He shouldn't have been able to push me in the river."

"Maybe he's changed his contract?" Jane said.

"I read that thing," Tito said. "No way he could do that. And I think murder is pretty much covered as not okay for the teachers."

Brynne wrinkled her brow. "He's not a teacher now," she said. "He's acting principal. We haven't seen the principal's contract. We don't even know if he has one."

"Even if he is so allowed, why kill an ally?" Caden said.

Tito opened his mouth as if to speak. Then he closed it. Then he opened it again like a blabbering word fish. "Ms. Primrose is bound by the rules, too, right? Now and when she was principal?"

If she wasn't, Caden was certain Rath Dunn would have long ago been her breakfast. Caden, Brynne, and Jasan would have been lunch, dinner, and dessert. "It seems so."

"She still ate people," Tito said. "No one survives that, right?"

A vision of Scribe Trevor's boots flashed in Caden's mind. Most definitely, he hadn't survived. "No one survives being eaten by an Elderdragon," Caden said, a bit shakily.

Tito nodded to himself. "She's eaten banished villains who she didn't pick to teach or who didn't fulfill their contracts. And she also threatened to eat you a bunch of times before you made that pact with her," he said. "You all have one thing in common."

"Jasan, Scribe Trevor, Brynne, and I have nothing in common with the rightfully banished."

Brynne, however, seemed to brighten up the way she did when an epiphany hit her or she stole something expensive. "That's not true, prince," she said. "We're all from the Greater Realm. That's what we have in common. We don't belong here."

"So," Tito said. "Maybe as long as Rath Dunn is principal, he can kill people from your world? It's in the wording. The contract said employment could be terminated. Maybe that includes the person along with their job. Maybe it supersedes the local law in the contract."

What had Ms. Primrose told Caden about him and Brynne soon after they'd been enrolled? "Ms. Primrose said Brynne and I were in her youth program. She said she'd free us when we graduated. If we behaved."

"Yeah," Tito said. "I'm guessing the principal can terminate you, too." He wrapped his knuckles on the green binder. "You know, if your grades are bad, or if you have an attitude problem, or whatever."

"So he has to sacrifice a teacher," Caden said. "Or me or Brynne."

"Yeah," Tito said. "And you're the one with the bad grades and attitude."

"I don't have an attitude," Caden said.

Brynne sniffed as if he'd said something funny.

So Rath Dunn needed to sacrifice Brynne, Caden, or one of his teachers; and he seemed as likely to sacrifice an ally as an enemy. Could Caden trust some of the teachers to help them? Not all of them were on Rath Dunn's side.

Since this morning, Rath Dunn's words kept ringing in Caden's ears: *"You can't save anyone."* The taunt made him feel sick. Worse than that, helpless.

That was what Rath Dunn wanted, wasn't it? That was why he kept saying things like that to Caden—to discourage him, to kill his morale. Words had power. Caden was gifted in speech; he understood that. He wouldn't let Rath Dunn's taunts keep him from fighting.

"We need to do more than observe the teachers. We need to question them," Caden said.

"The spell's set for Monday at dusk," Brynne said.

Caden walked over to the window. "Then we'll question them Monday morning at school."

Brynne, Tito, and Jane began to discuss the merits of his idea while he looked out. The mountain made a darker outline against the dark sky. Mountains, even small Ashevillian ones, made him feel more at ease when his mind was full of difficult thoughts.

Whoosh. Whoosh!

Something zoomed past the window. What was it? Caden fell into a defensive stance. It was no trick of the eye. He kept his sights on the window. Something had been there. He was certain. "There is something outside."

14

THE UNIDENTIFIED FLYING OBJECT

"It's called a mountain," Tito said.

Perhaps Caden preferred it when his foster brother's attention was captured by numbers or studies. Caden pressed his face to the glass. "No, there is something flying out there."

"A bird?" Tito said. "Or—"

Before he could finish, the thing charged the window. It knocked it with a loud *whap*. The thing banged the window again. Suddenly, Tito, Jane, and Brynne took the outdoor threat more seriously. They gathered closer.

"It's going to break the window," Tito said.

That, Caden could prevent. He unlatched the lock, slid the window open. Among the four of them, they could defeat whatever monster attacked. Caden jumped back into a defensive stance. Brynne did as well. Tito curled his hand into a fist. Jane grabbed scissors from the desk and held them like a dagger.

The creature sped inside. It didn't attack, though. It landed at Caden's feet, and he saw it wasn't a monster after all.

"It is a bird," Tito said. "Ha. I was right, bro."

Yes, Tito had been right. It was a bird. A small falcon of some kind. Its feathers were tawny and white. Its eyes golden and sharp. Something silver glinted around the bird's right wing as it hopped toward Caden.

Caden bent down to get a better look, then gently reached out and pushed back the falcon's feathers. They were tinged with the slight pink of dried blood. A silver chain of paper clips was wrapped around the wing—familiar, magical-looking paper clips. Carefully, he touched one. It hummed with enchantment.

He pulled back his hand, stunned.

Jasan's right hand was attached to his body with a chain of magic paper clips. If Jasan removed the chain, his hand would fall off. It had been severed from his arm by the blood dagger. No wound made with the dagger would ever truly heal and would reopen in the dagger's presence. Without the paper clips, Jason would bleed to death.

But enchanted items were rare things. It was unlikely more than one chain of enchanted paper clips existed. Caden didn't know what to think. The silver paper clips shimmered. "Lady Jane," Caden said, "did you enchant more paper clips?"

"I don't do repeats," Jane said.

Caden reached into his pocket, pulled out his cell phone, and called Jasan. No one answered. His stomach dropped. Why was the chain of paper clips that kept Jasan's hand attached wrapped around the wing of this Ashevillian bird?

Jasan wouldn't remove the paper clips willingly. Even if someone overpowered Jasan and removed the paper clips, why would they wrap them around a bird's wing?

The bird hopped, then flew to Caden's forearm.

If Jasan were a bird, he likely would look a little like this one: powerful and fast, with gleaming feathers and golden eyes. Caden calmed some. Now that he thought about it, there was only one reasonable answer. "This bird is Jasan." Caden turned to Jane, Tito, and Brynne. "It's the most logical explanation."

Brynne nodded.

Tito, however, did not. "You think this bird is your brother?" Tito said. "How is that logical? I don't think you know what logical means."

"I know what all words mean," Caden said. The falcon jumped to his shoulder. "Are you Jasan?" Caden asked. The falcon bent its head down and found a feather to pick.

"If he was fully transformed, he might be confused," Brynne said.

Jane reached out to pet him. "He's a pretty falcon," she said.

Pretty was a description Caden's other brothers occasionally used to tease Jasan. He wouldn't consider it a compliment, even in bird form. *"Kak, Kak, Kak!"* Jasan squawked. He hopped closer to Caden's head and out of her reach.

"Um," Tito said. "I've seen a lot of weird stuff this last year, and your brother does keep those paper clips wound around his right wrist, so I can accept he's a bird. But, bro, why is your brother a bird? How does someone even turn into a bird?"

"It happens," Caden said.

"What happens?" Tito said.

"Many spells and curses can cause transformations or partial transformations," Brynne said. "It's not so unusual. Certain magical fogs turn people into frogs."

"The frog fog?" Tito said.

"Yes," Brynne said.

"Sure, okay," Tito said, and pointed at Jasan. "Is there a bird fog?"

Brynne scrunched up her face. "Not that I'm aware of."

Most transformations only lasted for a limited amount of time. Caden turned to Brynne. "How long will this last?"

"It's hard to say," Brynne said. "Not without knowing the power behind it: who cast it and why." Then she fidgeted and chewed on her bottom lip. "However, you did tell

Ms. Primrose she could share Prince Jasan's house. If she moved her treasures there tonight, perhaps she and Prince Jasan clashed."

Could it have been Ms. Primrose who transformed Jasan? Caden considered the falcon on his shoulder. "Why would she turn him into a bird?"

"Because she can't eat him due to your pact. Maybe he's less appetizing in bird form, and the pact is easier to follow," Tito said. "Or maybe she's punishing him for something else. She threatened she'd get creative."

Brynne glanced at Tito, then Caden. "When did she threaten that?"

"In an incident neither Tito nor I talk about," Caden said.

The cold wind blew in again. It ruffled Caden's hair and Jasan's feathers. Caden felt a frown pull at his lips. Jasan dug his talons into Caden's shoulder. Jasan was their strongest ally against Rath Dunn and the biggest threat to his villains. How could he fight if he was a bird? How could he follow Ms. Jackson when he had the body and mind of a bird?

Jane spoke in her calm and cool manner. "Maybe Ms. Primrose transformed him for Rath Dunn. When he's a falcon, he's not that much of a threat to Rath Dunn or his plot."

That seemed like a possibility. Did that mean Ms. Primrose was helping Rath Dunn? Wasn't she as angry with Rath Dunn as Caden? Then again, in the past when

Caden pleased her, she rewarded him. When Rath Dunn pleased her, she rewarded Rath Dunn. Caden thought she'd begun to forgive him, to consider helping him. Was the same true of his enemy? She'd said she was tired of moderation. Maybe all those extra people she'd eaten had begun to expand her appetite. Or maybe she'd had no choice.

That night, Caden hid Jasan in the attic bath-closet with a small tray of water to sip and the shower-stall floor to nest within. Jasan, of course, was unhappy. Being a bird didn't seem to change his temperament, and the bath-closet was nothing like the grand rooms and ornate pools of the Winter Castle bathrooms.

"*Kak!*" Jasan squawked.

Tito stared down at him. As did Caden. The small room was crowded this night. "He better not wake up Rosa," Tito said. "She isn't going to be happy about a bird in the shower."

"Better she find bird-Jasan than human-Jasan, though," Caden said.

"Huh. You might be right on that one, bro," Tito said, and yawned. His eyelids kept fluttering closed; his whole body looked slumped and tired. Tito had used much mental energy on his map and binder information. He needed to sleep.

"Go rest," Caden told him. "I'll keep watch over Jasan."

After Tito stumbled toward the bedroom, Jasan hopped

around the shower stall, stopping to sip water, then tapping his beak on the drain. Such was fate's folly that Caden's only relative in Asheville was currently a falcon. "Chadwin's dead, Maden's a traitor, and you're a bird," Caden said. "A noble-looking one, but still a bird."

"*Kak!*" Jasan said.

"If you're not quiet, Rosa will hear you." Talk of Rosa brought back thoughts of mothers. Caden sank down to the floor so he could rest against the wall. Jasan knew about the second queen. He was the only one Caden could ask, so Caden leaned toward him and said, "Since you are trapped in the stall, I have questions. Who was my mother? Why is it such a secret?"

Jasan squawked again, then pooped beside the drain.

Caden sat back, pulled down a green towel, and leaned it across his shoulders. He didn't want Jasan hopping and pooping on him in the middle of the night. Part of Caden liked talking to Jasan in bird form. It was like talking to Sir Horace. "You should tell me about the second queen."

If Sir Horace were crammed in the bathroom with Caden, he'd have snorted in certain agreement. As for Jasan, he twisted his bird head around and plucked at a loose feather. He didn't appear to be listening.

"I suppose I should ask you when you're human."

Truth be told, however, that was hard for Caden. His father and brothers, the servants and guards, had refused his questions so many times when he was younger, he felt uncomfortable asking. No one wanted to break the king's order of silence, including Caden, and he'd been reluctant to push it. Jasan, however, no longer cared about that kind of thing.

"Despite the king's wishes, I deserve to know."

Caden leaned his head against the sink. His head felt heavy, his limbs spent. He hadn't realized he'd fallen asleep until he was waking up. Immediately, he knew something was amiss. One, he wasn't in his bed. He was cramped in a corner of the tiny Ashevillian bath-closet. Two, he had a green towel as a blanket and a wall as a bed. Three, someone was yanking the towel off him with amazing speed.

That's right; he'd slept next to the sink. Jasan was a falcon. Suddenly, Caden was alert and awake. He looked up at the tall figure standing over him.

Jasan—his nonbird brother Jasan—scowled down as he tied the green towel around his waist. There were no sounds of movement in the house. All was quiet in the way of early morning, of when daylight was still a whisper on the horizon and most of the world was asleep. Caden let go a sigh of relief. His brother no longer had wings; he was back to his normal, surly self.

Caden spoke quietly and in Royal Razzon. "You were a falcon last night. Do you know who transformed you?" Caden said.

"Ms. Primrose."

Caden had suspected as much. "But why?"

"Maybe because she's a bad roommate," Jasan said pointedly. "She disintegrated my couch to make room for shelves. She put her beads atop the . . . the . . . *television.*" "Television" he said in English. There was no Razzonian word for it. Jasan frowned. "She won't give me control of the *television* either."

"I don't believe she'd transform you for that."

Jasan was quiet, and Caden knew there was more. "Don't try to understand a dragon's motives" was all Jasan said before he leaned over the sink, glowered into the mirror, and pulled a stray feather from his hair. "I think I ate a frog before I flew at that window."

Caden felt for the poor frog. Then it occurred to Caden that his brother remembered eating one. "Do you remember your time as a falcon? You didn't seem your human self to me."

Jasan turned on the faucet, cupped water with his hand, and gulped it down. He removed a second feather, one matted into his hair behind his ear, then said, "I wasn't my human self then. But if you're asking if I remember you prattling on about the second queen now that I am? Yes."

Caden felt strangely ashamed, like he always did when he asked about her, like it was his fault no one talked about her. But if there was ever a time and person who would tell him, the time was now and the person was Jasan. "Then tell me about her."

"No good comes from you knowing."

"No good comes from ignorance either. You no longer care about Father's orders, and I want to know. I'm part of her as much as I am part of him."

Jasan shoved away from the mirror. He pursed his lips and peered at Caden. He was considering it; he really was. What could Caden say to make him actually tell him? Something meaningful to Jasan. Something Jasan would understand. Which emotion, which words, would his brother respond to best? Jasan loved the first queen. That was where Caden could connect with him.

"You knew your mother," Caden said. Jasan also knew what it was like to have everyone against you; he'd been framed, after all. There was some similarity to the kingdom refusing to give Caden information. "Think what it would be like not to know her and to have others know but refuse to tell you about her." Most of all, Jasan was protective of Caden. "Someday someone will tell me. Better it be you than some villain or rival."

Jasan huffed and shook his head. Finally, he said, "I'll only tell you once."

This was it. Caden held his breath. He dared not breathe or speak lest Jasan change his mind, lest Rosa wake up and charge into the bathroom before Jasan was finished, lest anything interrupt this moment.

15

THE SECOND QUEEN

"You know Father doesn't like your gift of speech," Jasan said. "He tolerates you using it to translate and communicate, but he shuts down anything deeper than that."

That was true, and Caden had just used his gift on his brother. He'd actually been practicing his charms on others, too. How disappointed King Axel would be. Caden's cheeks heated in shame. "I know my gift isn't good like the rest of yours."

Jasan snorted like Caden was being ridiculous.

Why was Jasan bringing this up? Did he know Caden charmed him? "What does my gift have to do with the second queen? You said you'd tell me about my mother, not talk about my lesser gift."

"Stop complaining and listen," Jasan snapped. "It has

everything to do with the second queen." Jasan crossed his arms and sighed. "I don't know all the details, but I remember that the second queen was charming. Father was taken with her. Valon and Maden were taken with her. The whole kingdom adored her."

That was a surprise. "Did you adore her?"

"I was young. I had recently lost my own mother," Jasan said. "She comforted me." He glowered like he didn't want to admit it. "I trusted her. We all did."

Caden felt his brow crinkle. If his mother was so well liked, why was her memory shunned? Where had she gone? Why would no one talk about her?

"But that was our mistake. She was a silver-tongued imposter. Nothing she'd ever said about herself was true. Her loyalty did not lie with Razzon or with our family, only with herself. Father caught her in the royal treasury one day, and her lies began to fall apart. Part of the treasury was gone. Stolen. Not long after, she ran away and sought refuge in the Autumnlands. That's all I know. A few months later, you were brought to us via a messenger."

All that made it sound like the second queen could charm people. Like Caden supposedly could. "She was gifted in speech, too?"

"No, I think she was just naturally captivating," Jasan said. "Our gifts make our natural talents stronger—I would be fast, Lucian stealthy, Maden strong, and Valon a natural-born leader without them. But since we were gifted, our talents are exaggerated. When the royal gift bestower granted you with the gift of speech, all Father could see in it was her. No doubt you were gifted that because you had inherited some of her talent for language and manipulation."

Manipulation? Caden had always thought of it as charm. Manipulation sounded worse, sounded dishonorable and dishonest.

Jasan snorted. "Father was furious."

Caden felt his shoulders slump. "So this is why the king doesn't like my gift. It is the gift of charlatans."

"Speech is also the gift of diplomats and orators. All our gifts have their potential to lead us to a bad place. My temper is far too fast. Valon, gifted in leadership, is far too domineering. Lucian, gifted in stealth, is beyond secretive. And Maden is strong but power hungry. It turns out it was he the king should have worried about." Jasan laughed wryly. "Our gifts are what we make them."

"Father wouldn't want me making mine into anything."

"Father is sometimes wrong," Jasan said.

If there hadn't been feathers sticking out of Jasan's ear and eyebrow, and they hadn't been crammed between the shower and sink, Caden would have found his brother quite sage then.

When they walked into the attic bedroom, Tito stirred. He pushed off his purple quilt and rubbed his eyes. "Oh," Tito said. He sounded surprised. "You're human again, huh, Mr. Prince?"

Jasan's brow creased. He looked to Caden to translate, which Caden did. Then Caden added, "Jasan needs clothes. And you should show him the map and the binder."

Tito stared for a moment. "He was a bird. Got it. Now he needs clothes. Got that, too." But he seemed to get anxious. "Why don't you show him the binder? Then he really should go before Rosa finds him, okay?"

While Tito searched for clothes big enough to fit Jasan, Caden showed him the map.

"We need to know more," Jasan said in Royal Razzon.

Caden agreed. "I can question the teachers." The king might not approve of Caden's gift, but Jasan did. "I'll use my gift for our benefit. One of them will know. I'll convince them to tell me."

"That might work," Jasan said. "If you do it right. And you'd best be careful."

"I will," Caden said. He felt a large smile spread across his face.

Jasan sighed.

"Are you guys having a moment?" Tito said. He pulled out a pair of gray sweatpants with a split at the side seam from his clothes mound and handed them to Jasan. "You look like you might be having a moment."

Jasan took the sweatpants with a slight frown. Then he caught Tito's gaze. "Thank you, Sir Tito," he said in English.

Tito seemed unsure of how to deal with Jasan's intensity.

"Uh, yeah, no problem." He gestured to the door. "Caden, tell him he should leave now. Rosa will be awake soon."

But Jasan was already changed and at the attic window. Brisk mountain air blew inside. "I'll see you again on Monday. Until then, practice your sword techniques, go over the information on the spell. If you figure out anything more, call me immediately." With a nod good-bye, he jumped out and scaled down the house.

"You know," Tito said, "your brother is a bit of a show-off."

But Caden's mind felt too cluttered to tell Tito why he was wrong. So Caden's mother had also been good with words and languages, and she'd betrayed the king and Razzon. That was why the king didn't like Caden's gift. It reminded him of her treachery. Did that mean the second queen was really so bad, though? Just because she ran away?

And apparently took part of the royal treasure. Caden cringed.

"Hey," Tito said. "Are you listening to me?"

"Not really," Caden said.

Stealing didn't necessarily mean she was evil, though. Just a thief. Caden wouldn't judge his mother by his father's standards. The king had wrongly judged Jasan and Maden; maybe he'd wrongly judged her. Once the king made up his mind about something, he never changed it. Jasan said that sometimes their father was wrong. Maybe they were all wrong about the second queen or, at least, not completely right.

One day, Caden vowed, when he found his way home to the Greater Realm, he would find his mother. He would ask her why she'd done what she had. He would decide himself what type of person she was.

16

THE DEAL

No new information was gathered before Monday, Caden was only three days away from his curse, and the second part of the spell would happen at dusk. To find out where the next part of the spell would be, they'd need someone to tell them. The teacher Caden decided to approach was short, stout Mrs. Grady, the eighth-grade math teacher. She was a close ally of Rath Dunn, had been trusted with his classes when he'd become principal, and had kept giving Caden failing grades. He would see her in math class.

Midafternoon, Caden sat in her classroom and watched as she wrote problems on the whiteboard. She had to stretch to reach the top of it. Her biceps bulged as she moved the marker.

Tito sat in the desk to Caden's right. He diligently copied the notes with his blue pen. Jane sat to his left. She doodled a picture of the Great Walking Oak, the Elderkind who protected the Springlands. Brynne was in the back. She refused to sit near the front.

Caden leaned toward Jane. "She's Rath Dunn's ally," he whispered. She'd been one of the villains who had held Scribe Trevor in the principal's office. "Likely, she knows about the spell." Then he leaned toward Tito. "It is Mrs. Grady we must question."

When the bell rang to release them for lunch, most students rushed out. Caden lingered. He nodded for Tito and Jane to head toward the cafeteria. In the back, Brynne packed up her things one pen, one pencil at a time. She was slow on purpose; she stayed to be backup. With the exception of cursing Caden with compliance and possibly ruining his life, she was a good partner.

Mrs. Grady had her back turned. She swiped the eraser across the board and the numbers disappeared. For one so short, she seemed powerful and quick. Not quick like Jasan, but quick enough to be dangerous.

Caden cleared his throat. "Mrs. Grady?"

She spun around. Caden was a bit taller than she was, so she had to look up. "What do you want?"

He'd been in her class almost a month and they'd never spoken. Usually, he talked to everyone, but he'd had nothing to say to her. Like Rath Dunn, she'd laughed when Scribe Trevor died. Some of his anger resurfaced. How does someone laugh when someone else is eaten by a dragon? How could Caden charm someone who would do that?

No, "charm" wasn't the right word. That's why his gift didn't always work. He always tried to win over people when he spoke to them. To get what he wanted, he shouldn't try to charm her; he should try to manipulate her. How, though? He knew little about her. That, however, was a fact that he could remedy. The best way to learn about her was to talk to her.

"Rath Dunn won't hesitate to kill you," Caden said. "Why follow him?"

Her brow was heavy, her voice deep. "Go to lunch, prince."

Brynne got up and sauntered toward to door. "It sounds like she enjoys being his lackey, Caden," she said.

Mrs. Grady squeezed her hand into a thick fist. "I'm no one's lackey." She pointed at the door. "Get out, girlie."

Brynne cast her a glare that could scare a fear wraith, then stepped toward the hall. "I'll wait for you outside." After she left the room, he saw her shadow just beyond the doorway.

"You get out, too," Mrs. Grady said.

Caden wasn't ready to leave. "You've yet to answer my question. Why follow Rath Dunn?" he said. "Do you admire him? Serve him? Worship him?"

She snorted, obviously offended. "You really want to know why? He's the best gamble in town," she said. "Do you think your brother or the other teachers have a better chance of surviving this game? I don't. Let me give you some advice. Always align with the winner."

"The winner?" It sounded like all Mrs. Grady cared about was herself, not Rath Dunn's plot, not the school, not either realm. She just wanted to stay alive by whatever self-ish means possible. Caden crossed his arms. "Three days ago Rath Dunn sacrificed Mr. McDonald to the river. He has to sacrifice a teacher again tonight. You might be next. You're expendable."

"Your brother would be a better choice. Don't you think?"

"My brother is fast and smart and inconvenient. Rath Dunn might want him dead, but he wants the spell done as easily as possible. Nothing about Jasan is easy."

That seemed to give her pause. "What is it you want?"

Caden lowered his voice so no one else would hear. "I have a deal for you."

She full-out laughed at him. "What could you offer me?"

"A better gamble. A hedged bet." He took a deep breath and hoped he was reading her properly, that she cared about herself only and not about power or returning to the Greater Realm. "Tell me what I want to know, and, if Rath Dunn fails, if the school returns to Ms. Primrose and no barriers are broken, I'll convince Jasan and her to pardon you, to leave you be. I'm gifted in speech; I can do it. Then whoever wins the game, you survive. That's what you want, right? To survive."

Mrs. Grady looked up at him with interest now. "I've always enjoyed playing both sides."

"Rath Dunn deserves to get played." When he said it, Mrs. Grady's lips turned up in a tight grin. He could tell she liked the idea. Caden continued. "And if we fail to stop him, our deal will forever be buried. Never will I tell a soul." He considered. "Point of fact, I'll likely be dead."

"How do I know I can trust you if you don't die?"

Caden straightened his posture; he raised his chin. "I am a future Elite Paladin, a prince of Razzon. My word is my bond. I will not break it. Not now. Not ever."

She leaned back against the whiteboard and looked up at him. "All right," she said, and her voice dropped to a whisper. "You've got my attention. What is it you want to know?"

Caden met Brynne in the hall, and they hurried to the lunchroom. As they walked, he whispered, "Downtown, on a side street, away from most onlookers."

"Are you certain?"

Caden handed her a piece of paper. "That's the address. Rath Dunn is calling it a teachers' appreciation dinner."

Since the halls were empty, Caden pulled out his phone and called Jasan. His brother didn't answer. Caden tramped down his worry and left a message. Certainly, Jasan would be impressed that he'd found out the location of the spell.

They passed by the science room just as Mrs. Belle, the science teacher, came out. Her shirt was wrinkled but clean; her long hair was set in a messy bun. Her nails, as usual, shone like elvish rubies. There wasn't a chip or dull spot on them. She was one of the teachers against Rath Dunn.

Although a villain, although undependable, Caden felt safe with her, and she was nice to him in class. "Hello, Mrs. Belle," Caden said.

Mrs. Belle smiled. "Good afternoon, Caden," she said, and locked her door. "Brynne."

Brynne nodded at her coolly. "Mrs. Belle." She'd never warmed to Mrs. Belle. Caden suspected it was because Mrs. Belle had given her a B on her first quiz. No matter. Spellcasters were known for magic, not manners.

Caden, however, liked Mrs. Belle. Suddenly, he knew he had to warn her. She was a potential sacrifice. He checked to make sure no other students were in hearing range and spoke carefully. "Stay away from downtown tonight."

Mrs. Belle's smile became forced. "There's a dinner tonight. I'm expected to attend."

"Rath Dunn is going to sacrifice someone tonight."

"Are you sure?"

Brynne shrugged. "If you don't believe us, feel free to go and find out."

Caden shot her a glare. "Avoid it if you can. Or wait until after dusk to arrive. Rath Dunn needs to sacrifice someone who works at the school." The fewer possible sacrifices, the better. "Warn as many others as you can, especially those you think aren't allied with Rath Dunn, but tell no one we told you."

"I stay indoors after dark anyway," she said. "I don't like to be out so close to nightfall."

Brynne eyed her suspiciously. "Why not?"

"Ladies must have their secrets," Mrs. Belle said. She turned back to Caden. "I'll stay away. No one will know you warned me. You can trust me."

Caden's third-born brother, Lucian, was gifted in stealth. He scouted and spied more than any of Caden's other brothers. Once, he'd told Caden never to trust those who offered it easily. Caden frowned. "I don't trust you," he said, "but I don't want you hurt."

"And I don't want you hurt." Mrs. Belle reached into her pocket and pulled out a sheet of her dead-looking yellow smiley face stickers. "Rath Dunn will never know you warned me. *He* has no right to rule over Ms. Primrose. *She* is something greater."

"Why would you say that?" Caden said.

"This school shouldn't be run by a mere human," Mrs. Belle said. Then she raised her red-painted nails to her mouth like she'd said too much. "Oh my, never mind that. Here. For you, for helping me." She gave Caden a sticker, then laughed too loud and too fast as she walked toward the cafeteria. It was a strange, inhuman sound.

Caden stared at the sticker. It wasn't much of a gift.

"Why didn't I get one?" Brynne said, so Caden stuck it

on her back on their way to the lunchroom.

As they entered the cafeteria, Caden asked, "Why don't you like Mrs. Belle?"

"I just don't," Brynne said.

Caden grinned at her. "Perhaps you are jealous because she likes me more than you?"

"If you must know, she's creepy," Brynne said. "And not everyone likes you."

"Most people do," Caden said. "You know, sorceress, a girl left notes of affection in my locker last year," Caden said. He felt his cheeks heat. Why was he saying this now?

Brynne pretended not to care. "Is that so?"

"It is so. Tito told her I liked someone else."

"Why should I care?"

That wasn't a statement that she didn't care. "I suspect you might, that's all," Caden said.

Brynne fidgeted. She looked down. When she looked back up, she also wore a challenging smile. With Brynne, even an awkward conversation could turn into a competition. "I've had notes in my locker. I've had boys tell me they like me before."

If Caden made her feel more uncomfortable than himself, it would be like winning. "I understand that," he said. "Because sometimes you're likable."

"Am I, prince?"

"Sometimes," Caden said as they sat down at the middle table. "Not often, though."

Jane placed a tray of braided rolls, roasted squash, and

chicken on the table. She would throw it away at the end of lunch, untouched. Such was part of her war with Ms. Jackson. She glanced at Brynne and Caden and seemed thoughtful.

Tito plopped a similar tray beside her. He would eat his food. "What are you two doing?" he said as he sat down.

Caden straightened his posture and ignored the flush he felt reddening his cheeks. "Waiting for you," he said.

"Sure," Tito said.

Caden cleared his throat. "We need to get downtown tonight. Officer Levine is an honorable and noble sort," Caden said. "I'll ask for his help."

"And," Tito said, "as soon as he finds out there is a freaky spell that involves human sacrifice, he'll lock us all in Rosa's attic. Bro, what are you thinking? It's great he believes you, but that means he's not going to want you near any of the villains."

"I think Tito's right, Caden," Jane said. "He thinks we're children."

"Then how will we get downtown?" Brynne said.

"Easy," Tito said. "We'll take the bus."

"Or," Caden said, "we could take Sir Horace."

"Your horse is great and all," Tito said. "But he's going to stand out downtown during rush hour. Let's take the bus this time. Trust me."

Caden wanted to ride Sir Horace. However, "I do trust you."

Brynne laughed, but it sounded a bit hollow. She twirled a strand of her short hair around a fingertip as if willing her hair to grow longer. The fate of her magical locks was also at stake. She saw Caden had noticed and let go. "Tonight, then," she said. "Let us stop a spell."

"And a witch," Jane said, and rubbed her eyes.

This camaraderie Caden could get behind. He grinned and set his fist on the table. "And a tyrant."

17

DOWNTOWN AT DUSK

After school, Caden sat on Rosa's porch. He listened to the metal sculptures go *clink, clink* in the autumn breeze and tried to call Jasan. Again, Jasan didn't answer. He tried calling Ward, too, as Jasan lived in the town house next door to Ward and his parents, Manglor and Desirae.

"Haven't seen him," Ward said. "Pa's not been home all afternoon either."

"Call me when either returns."

Both Jasan and Manglor were missing. Had his message gotten to Jasan? Did he know where the spell was going to be cast? If he'd been able to follow Ms. Jackson, maybe he and Manglor planned to stop her before tonight. With Jasan not answering his phone, however, Caden worried.

Jane stood by the railing. The wind blew her hair away

from her ears. She tried to pat it back down but soon gave up. "Rosa's starting dinner," Jane said. "If we're going to go, we should go soon."

Brynne sat down. "First we need a plan."

Tito plopped down beside him. "What Brynne said."

Clouds of three shades of dark gray hung low near the mountain, and while the day was still bright, it wouldn't be for long. "Then let's make one. And let's go."

Feigning they were going to run the mountain, Caden and the others instead ran through the woods to a mapped-out bus stop. There Jane paid for passage. They rumbled into the downtown just before sunset.

The clouds turned a spectacular orange. The rectangular buildings cast long autumn shadows down the alleyway. The cafés were full of people eating vegan food under umbrellas and awnings. A group of old men played guitars and sang bluegrass songs near the craft store. Everything looked and sounded like evening, all looked and sounded like it should.

"Sir Horace would've been much faster," Caden said as they hurried away from the bus.

"We know, bro," Tito said. "Faster, better smelling, and more comfortable. We heard you the first five times."

"Next time he comes with us," Caden said, and scanned the road. He saw no sign of Rath Dunn or Ms. Jackson. Nor did he see Jasan, Manglor, or any of the teachers. "Where are they?"

Tito fiddled with a map on his phone. "Down the block and left on the side street."

When they got to the end of the block, they stopped and moved more slowly, more furtively. Caden spied many of the teachers down the side street. They lounged at sidewalk tables. Red umbrellas shaded them from the fading rays of daylight. Only a few people were missing from the group: Mrs. Belle, who was supposed to have warned the others not to come; Jasan, who was supposed to be stopping the spell; and Manglor, who was allied with Jasan.

"Do you see anyone?" Jane squinted toward the villain assembly. "All I see is a red blur."

"Those are umbrellas," Brynne said, and worry creased her brow. "Your eyes seem worse, Lady Jane."

"All the more reason to stop this spell and make the villains pay," Jane said.

Stout Mrs. Grady hovered near the edge of the group. As did the large school nurse; the sixth-grade gifted teacher, Mr. Limon, with the strange brow; and the lanky sixth-grade English teacher, Mr. Frye. They seemed ready to escape if things went bad. Mr. Wist, the banshee, had his mouth open. He looked as if he was sucking in the winds. Mr. Bellows fidgeted at a table near the front. There was a large, heavy-looking bag at his feet. Ms. Levers, the wraith, sat near the back with Mr. Faunt, who scraped his razor-sharp nails on the wood, the same nails that had helped hold Scribe Trevor in place the last day of summer session.

Ms. Jackson and Rath Dunn stood off to the side seeming much in control of the others.

On the street in front of the café, cars puttered by, many with their headlights shining. Where was Jasan? Manglor? They should be here stopping the spell. They weren't here, however. But Caden, Brynne, Tito, and Jane were here, so they would have to be the ones to stop it.

"We need to be quick and efficient," Caden said. "Otherwise, someone will die at dusk."

Quickly, they formed a plan. While Caden and Brynne distracted the teachers, Jane and Tito would steal Ms. Jackson's vial. No vial, no spell ingredient. No spell ingredient, no spell. And Jane and Tito were locals. Rath Dunn couldn't sacrifice either of them. That didn't mean they couldn't get hurt, though.

"Sir Tito, Lady Jane." Caden made sure his voice was firm, his manner commanding. "Be careful."

"We will," Jane said.

"Yeah, you and Brynne be careful, too, your bossiness," Tito said.

Jane and Tito went to loop back around the block. They would approach from the opposite direction. Brynne and Caden walked down the street. It was time to confuse a tyrant, a witch, and a pack of villainous teachers.

Ms. Jackson noticed Caden and Brynne first. She pointed up the street and said something to Rath Dunn, who chuckled and waved. Caden, ever polite, waved back.

The winds had started to pick up, and an orange oak leaf soared past Caden's cheek.

A blue car passed them on the small street. Its lights were too bright. Bright lights, as Tito called them. As it rolled by, the headlights illuminated symbols on the road, on the buildings, on the sidewalk. The bricks were aglow with runes. The asphalt looked like a long gray scroll painted in magical ink. Caden felt as if they had walked into a book, and an evil book at that.

Then the car turned and the symbols disappeared.

"Did you see that?" Caden said.

"Ritual magic runes," Brynne said angrily. "Everywhere. I've had enough. It's time."

She reached out her hand. There was no better distraction than magic, and she was set to use her telekinesis spell. Oh, how Caden hoped she didn't topple one of the rune-covered buildings. Suddenly, there was a buzz of sorcery in the air. It felt like electricity and heat. Then Brynne pushed forward with her palms, and all that energy surged toward the teachers and tables.

The tables flew up and clattered into the café windows. One went tumbling down the road. The red umbrellas hit the ground. Mr. Faunt toppled out of his chair. Mr. Bellows grabbed for his heavy-looking bag. The banshee opened his mouth as if to scream. Mrs. Grady slinked away from the others. Rath Dunn stumbled but stayed on his feet. As for Ms. Jackson, she remained standing.

In some ways, magic was like other fighting disciplines. Some people could defend against it better than others, and practice improved anyone's defense. It was no surprise the witch was least affected. Caden took some satisfaction that Rath Dunn had at least stumbled.

As Rath Dunn returned to his feet, he caught Caden's gaze and called, "Come here, boy! Now. Bring the little sorceress with you."

Orders. He was still testing Caden. Caden wasn't bound by them yet, but he took a step forward. Hopefully, Rath Dunn would be confused. "Distract them more," Caden said. "Send something else flying."

"I've got a better idea," Brynne said with a bright grin. "I'm going to light something on fire."

Brynne's control of pyrokinesis, of fire magic, wasn't so great. Her firewall had been more contained than the time she lit a mountain ablaze, but only a little bit. Caden snapped his attention to her. "Telekinesis was the plan," he said. "There are too many people here for fire magic—"

But Brynne already waved her hands, and they glowed with power. Her brow was wet with sweat; her concentration seemed intense. The last standing umbrella burst into flame. An impressive, controlled burn. Rath Dunn stepped back, raising a hand to shield himself from the heat. Ms. Jackson cocked her head as if considering the fire. Mr. Faunt stood and pointed. The others gawked.

"I practice magic as much as you do swordplay," she

said. "Give me some credit, prince."

Behind the spectacle, Caden saw Tito and Jane creep up behind Ms. Jackson. All they had to do was find the vial and grab it. She'd had the previous green one on her. Likely, the same would be true of this one. Still, Jane and Tito needed to hurry. The burning umbrella would only distract for so long.

Tito, however, seemed distracted. Something caught his attention under the table to his right. He whispered something to Jane and scooted in that direction. She crept closer to Ms. Jackson. What were they doing? The plan was to stay together, grab the vial, and run.

Whatever Tito and Jane were doing, Brynne and Caden had to keep the villains' attention, and Brynne couldn't risk another spell with Tito and Jane in the midst of the spell area. Magic was only one form of distraction. Words were another.

"Let's get closer," Caden said. He ran down the street, Brynne running fast behind him. Time to warn the villains; time to cause dissent in the ranks. "He's going to sacrifice one of you! As he did Mr. McDonald!"

The villains chuckled and pointed, seemingly amused by Brynne's magic after the shock of it had worn off. Didn't they understand that Rath Dunn couldn't be trusted?

Caden tried again. "Run!" He put all the urgency he felt into his words. "Run away!"

His words seemed to make several of them nervous—

Mr. Limon rubbed his brow, Mr. Frye shifted in his seat, the nurse clenched her giant fist—but only Mrs. Grady slunk away. Then Ms. Jackson reached into her pocket and pulled out a vial. The liquid inside was black and sparkling like a night with a thousand stars. She smiled and held it up.

Jane was near enough to touch her, to grab the vial. Firefox fast, using fighting form seven, Jane knocked Ms. Jackson back and snatched it. Ms. Jackson's expression darkened as she stepped Jane's way. Jane needed to make haste and get away.

But where was Tito? Caden scanned the area. Then he saw him. Tito pulled a large cage from under the table. What was Tito doing? Before Caden could figure that out, Rath Dunn turned toward Tito. As did Mr. Faunt.

One of Caden's friends was too near a witch, one too near a tyrant and a banshee. "Run," Caden yelled again, this time to Jane and Tito. "Run now!"

They bolted. Jane made it away, but Mr. Faunt lurched from where he stood and used his long, sharp nails to latch onto the cage Tito had nabbed. The two of them tugged it back and forth. Why was Tito fighting Mr. Faunt over a cage?

Neither Ms. Jackson nor Rath Dunn ran after Jane. "Why aren't they chasing Jane?" Caden said.

Brynne stood beside him. Then she inhaled sharply. "Because she's got another vial, Caden." Her words got faster. "Of course they'd have more than one. With the amount they stole of each ingredient, we should have known there would be backup vials." She clenched her fist. "I'll stop her," she said, and sprinted into the fray.

Caden chased after her.

They were out of time. Ms. Jackson raised the new vial—it was just as dark and sparkling as the first—and started to speak. "Wind roar, sky break, let these magical locks continue the spell, and link not only water but air as well."

Magical locks. The spell ingredient that had been taken from Brynne.

The colorful clouds darkened. The light dimmed. The wind whipped past Caden's face and roared past his body, taking leaves and napkins and trash with it. People on the sidewalk shouted. Mr. Faunt let loose the cage, and Tito fell backward and downhill. The cage rolled with him and the door popped open. The sounds of traffic stopped.

The wind began to rage just as the river had three days prior.

18

THE BELLOWING WIND

The burning umbrella came loose from a table. It zoomed past Caden, tumbling up into the angry sky like a fiery spear. The debris that funneled up with it caught fire. Mr. Faunt used his long nails to latch onto the brick wall. The nurse and sixth-grade teachers ran out of sight. Ms. Levers, the wraith, did the same.

Mr. Wist was unaffected by the winds. Certain proof he was a banshee. He turned down the street and walked toward the cage. Whatever was inside, zoomed up and flew straight at Mr. Wist's face.

Jane ran to Tito and grabbed his hand. She pulled him toward the cover of the alleyway. Tito started to yell. His voice barely registered over the winds. "The cage! The cage!" The wind had turned Tito insane. Then Tito said, "Bird! Jasan!"

Then Caden knew what and who had been in the cage. Jasan—the bird version. Mr. Wist seized Jasan by his talons. With his prize obtained, Mr. Wist turned and flung Jasan at Rath Dunn. Was Jasan the sacrifice after all? He was in bird form, but in truth he was a human. Would he satisfy the spell? Caden wouldn't wait to find out.

A metal trash can banged down the street. Caden jumped to miss it. He skidded to a stop on the sidewalk next to Brynne. Rath Dunn braced against the winds and his red coat whipped behind him. Mr. Bellows stood to the right of him. Ms. Jackson to the left.

A nearby yellow awning ripped from its overhang.

As Rath Dunn caught Jasan, he said, "Watch, son of Axel, as Prince Jasan, once champion of Razzon, fulfills my purposes and—"

Before he could finish, bird-Jasan clamped his powerful beak down on Rath Dunn's hand.

Rath Dunn flung his arm left and right and knocked Jasan away. Caden darted for his brother. He reached up and pulled Jasan toward his chest. Jasan struggled in Caden's grip.

Rath Dunn jumped back. His sweater was ripped, his hand bleeding. He gestured to Mr. Bellows. "Take care of those students," he shouted. "Of course, if you can't save them, you can always reanimate their bodies."

Ms. Jackson turned as if to leave. Mr. Wist was already walking away.

Mr. Bellows surveyed Caden and Brynne with grim excitement. He held on to the side of a flipped table to keep from being blown back. "I don't know which of you I want to reanimate first."

Brynne raised her hands as if to fling Mr. Bellows against the building. But she stopped suddenly. She shifted her gaze upward and gaped.

Jasan sensed Mr. Bellows was a threat. He wriggled from Caden's hold and charged through the winds. Mr. Bellows dived for his heavy bag. Before he could grab it, though, Jasan screeched and dived at his hand.

Caden darted for the bag, beating Mr. Bellows to it. The zipper was opened. Inside, Caden saw bones. Those of some poor, hapless creatures Mr. Bellows planned to reanimate and use. With all his might, Caden swung the heavy bag into the street.

Not only leaves and napkins, but larger things flew. Branches. A tabletop. It had gotten so dark, he could see only partway across the street. The winds caught the bag and carried it out of sight.

"Caden." Brynne pointed up. "We need to go! All of us!"

Caden gaze turned skyward. A wind funnel hovered directly above them.

Mr. Bellows noticed it, too. He scrambled backward, falling onto the sidewalk, but as he stood, the winds started to lift him. Jasan, too, couldn't fight the winds. His wings were no match, and he began to rise toward the sky.

"Any of us will satisfy the spell!" Brynne yelled from behind Caden.

Suddenly, Caden felt weightless. He twisted toward Brynne. She wound her left arm around a nearby streetlight. With the right, she grabbed for him. Caden reached back. She gripped his hand tighter than he thought possible.

Caden felt the spell pull him toward the sky. Only Brynne's grip tethered him to the ground. He turned back. Mr. Bellows clawed against the cement. He wouldn't be able to hold on, though. If Caden stretched he could reach him. Not that Mr. Bellows was someone Caden wanted to save, but if Mr. Bellows fell prey to the spell, the sacrifice would be satisfied. The second part of the spell would be complete.

With a blackened, dead-looking hand, Mr. Bellows dived for Caden's hand. But in bird form, Jasan must have taken it as an attack. He darted over Caden and Brynne, toward Mr. Bellows, beak open, a mighty squawk on the wind.

"Jasan!" Caden yelled.

If Caden let go of Brynne's hand, he'd be sucked into the sky. If Caden didn't grab Mr. Bellows and Jasan, so would they. But Caden only had one free hand. He could only save one. There wasn't a choice. Of course he reached for his brother.

Caden seized Jasan by the talons. The whirlwind pulled them, and they tilted toward the sky. Mr. Bellows flew upward but grasped onto the rippling fabric of a partially torn awning. One of his shoes flew off, up, and into the spiraling winds.

Brynne gripped Caden's hand tightly. "Don't let go! Don't let go!"

Caden's hands hurt—his right where Brynne held it, his left where he held Jasan's sharp claws. But he would never let go.

The streetlight Brynne hugged flipped on, which meant it was getting darker. It bathed them in yellow light. If they could all hang on long enough—he, Brynne, Jasan—and if Mr. Bellows could keep hold of the yellow awning—dusk would pass. Part two would end without a sacrifice and be incomplete. The winds increased. Caden was midair, caught between Brynne and Jasan. Jasan started to slip from Caden's fingers.

Rip. The yellow fabric Mr. Bellows grasped tore from the building. Mr. Bellows sped upward into the sky, a trail of ripped yellow fabric zooming behind him, and disappeared into darkness.

Like an extinguished candle, the winds stopped. *Whap.* Caden fell face-first onto the sidewalk. Jasan fluttered out of his hand and flew down beside him. Brynne kept hold of Caden's hand.

Items were strewn around them: A large branch to

Caden's left, a dented Ashevillian trash can to his right. On the street, cars were overturned. High above, it sounded as if the winds still raged. Jasan pecked lightly at Caden's cheek.

Debris also fell from the sky. Caden grabbed a broken leaf. It was cold and covered in blue ice, but one side was melted and burned. It was a blizzard oak leaf from the great forests of the Winterlands. Caden stared at it. It was rare for the blizzard oaks to burn. And there were no blizzard oaks in Asheville.

Caden was still staring at it when something crashed down an arm's length from him and stuck in the sidewalk. It was charred and ash covered. When Caden reached out, heat emanated from the item, and he pulled back his hand. There was something about the shape that was familiar.

Caden pulled his hand from Brynne's and pushed up to his knees. She still had her arm wound around the streetlamp and seemed content to keep it there. After a moment, she cleared her throat. "Are you all right, prince?"

Caden also had to catch his breath. "As well as can be," he said, and pointed to the item. "What is that?"

"Carnage?" Brynne said.

Caden handed her the blizzard oak leaf. It was rapidly melting. Soon it would be little more than blue water. Brynne blinked at it, and her brow creased. "This is from the Greater Realm."

Jasan hopped and landed on Caden's shoulder. "I

know," Caden said. Maybe the item in the sidewalk was as well? Did that mean more cracks had formed between the realms? Was the tornado a portal, part of the rip that would connect the realms? Maybe the river was the same?

Caden used his coat sleeve to protect his hand and yanked the item from the cement. It was metal. That he could tell through the coat. It was shaped a lot like the Winterbird emblem of the Elite Guard. He turned back to Brynne to show her. "What do you think—" He stopped and couldn't help but stare.

Brynne unwound her arm from the post. "Why are you looking at me like that?"

Caden put the item in his pocket. His coat would keep it from burning him until it cooled down enough for him to clean it off and investigate. There really was no good way to say what needed to be said. "Your hair," Caden said.

"Well, if it won't grow, it won't grow," she said, but he could tell she was upset. "It doesn't look bad short." She waved like it was nothing. "It's fine."

When Caden told her, he feared she might explode. Caden scooted back and ignored Jasan as he pecked his cheek again. "Brynne," he said as gently as possible. "Your hair isn't short"—he took a deep breath—"it's gone."

19

THE FALLEN EMBLEM

rynne reached up and patted her head. She became more fervent as she searched for what wasn't there. Her face went as white as a frost spirit. Her lip trembled.

Mr. Faunt peeked out from his hiding place, then scurried away. Mr. Wist had left, as had Ms. Levers. Downhill, Caden saw Rath Dunn and Ms. Jackson getting into his red Audi. A building alarm wailed.

"Caden! Brynne!" It was Jane. She ran out from an alleyway, Tito behind her. "In her hand, she still grasped the vial she'd taken from Ms. Jackson. The once sparkling contents looked as if they'd turned to ash. The vial was cracked. "Are you all right . . ."

Her voice trailed off as she saw Brynne. Tito seemed to force himself not to stare.

"Did you get your brother?" Tito said, and turned

to him. "He was in the cage. I tried to run with him, but Mr. Faunt latched onto it." When he noticed the falcon on Caden's shoulder, he let out a relieved sigh. "Oh good."

"We're okay," Caden said, though his voice sounded weaker than he expected. "Mostly."

A melody began to play—one with drums and trumpets—and the music came from Brynne's pocket. Her phone was ringing. Then Jane's rang. Then Tito's. Finally, Caden felt his phone buzz. He pulled it out. It was Rosa. Their absence had been noticed.

After the incident on the last day of summer school, Caden had promised never to avoid her calls. He tapped the answer icon. "Rosa?" he said.

"Where. Are. You?" She sounded furious.

"There was a tornado," Caden said. "Downtown. Brynne's hair blew away. And my brother got turned into a bird again."

Wait. Did Rosa know Jasan had been turned into a bird? Caden couldn't remember at that moment. Maybe he wasn't explaining things well?

"Caden," Rosa said. Her fury had shifted to worry. "Where exactly are you?"

He told her. Looking around at the damage from the spell's winds, Caden doubted the bus would be running to take them home. "Please come pick us up."

"I'm on my way," Rosa said.

They sat on the curb and waited. Brynne had her face

buried in her hands. Jane rubbed her back in slow circles. Caden sat with his posture perfect and petted Jasan on the head. Tito looked terrified.

"She's going to kill us," Tito said.

"She won't," Caden said.

"Bro," Tito said. "Even Rosa has limits to how much she'll put up with."

"She considers you her son; she won't give up on you."

"Then she should adopt me," Tito snapped, but he looked like he immediately regretted saying that out loud.

"You should tell her that," Caden said.

Tito rested his chin on his hands. "That would be embarrassing for me and uncomfortable for her. It would be bad for all of us." He shrugged. "Even if she'd consider it, she couldn't just adopt me. What about the three of you?"

"I have a family," Caden said. "So does Brynne."

Jane leaned over. "I don't want to be adopted. I like things as they are. So I'm okay, too."

"You're just saying that." Tito sat back straight. "Look, don't tell Rosa I said I wanted to be adopted." His voice was harsher this time. "Got it?"

Jane nodded.

"I understand," Caden said. He decided that, like Brynne, Tito needed someone to rub his back. "There, there."

Tito scrunched up his face. "Don't do that."

That's when Rosa drove up, steering her pickup around

the debris. Officer Levine drove up behind her in his patrol car. Immediately, Rosa got out and ran to them. She scanned the overturned cars and the scattered tables. "Are you all right?" she said.

Tito stood up to greet her, and she pulled Tito into a hug.

"Yeah," Tito said.

"Brynne needs you," Jane said.

Rosa let Tito go. She turned to Brynne, paused, and blinked at her.

"Rosa . . . ," Brynne said, and stood. Her voice cracked. "My hair."

For a brief moment, Rosa didn't seem to know what to say. Then she drew Brynne into her arms. "It's all right," she said, and gently ran a hand over Brynne's bare head like she couldn't process what had happened. "It's all right," she said again. "Let's get you checked out at the emergency room."

Officer Levine strode over as well. He surveyed the scene with concern and caution. "What happened? They okay?"

Brynne pushed away from Rosa and threw up her hands. "My hair blew away."

Rosa pulled Brynne back to her, but frowned like she couldn't figure out how someone's hair could blow away in an evening windstorm. "They seem mostly okay."

"More happened than Brynne losing her hair," Caden

said. "Part two of the spell is complete. Mr. Bellows was sucked into the wind funnel."

Officer Levine glanced up at the swirling sky with a deep frown. "I'm not sure there'll be any evidence. We didn't find anything of Mr. McDonald in the river."

"*Kak!*" Jasan said.

Caden motioned to him. "Also, Jasan has been transformed into a falcon."

Rosa's eyes went wide at the bird on Caden's shoulder like she'd just noticed him. "Where did you find that animal?"

Caden looked at her, confused. "It's Jasan."

But why was he a bird again? Near the joint of his right wing, where the paper clips connected it to his bird body, Caden saw blood. The enchanted paper clips didn't completely negate the effects of the blood dagger. Likely, Caden's arm bled again, too. And where was Manglor?

Suddenly, Brynne looked up from Rosa's embrace. Her cheeks began to blaze. It never took Brynne long to move from despair to fury. "Someone is going to suffer for this."

Rosa squeezed her tighter. "It's only hair."

"But it's my hair," Brynne said.

The villains had used Jane's tears, and she'd lost them. They'd used Brynne's hair, and it had blown away on the wind. If they had the opportunity, they'd also use Jasan's blood and then . . .

Jane could live without tears, Brynne without hair. But what would happen if Jasan lost his blood? Caden felt his heart drop. Jasan couldn't live without his blood. If the next part of the spell happened, Jasan would die. It wouldn't matter that Caden had saved him from the wind funnel. He'd die either as man or bird.

Already, Caden had lost sixth-born Chadwin. And though still alive, it felt like he had lost second-born Maden, too. He couldn't lose another brother; he couldn't.

"I'll take Brynne to the doctor," Rosa said, drawing Caden out of his thoughts.

"I'll drive the others home," Officer Levine said.

"Thank you, Harold," Rosa said. "Caden, leave the bird for animal control." She sounded as if she expected no argument, as if she expected him to obey.

However, Caden would never leave his brother for animal control. He raised his chin. As he was gifted with speech and Jasan with speed, their father was gifted with resolution. He was headstrong and unrelenting in a way beyond description. It had to be experienced to be understood. Caden might not be as resolute as his noble father, but he'd seen how effective being unyielding could be.

Caden didn't falter. "No. He's my brother." To prove his point, Caden brushed Jasan's wing and showed her the paper clips. "Just like Jasan. You see."

"That's a bird," Rosa said.

It was true. "He's a bird for the time being. He'll turn back."

Rosa rubbed her temple, then glanced at Brynne's bare head again. She'd witnessed Jane's eyes go bad. Brynne was now bald. It was time for Rosa to believe him.

"Rosa," Caden said. "It's time to accept that things in the world are not what they seem. Why can't you keep us from school? There have been countless disasters there. Jane was kidnapped. A building fell on Tito. Yet each day you drive us back. That doesn't seem like something you'd do lightly. Why do Jasan and I speak a language you've never heard?" Caden showed her the cut on his arm. "Why won't this heal? It's because I speak the truth. You need to accept it."

Rosa didn't dismiss his words this time. "I need to think about everything." She turned to Officer Levine. "Do you believe this?"

"Yeah," he said. "I do. And I don't like the mess these villains have brought to my town."

Some people needed undeniable proof. Rosa still seemed hesitant, but not as much as before. "We'll talk more about this at home," she said. "I still need to take Brynne to the emergency room." With a deep inhale, she added, "Assuming there'll be no more . . . spells . . . of any kind tonight."

"There shouldn't be," Caden said.

That was how Officer Levine, Caden, Tito, and Jane ended up in the patrol car—Caden in the front seat, of course, Jasan in his lap, and Tito and Jane in the back— while Rosa drove Brynne to get checked by an Ashevillian doctor. Sadly, Caden doubted there was any treatment for magically induced baldness.

Officer Levine drove carefully. He gestured to the falcon in Caden's lap. "What happens if those clips come unwound?"

"His hand falls off," Caden said.

"I think you mean wing," Tito said.

"Not funny, Tito," Jane said.

Caden meant hand or wing. It didn't matter. "It's a magical wound that will never heal. He'll bleed to death without the clips." He squared his shoulders and sat straight against the seat. "He'll die."

Officer Levine reached over and patted his shoulder. "We won't let that happen, son."

Outside, all traces of daylight had faded. Like pinpricks in the dark sky, stars started to flicker. The part-moon peeked from behind a small mountain. Another day and it would be half-full and Caden would be cursed. Maybe they should have chosen to break Caden's curse. Neither Caden nor Brynne had yet to find the information Ms. Primrose gave them about the spell useful.

Caden reached into his coat pocket. The item that had fallen was still warm, but he could touch it now. He pulled it out and wiped off the ash with his sleeve. Shining silver and gold came into view. The item wasn't just shaped like the royal Winterbird emblem. It *was* the royal Winterbird emblem—the ornate version of the symbol on the dress uniform of the royal family. Caden cleaned the upper-wing area. Five mountain sapphires. This was his brother

Landon's emblem, fifth-born and gifted with fortitude.

Officer Levine glanced at the item. "What's that?"

Caden's hand began to shake. "It doesn't mean anything," he said. "I don't think it means anything."

"Are you sure?" Officer Levine said.

"No," said Caden.

The emblem had cooled, but it burned in his hand. Ms. Primrose told Brynne the spell that happened here was mirrored in the Greater Realm. Were there sacrifices there as well? Caden's family, his people were in danger. Jasan had said they needed to find a way to contact Razzon. His brother was right. They needed to warn the king and the kingdom.

But why had Ms. Primrose turned Jasan into a bird? Was it to help Rath Dunn? Caden couldn't believe it was only because they'd fought over what to watch on television.

Ms. Primrose needed to explain herself; she needed to help them, not Rath Dunn. Caden should ask her. He should be the one to charm the dragon. That aspect of his gift was getting stronger, wasn't it? And Ms. Primrose had always been more impressed by it than most.

It was evening, so Ms. Primrose was likely at Jasan's town house admiring her treasures. "We need to go to Jasan's town house. I need to talk to Ms. Primrose."

"Are you sure about that?" Tito said.

"Yes," Caden said.

Officer Levine slowed the patrol car at a stoplight. Ashevillian stoplights were strange things. Red meant stop. In any other world, red always meant charge. "And Ms. Primrose, aka the Elderdragon, just happens to be at your brother's town house?"

"She needed a place to display her treasures," Caden said. "Just hurry to Jasan's house."

Officer Levine hesitated.

"I need to ask her something. That's all," Caden said. "Please. Trust me on this."

Officer Levine peered at him. Finally, he said, "Okay," and as the light changed to green, he directed the car left toward Jasan's home. "But I'm coming with you." He paused. "Not because I don't trust you. I just don't trust her."

Caden wasn't sure he trusted Ms. Primrose either. He jammed the emblem into his pocket and turned to the window. The emblem could have fallen from Landon's wardrobe and somehow gotten sucked into the winds from across realms. But what if it meant something more sinister? In Asheville, Ms. Jackson's spell required a sacrifice. A connecting spell in the Greater Realm likely did as well.

Caden's heart was heavy not only with worry for Jasan and Asheville, but with worry for Landon, with worry that the blizzard oaks were burning in the Winterlands.

It was time Ms. Primrose stopped playing games and aided them. Her essence was also at risk; it was an ingredient in the spell. Wasn't that a good enough reason for her to help them stop the villains? What would happen to her when that ingredient was used? Caden didn't understand her.

She is an Elderdragon, he reminded himself. Don't try to understand her in human terms. Listen to her and figure out what to say. He could do that. He needed to do that.

20

THE DRAGON IN THE TOWN HOUSE

The night had turned cold and remained windy. Officer Levine parked in front of the town houses. They were painted in pale yellows, pinks, and blues; and the colors were faint under the moonlight. Small streetlights brightened the parking lot.

Ward and his parents, Manglor and Desirae, lived in the pale-pink town house. Ward's mother was a local, but she knew of the Greater Realm. There was a light on inside their home.

Manglor was their ally, and he'd also been missing. As Caden and the others exited the car, Caden saw something lumbering behind the pink town house's curtains, something large, bent over, and with a monstrous shadow.

Maybe Manglor hadn't come because he and his family had been devoured by a home demon? Evil creatures summoned them, and they preyed on families after dark. Desirae's plastic Ashevillian gnome smiled at Caden from their lawn. Maybe the gnome had summoned it.

Caden rushed to Ward's door, Jasan flying at his shoulder, and pounded on the door.

"Wrong house!" Tito called.

"Just keep an eye on the gnome," Caden said.

"Maybe you should go to the emergency room, too," Tito said.

Caden ignored him. He tried the doorknob. It rattled in his hand, locked. Caden hit the doorbell. It chimed again and again. Caden stopped midpush when the stoop light switched on.

"Just a moment," Desirae called from inside.

She didn't sound like she'd been devoured by a demon.

When she opened the door, Ward stood next to her. Behind them hulked the biggest dog Caden had ever seen. The dog regarded him with a curled lip and a low growl and looked like he would rip apart anyone who threatened Ward or Desirae.

"That a mastiff?" Officer Levine said.

"We thought it was a monster," Caden said.

Officer Levine put a hand on Caden's shoulder. "Son?"

"I mean," Caden corrected, "I thought it was a monster. I feared the evil gnome summoned it."

It seemed Jasan agreed. "*Kak!*" he squawked. Caden

rubbed his ear. That was loud.

Something began to make sense. Jasan was missing, then turned up as a bird. Manglor, too, was missing, and now a giant dog stood in his living room with his wife and son. Caden pointed. "Is that Manglor?"

Desirae hesitated. "My husband should be back tomorrow before class. Ms. Primrose informed us."

That sounded like a yes. "You know what she is?" Caden said.

"I do, and I know she's dangerous."

Caden looked at Desirae, then at Ward. "Why would Ms. Primrose turn Manglor into a dog? And Jasan into a bird?" He felt frustration overcome him. When she'd eaten Scribe Trevor, she'd been forced to do it. Did the same rules apply to animal transformations? Caden didn't really think so. "Why is she working against us?"

"I don't know." Desirae smiled. "He and I were going to talk after I got home from work. As you can see, that's not yet possible."

It had struck Caden as strange that Jasan would be foolish enough to get turned into a bird over a television program argument with Ms. Primrose. Despite his quick temper, he wasn't foolish. Too many important things were going on to risk safety over roommate squabbles. Maybe Jasan hadn't told Caden all he knew about what was going on in Asheville, about what was going on in the Greater Realm.

Caden and Brynne had been stranded three months longer than Jasan. That was three months longer that Jasan was in the Greater Realm. It was possible he knew a great deal more about what was happening there.

Officer Levine squeezed Caden's shoulder. "You still want to go next door?"

"I do." Caden would just have to ask Ms. Primrose what happened. And unlike Jasan and Manglor, Caden wouldn't be turned into a bird in the sky or dog on the ground. He was gifted with words.

Caden paused at the door to Ms. Primrose and Jasan's town house and turned back to Officer Levine, Tito, and Jane. "Remember," Caden said. "No matter what, be polite."

"Bro, Ms. Primrose loves me," Tito said, and walked past him. "And I'm a local."

"Me, too," Jane said.

"I was born in Boone," Officer Levine said. "I'm guessing that counts."

"Fine," Caden said. "But if you get turned into a helpless carrot-eating Ashevillian rabbit, it's your own fault."

Caden glanced at his shoulder and at his feathery brother upon it. "As it is your fault you and Manglor got transformed." He reached up to scratch the side of Jasan's head. "What haven't you told me?"

Officer Levine knocked. The light within came on and shone through the curtain. The door opened on its own.

"I guess we can go inside?" Tito said.

Caden walked through the doorway. Jasan's talons dug into his shoulder. Officer Levine, Tito, and Jane followed.

"It's cold," Jane said.

The town house looked different than the last time Caden visited. There were display shelves in the small hall; beads and baubles and shiny things filled every space shiny things could be. Caden peeked into the kitchen. Bowls of buttons and rocks were lined up on the granite counter. Jasan's candy bars were stacked in a small corner section. Despite the massive amount of *things*, it was clean and organized.

Caden was careful not to knock over anything and kept Jasan close as he walked down the short hallway. Tito, Jane, and Officer Levine followed, single file, until they arrived in the living room.

There were more shelves. And more things. As Jasan had mentioned, the couch was gone. In its place was a large wooden table. The legs looked like tree trunks, the top polished with a silvery finish. In neat, straight lines atop it, was every type of cheap trinket imaginable. He saw a large television tuned to the craft channel and a cushy chair by the fireplace. The fabric was striped blue and silver. On the floor beside it stood a bird perch. Ms. Primrose sat in the chair.

"I like what you've done with the place," Tito said.

Jane stood near the table and reached out toward a row of metal buttons. "These are nice."

"I just polished them," Ms. Primrose said, but she didn't sound friendly.

Jane pulled her hand back. "I could enchant one for you."

"Why would I want that, dear?" Ms. Primrose said. "Those are perfect as they are."

Officer Levine walked around the room like he was cataloging all the oddities in it. He peered at Ms. Primrose. "Ma'am," he said. "We need to ask you some questions."

"Oh?" she said.

A painting hung over the fireplace mantel. It was brightly colored like a burning sunset and stood out against the cool blues and silvers of the walls and furniture. The image of a mighty red-and-gold dragon was painted on it. The dragon looked smart, looked merciless.

Ms. Primrose snapped her fingers as if to get Caden's attention. "I hope you haven't come to harass me like your brother." She peered down at Jasan. He squawked. "He's bothersome even as a bird."

It was important that Caden not lose his temper and that he not yell and demand she explain herself. As he'd learned in the hall with Tito, Ms. Primrose had to be shown respect. "We're not here to make demands; we're here because times grow dire." He paused to emphasize the problem. "The second part of the spell has been completed. Why have you transformed my brother? Why Manglor? They fight to stop it."

"Why would I care if they stop it?" She pointed at Jasan. "That one wouldn't stop squawking in my ear about spells and help and contacting his home. I couldn't eat him. So I transformed him into a bird. This is the second time he's irritated me." She sighed. "And Mr. Manglor kept growling that I needed to do something. Like a dog. Now he is one."

It was important not to get frustrated, to remain calm, to be polite. Caden spoke with as much respect as he could muster. "You're helping the enemy."

"I'm without ally or enemy, dear," she said. "I just am. If the spell is stopped and Mr. Rathis fails, I may get my school back. Maybe I'll get to gobble him up. I'm sure he'd be dark and rich and tasty." The silver in the room started to glow. Scales on her arm shimmered the same lustrous color.

"And if it isn't stopped?" Caden said.

"If the barriers break between worlds, I can see my home again. I am not the one pursuing that end, so I break no bonds by returning. There Mr. Rathis promises to let me rage." Everything in the room turned blue. "It's been many years since I've let myself loose like that." She rubbed her stomach. "I've already let my dress out. Feasting is beginning to appeal to me."

Jane pulled her eyedrops from her pocket. She squinted toward Ms. Primrose. "But don't you want us to stop the spell, Ms. Primrose? Look what has happened to my eyes.

What will happen to you? Your essence is also an ingredient; you'll lose it."

She chuckled. "I have essence to spare."

Caden looked at the silver and blue decorations. He thought about her silver and blue scales, how sometimes she was nicer than at other times. "You mean your Silver side and your Blue side," Caden said.

She stretched out her legs. "Yes, and embodying two contrasting souls is exhausting. Mr. Rathis has suggested to me having only one would be freeing. I'm not happy he's taken over my school, but he makes a good point."

"Which side would you lose?" Caden said.

Her gnarled hand flashed with blue scales. "Well, I have been feeling rather Blue lately." Her Blue side was vicious. Caden couldn't imagine how terrifying it would be without some Silver to moderate it. Ms. Primrose seemed deep in thought. "Eating people always favors that side, and I have eaten so many recently."

Officer Levine seemed uneasy with the turn of the conversation. "Eating a human being is against the law."

Ms. Primrose shook her head. "Not if they break my contract. Then they can be terminated." She licked her lips as if remembering tasty morsels. "And eaten."

"Does that mean you've eaten people before?"

"I don't think I appreciate your tone."

Officer Levine was using his policeman tone. "Just answer the question, ma'am."

"Dude," Tito said, and leaned closer to Officer Levine. "She's no help to us if you arrest her."

Caden highly doubted Ms. Primrose would let herself be arrested; she'd broken none of her rules—those were the ones that mattered to her. Best Caden distract Ms. Primrose from Officer Levine before she transformed him into a simpering rodent or purring cat, and find a way to ask her for help. If she was no one's ally and no one's enemy, then there was no reason for her not to help Caden. When she was pleased, she helped. When she wasn't, well, that's when she turned Jasan into a falcon and Manglor into a mastiff. What did he have to say to get her to help, though?

"Ms. Primrose," Caden said, and motioned to the painting. "The artwork is . . ." What was there to say about a painting of a gold-and-red dragon? "Interesting." She was the Blue Elderdragon and the Silver Elderdragon. The dragon in the picture was red and gold. "Is that another of the mighty Elderdragons?"

"There are others?" Tito said.

"There is one other. Or there was," she said.

"He's not alive anymore?" Caden said. "What about the other Elderkind."

Ms. Primrose sat back in her chair. She seemed far away for a moment. "Even creatures such as us age, dear. We are not eternal. I'm the last one."

"They're all gone? Even the wise Walking Oak?" Jane said.

That brought Ms. Primrose back to the present. "Wise?" She shook her head. "Try asking that obnoxious tree anything." She harrumphed. "It was always 'I'm stumped, I'm stumped' or 'Leaf me alone.'"

Tito snorted. "That tree sounds awesome," he said.

Jane smiled.

"Doubt this so-called tree ate anyone," Officer Levine said, and sounded far less amused.

From the tight line of Ms. Primrose's mouth, she wasn't amused either. Then her face softened. Some of her skin shone in silver scales. An emotion Caden hadn't seen before crossed her face. It was so odd on her, so unnatural in her pale-blue eyes, it took him a moment to catalog it. But then he knew it. He'd seen it in the mirror when he'd thought about Chadwin. He'd seen it on Jane's face when she spoke of her mother.

Suddenly, Caden knew how he could connect with her.

The tree might have been obnoxious, but it seemed she missed it. The Red and Gold Elderdragon might have been difficult, but she put up a painting of him over the fireplace. Missing someone was an emotion Caden understood. He missed his father, his brothers. He missed his home. Perhaps Ms. Primrose missed hers, too. When Caden saw hints of those softer emotions, he often saw her softer side, her Silver side. Just like he did when he amused her.

Maybe he could say something to make her feel better, and, according to her, the tree enjoyed wordplay. Caden could do that. "The Walking Oak probably just didn't like people *barking* questions at it."

Everyone stared at him. Then Ms. Primrose blinked and Office Levine frowned. Tito peered at him, his mouth half open and crooked, a confused look on his face.

Jane squinted like she couldn't quite see him. "Caden," she said, "did you make a joke?"

"I think we can all agree 'no' to that," Tito said.

"You're mistaken, Sir Tito," Caden said, and raised a brow. "Humor is the *root* of good interaction." He turned to Ms. Primrose. "Don't you agree? It shouldn't be kept in a *trunk*."

Ms. Primrose sighed. "I suppose the tree would have liked you."

Caden stood straighter, and Ms. Primrose would like him again, too. She couldn't be manipulated with anger or greed or jealousy. Truly, she had to be charmed. "Most do like me," Caden said. "Even trees." But it wasn't the tree's portrait Ms. Primrose had hung over her fireplace. It was the Red and Gold Elderdragon. Caden felt confident now there were only two Elderdragons: Ms. Primrose, the Blue and Silver. And the mighty Red and Gold in the portrait on the wall. "The Red and Gold Elderdragon would have liked me, too."

"Well," Ms. Primrose said, her eyes clear and blue. "He did enjoy eating princes."

"I meant he would have enjoyed speaking to me."

She relaxed back into her comfy chair. While she looked interested, she honestly didn't looked charmed. Caden wasn't sure what else to say until Ms. Primrose said, "He didn't deign to speak lowly human tongues."

Oh. She wanted him to speak the forgotten tongue, to charm her in a language of power. Well, he would just do it then. Caden concentrated. He tried to draw the forgotten language into his mind. His head began to throb. He tried to say something, anything, but no words tickled his tongue. Caden brought his hand to his forehead.

Ms. Primrose stared at him with a stern expression. "You can't do it unless prompted, can you, dear?"

Caden swallowed. "Not yet," he said.

In some ways, he needed prompting to speak any language. The main difference was that with normal, non-forgotten tongues, he could summon them to his mind after hearing them only once. He'd heard the forgotten languages on several occasions. Those mystical languages, he'd never produced on demand. Although, he hadn't tried to speak them much. They were painful, powerful things—words that literally hurt.

"You should practice more," she said. "If you want to please me."

"I will," Caden said. If Caden couldn't ask for her help in the forgotten tongue, he'd do so in the local English. "Help us now, and one day I'll speak the forgotten language first."

Ms. Primrose narrowed her eyes. "It's not that easy."

Caden held her gaze. "You gave me a quest last spring; I completed it," he said. "You had no lair"—he motioned to the room—"I found you a new one. Have I not earned the privilege of being taken at my word?"

"I wasn't pleased with the outcome of your quest." With a loud sigh, Ms. Primrose laid her head back. "But you have proved yourself reliable. And you amused me with your talk of trees. One question." She lifted her head and waggled a finger at him. "No more."

What should he ask? The emblem in his pocket was cool to the touch, but it blazed in Caden's mind. It had fallen from the sky. It was from the Greater Realm. What was happening there? If only Caden could talk to his father. The king would know what to do.

Ms. Primrose tapped her wrist. "*Ticktock*, young prince," she said. "I haven't got all night. I've beads to sort."

It was simple, really—they needed to know how to stop the spells in Asheville and Razzon. Caden focused back on Ms. Primrose. "How do we stop the next part of the spells? Both here and in the Greater Realm. Certainly you know."

"I suppose that counts as one question." She peered at him, her eyes intense and inhuman. "To stop the spell here, you must prevent the sacrifice. For at midnight tomorrow, blood will be spilled in Biltmore Forest. To stop the spell there, you must warn those there; you must use life force to make the connection."

They couldn't sacrifice life to dark magic. Caden started to object.

Ms. Primrose held up her palm to quiet him. "You can't contact anyone in any other realm without sacrificing life force, dear. That's just how it works."

"Huh," Tito said.

Ms. Primrose pointed a long fingernail at bird-Jasan. Caden reached up to keep Jasan from snapping at her. "If he learns to behave, I'll leave him human. Tell him not to test me again. Tell Mr. Manglor the same."

Ms. Primrose stretched and stood. Her shadow began to lengthen. Her fingernails turned sharper and longer. She looked from Caden to Jasan on his shoulder to Officer Levine in the corner, then to Tito and Jane by the silver bead table. "It's time you leave my lair." She pointed to the perch. "Leave my roommate, and I'll transform him back. In time." Caden felt reluctant, and it must have shown on his face, because she added, "Are you doubting me?"

Caden couldn't lie. "I apologize," he said, and placed Jasan on the perch. One thing about Ms. Primrose, she would do as she said.

There was nothing more to say, no more questions to ask. Caden hated leaving Jasan, but he didn't know if she'd change him back if Caden took him. He bowed, tugged Officer Levine by the sleeve, and they, Jane, and Tito hurried out the doorway.

They got into the patrol car. Caden was quiet. Despite

popular opinion, he didn't talk constantly. Two parts of the spell remained. Blood would be spilled, she'd said. The third vial used would be Jasan's blood, then, blood of son, and it would occur at midnight tomorrow in Biltmore Forest. The day after that, Caden would be cursed.

When Caden and the others returned, Rosa and Brynne were back from the hospital. Officer Levine took Rosa aside, and they spoke quietly. Caden joined Brynne, Jane, and Tito in the living room.

He kept his hand in his coat pocket and rubbed his thumb across the emblem's wing. Five sapphires. Landon's birth number. What had happened? Could Landon have been the sacrifice there like Mr. Bellows had been here? No, that couldn't be true. His brothers would look after one another.

Yet Maden was with them. He'd killed Chadwin. Could he have killed Landon as well?

Brynne sat on the living-room coffee table. Her head was bare and her expression a cross between fury and shock. A black-and-silver knit cap was beside her. "The

doctor didn't believe all my hair flew away," she said. "He said I have nonworking follicles." Then she glanced up at Caden. "I think now Rosa better understands how *you* feel when she doesn't believe *you*."

Tito plopped down on the green punishment couch. He motioned to her head. "It doesn't look so bad."

Brynne shot him a withering look.

Jane sat on the table on the other side of the cap. "Are you okay?"

Brynne crossed her arms. "I'm fine. Perfectly healthy. Just bald."

Caden didn't want to sit on the punishment couch unless being punished—that was often enough. The table wasn't a proper seat either. He stood beside the table and considered Brynne. A prince should say something to make his ally feel better. "You have a mostly round head."

Brynne turned some of her fury on him.

But better she was angry than upset. Truly, though, Brynne was pretty with or without hair. Caden simply needed to emphasize the splendor of baldness. "Your head looks like a ripe moon melon."

"I don't know if you're helping there, bro," Tito said.

"Obviously, you've never seen a ripe moon melon," Caden said.

"Obviously," Tito said.

Brynne reached down, picked up the knit cap, and pulled it on her head. "Because I'm cold," she said. "Not because I lost my hair and feel bad about it."

"I see," Caden said.

"Good." She stared at him for a moment, then scrunched up her nose. "You look weird."

It was Caden's turn to raise a brow.

"I mean, you look worried," Brynne said.

"I am worried," Caden said. He ticked off items with his fingers. "About your hair, about Jane's eyes. About Jasan. About Ms. Primrose. About Asheville." He swallowed and brought the emblem out from his pocket. "About this." Caden showed it to her. "Five sapphires," he said quietly. "It belongs to my fifth-born brother, Landon."

"What does it mean?" Jane asked.

"It might not mean anything," Brynne said, but she wasn't convincing.

"It might mean something terrible," Caden said, and looked away. Something terrible was actually much more likely. He took a breath to calm himself and turned back. "The only way to stop the spell there is to warn my family. Then they will know what is happening. They will fight." Caden felt helpless. "But Ms. Primrose said there was no way to contact home without sacrificing life."

There was an uncomfortable silence. Outside, the wind blew, and Caden heard the screen door knocking against the frame. Tito seemed thoughtful.

"Why not just sacrifice some plants and do the ritual spell thing," Tito said. Caden was taken aback. Brynne looked shocked. Jane shook her head no. Tito seemed confused. "What?"

"Ritual magic is dark magic, Sir Tito," Brynne said. "We can't sacrifice plants."

Tito pointed at his mouth. "We eat plants, but we can't sacrifice a few? Not even some grass?" He pointed at Caden. "Or spinach? How about mushrooms? Mushrooms seem all right. No one cares about fungi."

Brynne pulled her hat lower on her ripe moon melon head. Despite what she said, she seemed self-conscious about her lost hair. "Ritual magic corrupts the soul," she said.

"Although," Caden said, "one could say the same about sorcery."

Her sad expression froze. "One could," she said, and narrowed her eyes, "but he'd be wrong. And he might find himself stuck with a fluffy tail and fox ears for a few days."

Now Caden was also annoyed. It was her fault that Caden was forced to obey any order for three days of every month. "You've cursed me enough, sorceress."

Tito lay back and put his feet on the edge of the coffee table. His brow furrowed. After a moment, he said, "So no ritual magic? Got it. But you know, Ms. Primrose only said life force had to be used. She didn't say anything about ritual magic."

"Your point?" Caden said.

"Do you have to use ritual magic?" Tito said. "Is there another way to use life force?"

Brynne's face lit up. She and Jane exchanged a look. With talk of magic and spells, it was as if they were in perfect sync—a sorceress and an enchantress teamed up to protect their homes. A slow smile spread across Jane's face.

Caden, however, didn't know what they were thinking. "I don't understand."

Brynne's eyes were bright. "Maybe it *is* possible to sacrifice life force without sacrificing a life." Her voice couldn't contain her rising excitement. "Sir Tito, you're brilliant." Her gaze darted to Caden. She arched a brow. "Unlike some people."

Perhaps Caden shouldn't annoy her. Also. "How can you sacrifice life force without sacrificing a life?"

Jane squinted at him. "Enchantments contain life force. That includes those I've made." She pulled her eyedrops from her pocket. "Maybe we can fuel the magic with items I've already enchanted."

"Jane and I can work together," Brynne said. "We can make something similar to a Razzonian communication pool. Only not. A spell like ritual magic, but sorcery, and fueled by enchantments."

"I see," Caden said.

"It will work," Brynne said. "And we will warn the Greater Realm."

Officer Levine and Rosa returned from the kitchen.

Apparently, he needed to go back downtown when his shift started. Before he left, he patted Brynne on the shoulder. "You kids be good. Stay in and stay safe." He bent down and spoke to them in a hushed tone. "Just give Rosa a little time. She's trying to come to grips with the fact that I believe you kids and that Brynne just lost all her hair in the windstorm. I've had all summer to take it in. It's not easy to accept. Magic and villains and all."

After Officer Levine left and Rosa checked that everyone was all right, they headed upstairs.

"Call me if you need anything," Rosa called after them.

Caden stopped midstep just before the stairs and turned back. "You believe me now, don't you?"

Rosa furrowed her brow. "It's a lot to believe, Caden."

"You'll believe soon. And once you do," Caden said, and he offered his most charming smile, "you'll see my actions are only courageous and good like the Elite Paladins."

"I already know you're courageous and good whether I believe you or not, Caden."

Upstairs, Caden, Tito, Brynne, and Jane gathered in the girls' room. Tito brought his green binder, and they wrote down all the details of the downtown spell. The girls huddled together on the floor. In front of them they set out the Enchanted Stapler of Stapling, a hammer, and a cup of water.

The stapler shimmered, its enchantment obvious

close-up. The hammer, however, also glinted under the lamplight. The rubber handle looked smooth and finely molded.

Jane held up the hammer. "I enchanted it also."

"I thought you were going to stop," Tito said.

"I stopped doing big enchantments. This isn't a big enchantment," Jane said.

"What does it do?" Caden said.

"It smashes things," Jane said, as if this should have been obvious. Caden dubbed it enchanted item one hundred thirty-five, the Enchanted Hammer of Smashing.

"But why?" Caden asked.

Brynne's voice hummed with excitement. "We're going to sacrifice life force in order to communicate with the Greater Realm, right? Jane and I talked, and we think the best way to do it is to break an item that's already been enchanted. And our guess is that an enchanted item can only be broken by another enchanted item—an object with some sort of magic attached to it."

"Hence, the Enchanted Hammer of Smashing," Jane said. "We're going to smash the stapler."

"Only Rath Dunn's enchanted dagger could tear Caden's magical coat," Brynne said. "And Tito's magical necklace was only destroyed when a wall inscribed with ritual magic runes fell on him. We just need something to be the conduit from here to there." She pursed her lips. "In the Greater Realm, we use specially forged pools or mirrors."

"Then why not use a mirror?" Caden said.

"Tech is the magic of this world," Brynne said. "If we want to connect this world to the magic of our world, I think technology needs to be part of it."

Jane sat back on her heels, and she held up her phone. "What about my cell."

"It needs to be flat with a larger surface area," Brynne said.

Tito grumbled something and left the room. When he came back, he had his tablet. The one he cradled at night sometimes like a child's precious toy. "I saved up all summer for this," he said. "Will it work? I don't want it smashed."

Brynne and Jane exchanged looks. Then Jane said, "It's perfect."

Tito seemed reluctant to release it. "I don't want it smashed," he said again.

"Of course not, Sir Tito." Brynne reached up and took it from him. "The screen must be flat and undamaged for communication. We must connect it to the other realm like it would connect to another device."

"There are no computer tablets in the Greater Realm," Caden said.

"But there are reflecting disks, mirrors, and all forms of reflective surfaces," Brynne said, as if both Greater Realm magic *and* the local tech made perfect sense to her.

Caden remained skeptical. "I don't believe you understand all this tech."

She arched a brow. "You don't have to believe me to make it so."

Caden leaned over the tablet screen. He saw his royal self looking back. When he waved, his royal self waved, too. "We need to see the other realm, not ourselves."

"It's the camera function," Brynne said. "There's no life force in it yet. We haven't smashed the stapler."

He glanced up. "And how will releasing the life force of the stapler help us contact home?"

It was like she'd been waiting for the question. Her eyes were bright with magic and mischief. "Razzonian communication pools use telepathy sorcery—the mind magic of communication. The water and mirror of the pool enhance the connection, and help to visualize the person to contact. So we're making our version of a Razzonian communication pool. Sort of. But not. You see?"

There was a finite limit to the reach of such magic. Caden didn't see. "In the Greater Realm, such magic barely reaches the Summerlands."

Tito looked worriedly at his tablet, like he was regretting bringing it to the girls. "You've lost me, too."

"We're combining our magics with technology," Jane said. "It's cool."

Brynne nodded; she seemed lost in the wonder of magic and technology. "And my magic will be combined with the life force from the enchantments, too."

"And that's stronger?" Caden said.

"Yes," Brynne said, and held up the cup of water. "Now you two, move back, watch, and learn."

Looking troubled, Tito scooted against the yellow wall. He patted the spot beside him like he expected Caden to sit there. Royalty didn't usually sit on floors, but Caden supposed he could do so this once.

Jane made sure the tablet was secure. Brynne readied the water and hammer.

Tito covered his eyes. "I can't watch this."

"You give up your tablet for the good of all peoples. This is the action of an Elite Paladin." Caden reached out and squeezed his shoulder. "I'll watch for you, Sir Tito."

Brynne poured a small amount of water over the lit tablet surface. The water sat like a thin film atop the device. Truth be told, it did somewhat resemble a small, square Razzonian communication pool.

Tito peeked through his fingers. "I'm not all that wild about the fact you're pouring water over it." Tito was protective of his Ashevillian tech pieces. "I'm going to have to stick it in a sack of rice for a week." He brought his hands down and looked at Caden. "You know, to—"

"To draw out the moisture," Caden said.

Tito raised his brows. Brynne seemed surprised. Jane nodded.

"I know things," Caden said. He learned them watching television.

Brynne and Jane turned back to their work. It seemed

their plan ended with water on the screen.

"What now?" Brynne said.

"Well," Jane said. "We have to smash the stapler and get the energy out of it. So let's smash it into the water."

"But it won't put that energy into the tablet," Brynne said.

"Then we pour the water over it. After the smashing," Jane said.

"Oh." Brynne brightened. "That might work."

Brynne grabbed the half-full cup. "We need something bigger. I'll find a pan instead." As she walked past Caden, she tripped on a metal wrench and dumped the water on his head. Caden wiped wet hair from his forehead. Brynne smirked a bit and hurried out of the room.

"Bro, we need to stick you in a sack of rice, too," Tito said.

Brynne returned a moment later with a plastic tub of water. Now that Caden watched, she moved slower and less sure than usual. It had been a long day, and Brynne was easily drained by magic. She'd toppled tables and set umbrellas aflame already.

Brynne put the tub on the carpet. Jane placed the stapler in the water and lifted the hammer.

"Ready," Jane said.

"Smash it," Brynne said.

With a look of glee, Jane pounded the Enchanted Stapler of Stapling with the Enchanted Hammer of Smashing. *Bang.*

Splish. Bang. Splash. The metal head of the stapler dented.

"Girl's got some rage," Tito said, but he sounded impressed. Caden couldn't help but agree. Jane had been through a lot, and though she seemed so calm on the surface, underneath she likely had a lot of fury.

Ripples emanated from the stapler. The water's surface took on a silvery film.

"It's working," Brynne said. She was out of breath. "Quickly."

Jane set aside the hammer. She lifted the tub and poured the water over the tablet's screen.

"Please don't break my tablet," Tito said, clasping his hands together and rocking back and forth. "Please."

The screen stayed lit. Caden and Tito crawled back to the middle of the room. Like points on the compass, they each took a seat at one side of Tito's water-covered tablet. Beside Jane, the stapler lay in a dented heap. Caden peered into the water-drenched tablet, but all he saw was his water-soaked reflection.

"Nothing's happening," Jane said.

"Not yet," Brynne said. "Razzonian communication pools work by utilizing concentration, reflective quality, *and* telepathy magic. The camera is the visual connection. The sacrificed life force fuels the spell. But I have to magic us, too, so we can telepathically connect with those on the other side."

She touched Jane's forehead and Tito's shoulder. She

touched Caden's cheek lightly. She held his gaze for a moment, her finger lingered, and he felt his cheeks heat. Then the tingle of sorcery rushed through his body.

The water on the screen shimmered, and ripples radiated from the center. The glow of the screen turned soft silver. An image appeared, one that was certainly not a reflection. Caden, Brynne, Tito, and Jane leaned over and looked into another world—into the Great Hall of the Winter Castle.

22

THE CASTLE IN THE TABLET

Home. Caden saw home. For the first time in almost eight months, he saw his people.

Brynne placed her palm just above the water. "It's working. It's working, prince!" She grinned. "Hello! Hello!"

Everything within the hall was large and ornate. A midnight-blue wool rug with gold and silver silk trim covered the marble floor and stretched as wide and long as the hall itself. Elite Guards stood stationed along the walls, and there were many people: guardsmen, merchants, nobles. The sound of chatter and life made Caden feel as if he was there. He could almost smell the woody scent of the hearths that kept the castle warm, almost feel the cool drafts that wafted through the castle as doors opened and closed.

From the angle, they looked into the hall from the Mirror of the Sunsnake. Long ago, it had been a gift from

Summerlands diplomats. An image of the Sunsnake, the Elderkind that protected the Summerlands, was carved into the mirror's massive frame. Although old and valuable, the mirror wasn't magical on its own.

Suddenly a woman stopped and checked her reflection. An expensive, high-collared silver-and-gold frock covered her shoulders, and a Korvan battle staff was strapped across her back. Her hair was long and black, her skin pale like moonlight. Her eyes were as black as midnight yet twinkled like stars.

She appeared young, but Caden knew she was older. She'd magicked herself to look youthful and beautiful—not unlike a certain other sorceress he knew. The woman was the powerful sorceress Lyn. She was Brynne's mother.

Brynne's face lit up, and her hand began to tremble. "Mom! Mom! Mom!"

Lyn didn't respond or register that she'd heard. Instead, she fixed her hair and her collar. A slightly shorter figure stepped up beside her. His hair was cropped and black. His skin was dark like obsidian stone, and he had silvery eyes like Brynne. He carried a spellcaster's ax. It was Brynne's father, Madrol.

The staff and ax struck Caden as strange. It was rare that he'd seen Brynne's parents carry weapons. Like Brynne, their magic was enough to protect them. It was enough to warn others away.

"Daddy!" Brynne said.

Madrol, too, checked his reflection and smoothed his hair.

Caden raised a brow. "Vanity runs in your family."

"Jeez. Good looks, too," Tito said.

Caden glanced across at Tito. "They magic themselves, that's why."

"Hush, prince," Brynne said. She leaned closer to the water and screen. "Mom! Dad! Can you hear me! Can you see me?"

Neither Lyn nor Madrol gave any indication they heard or saw Brynne. Brynne pursed her lips. She leaned so close to the tablet, her head blocked most of it from Caden's view.

Why weren't they answering? "Try again," Caden said.

Brynne tried four more times. She yelled so loud that Rosa called up at them to quiet down, so loud Caden felt certain the mountain outside heard. Her parents, however, didn't. Brynne sat back on her heels.

Jane took her hand. "I don't think they can hear you."

Caden waved in front of the screen. "Or see us." He glanced at Brynne. She looked stricken. Her lip trembled, and he felt his heart sink.

On the screen, Brynne's parents gazed at each other. They too looked stricken. "We'll find her," her father said.

Were they talking about Brynne? After all, she'd been missing as long as Caden.

Lyn arched a brow and nodded. "And anyone involved in taking her from us will suffer."

Caden suddenly understood where Brynne's temper came from—her mother.

"And they shall suffer like none before them," her father replied. Or maybe it came from both parents. A double dose. That made perfect sense.

Her father took her mother's hand, and they walked toward the large doors that led to the king's strategy room. The Elite Guards moved to let them through. Caden watched, wanting a glimpse inside, wanting to see his father, his brothers; but an Elite Guardswoman stopped in front of the Mirror of the Sunsnake and blocked his view.

She had a golden complexion and greenish-yellow eyes. "That's Olive from Eagle Eye Village," Caden said. "Her mother named her for her eye color, and she joined the Elite Guard when her father got sick. Her sword skills need work; but her precision with a bow rivals my fourth-oldest brother, Martin, and he's gifted in accuracy."

Though likely hopeless, Caden tried speaking to Olive. She seemed content inspecting her eyebrows. As she stepped away, she kept her hand on her dagger. That was another oddity. Why would she be on guard while in the hall?

Brynne seemed to have collected herself. "The connection isn't complete," she said, and sniffed. She cocked her head. Her cap tilted. "But it's not fading either. Usually the magic is more fleeting."

"It's only our first try," Jane said.

But Caden was getting frustrated. The third part of the spell was tomorrow. They didn't have time to try things. This had to work. "We need to warn them and soon, not spy on them," he snapped.

"That's not helping, Caden," Jane said.

A figure in black dashed through the crowd. Brynne pointed to the corner of the screen. "Is that Prince Lucian?"

At the name of one of his brothers, Caden snapped his gaze back to the screen. How he wished to see them, to know they were okay. Lucian was third-born and gifted in stealth. When he moved, he was silent and became one with the shadows.

On the screen, a figure with desert-brown hair darted through the crowd. There was no wasted movement. Each step was precise. Caden felt relief at seeing the figure. But it wasn't third-born Lucian.

"That's Martin, my fourth-born brother." While stealthy Lucian was deadly with a dagger, accurate Martin was deadly with a bow and throwing dagger.

"Oh," Brynne said.

Lucian and Martin were born on different ends of the same turn of year, a mere ten months apart on the Ashevillian calendar. They were the skinniest and wiriest of all Caden's brothers, and they looked enough alike to be mistaken for each other.

"Lucian is shorter," Caden said. "He moves differently." Also Lucian's gift of stealth made him as hard to find in a crowd as in a dim-lit room. It took practice to spot him. Caden scanned the crowd. Again he felt overcome. Lucian was in the crowd. Caden pointed to what at first glance seemed to be a shadow trailing Martin. "That's Lucian."

Why was Lucian trailing Martin? Shouldn't they be side by side?

Caden didn't see fifth-born Landon, and his dented and charred dress emblem was still in Caden's right pocket. Nor did he see first-born Valon or traitorous Maden. But no black drapes hung in the Great Hall. If Landon was dead, if he'd been killed, the hall would be black with mourning drapes. Those things *should* have made Caden feel better.

But they didn't. The emblem had fallen from the sky mere hours earlier. The castle wouldn't have had time to hang black drapes yet. They might not yet know if fifth-born Landon was in trouble. They might not know if he was dead.

Chadwin had been stabbed in the night, and they hadn't found him until morning. Caden sat back and cleared his mind of thoughts of Chadwin, of visions of Landon in the same pose with a dagger in his back and blood around his body, of his emblem tossed into evil winds.

It was better not to remember finding Chadwin, better

not to imagine finding Landon. Caden took in a shaky breath. "It is good to see home, but it does not help us if we can't communicate."

More and more people passed down the hall: Elite Guards, regular guards, meadow gnome scouts, battle gnomes, Summerlands strategists. Then Caden saw something that truly worried him. The guards, gnomes, and scouts parted as a winged figure with a five-pointed spear marched toward the king's chambers. That was a war wraith. Why would the king ever bring a war wraith to the castle?

On the other side of the tablet, Jane sat cross-legged. She tapped her fingers against the floor. "I should just enchant the tablet to make the connection stronger," she said. "It has metal parts."

"No," Tito said. "You can't do that. You put too much life force into these things, you die. Remember?" He motioned to Caden, then Brynne. "The fantasy people said so."

"We don't know that I'd die," Jane said. "I'll try to put just a little life force into it."

This was the problem with enchanters. They wanted to enchant. And it was almost impossible to stop them. It's why they never lived very long. By fate's favor, Jane's elvish blood and Brynne's small-enchantment plan would help her live longer than most.

"It's too strong an enchantment," Brynne said. "The tablet is a complex device, and the magic is complicated, too. The more complicated the magic, the more life force it would take. Even as a half elf these enchantments shorten your life. If the stapler took off half a year, something to communicate across realms could take off half your life span."

"Wait," Tito said. "That stapler took off half a year?"

Brynne fidgeted. "I'm just guessing."

"Wait." Tito looked truly concerned. "How much life force did that cursed ladle take?" The Aging Ladle of Justice wasn't a complex item, but the curse attached to it was. Tito reached and touched his once-enchanted necklace. "How much did this take?"

"It saved you. Whatever it was," Jane said, "it was worth it."

Brynne slid her hand across the water on the screen's surface. "We need more life force for a stronger signal. We'll collect things Jane's already enchanted and use them all." She caught Caden's gaze. Her eyes flickered to his coat.

Caden tensed and pulled it tighter.

"Oh relax, prince," Brynne said. "I'm not eyeing your coat. You can get the Enchanted Whisk of Mixing, right?"

That item Jasan used to mix eggs. "I'll ask Jasan to bring it once he's back to his human self." Caden returned his gaze to the screen. It was good to see home.

Flick. The screen went black. The tablet powered down. What? Wait. "Why did it stop?" Caden said.

Tito grabbed the tablet and shook off the water. "Dude," he said. "The battery is out."

"What are you four watching?" Rosa said. She stood by the door in her purple robe. Her yellow shirt was visible under the too-short sleeves. She peered at the tablet and frowned. "And why is Tito's tablet wet?"

"It was necessary for the spell," Caden said.

"Spell?"

Brynne explained.

Caden couldn't tell if Rosa believed them or not. She seemed tired, exasperated, drained from the night's events. All she said was "Just be careful with Tito's tablet. He worked hard for it. All of you need to rest. Let's call it an early night."

Caden wasn't ready to sleep. He motioned to the drip-laden screen. "We saw the Winter Castle's Great Hall." He also stood. "When the device recharges, I'll show you my home."

Rosa looked skeptical. "We'll see." She kissed Jane on the head. "And don't forget to put in your eye gel before bed."

"I won't," Jane said.

She tempered her expression and drew Brynne in for a hug. "And let me know if you need me." There was nothing like a girl with no hair and lost parents to soften Rosa.

"I will," Brynne said.

Tito looked away like he was uncomfortable, though

Caden knew that wasn't the case. "Tito also wants a hug," he said.

"I don't," Tito said.

"Future Elite Paladins should always be honest, Sir Tito," Caden said, but Rosa had already pulled Tito close.

23

TO COUNTER A CURSE

While Tito and Jane hurried to get ready for school—
Caden had packed his bag and laid out his clothes
the night before; a true Paladin is always prepared—
Brynne texted Caden a smiley face and a winky face. It was
her code for him to meet her beside the house. They would
have to wait until after school to contact the Greater Realm
again, so he didn't know what she wanted.

Caden ducked past Rosa, who sat at the table with her
shoulders hunched like great thoughts weighed on her,
then headed outside. It was a crisp morning—the sky was
clear blue, the air dry. As always, however, Caden's coat
offered him warmth.

Brynne waited near the copper and pewter flowers.
Her hat was tugged snug down to her ears, and her cheeks
were rosy. There were hoofprints by her feet, a sign that
Sir Horace had been by during the night. When she saw

Caden, she smiled and twisted her hands together. "I know what to do about your curse," she said. "And I intend to fix it right now."

Wait? What? She knew how to break his curse. Caden felt a smile spread across his face. This was good news indeed. Brynne could fix him. Well, of course she could. Caden always had faith in his allies. "You can break it?"

She lifted her chin. "I'm taking a different approach."

Suddenly, Caden felt his faith being tested. He knew of no approaches to break a curse other than to break a curse. "That makes no sense."

"It does, Caden," Brynne said. "I've had this idea for a while, but I couldn't figure out how to time it right. I thought I'd need to act just as the curse descended on you, but that would be tricky, as the moon phases depend on day, month, year, and orbit."

That was Ashevillian science. Science, tech, and magic were her strong points. Caden sighed. "And?"

"And now I have figured out how to fix your curse without having to do it as the curse descends. I can do it today. Before the half-moon curse descends on you tomorrow."

All this sounded good. And suspicious. If she knew how to fix everything, why were her eyes wide? Why was she biting her lower lip? Caden stepped back. "For someone who's solved our great curse problem, you seem nervous and wary. How is it you will fix it?"

"If I tell you, you might say no."

"Then you should definitely tell me."

"I don't want you talking me out of it," she said. "Like I said, I need you to trust me."

Lucian, gifted in stealth, warned to be wary of such words. But that was when they came from strangers. Brynne was his closest ally. And if Caden considered Tito a brother and Jane possibly a sister, wasn't Brynne then his best friend?

His thoughts began to embarrass him. He looked away from Brynne and up to the mountain and morning sky.

He and Brynne had fought villains; they'd braved a strange new world together; they texted smiley faces back and forth. If she didn't want to tell him what she was about to do, he probably wouldn't let her do it if he knew. Future Elite Paladins, however, trusted their partners.

He returned his gaze to her. "I do trust you," he said. "You're my partner and my closest friend."

She went a bit rosy, a bit smug. "Maybe more than a friend."

This was why Caden regretted telling Brynne things at times. She always had to outdo him. He felt his cheeks heat but stood straighter. "Maybe. Definitely not a sister, anyway," he said.

"You've told me that before," she said. "So I win."

"It's not a competition."

"Of course it is, prince. That's what makes it fun."

Well, Caden saw no reason to argue with that.

"And today, I win," she said.

If he leaned forward and kissed her, even on the cheek, he wagered she'd lose. That's what he would do. In just a moment. Then he'd win. No future Elite Paladin should lose to a spellcaster.

Brynne arched a delicate brow. "Are you ready?"

Caden blushed. Kissing her would have to wait. "It seems not," he said. He took a deep breath. "But if you can fix my curse, do so now."

"Close your eyes, prince."

No doubt Caden would regret this, but he closed his eyes. For a moment, he stood in darkness. He heard the breeze blowing leaves from the trees. The cold bit at his cheeks and hands.

WHAP.

Brynne hit him, palm first, in the chest. He opened his eyes and looked at her. He felt magic tingle over his limbs. He fell to his knees, hitting the damp earth, no doubt dirtying his jeans. Whatever Brynne just did felt like a curse, not the breaking of one. "What did you do?"

She knelt beside him, face bright with anticipation. "How do you feel?"

Caden felt angry. "Like I did when you cursed me the first time."

Her smile lit up the morning. "That's good."

"No, it's not," he said. His bad feeling about this intensified. "Tell me what you did."

"As your compliance curse for the half-moon holds,

so shall you be resistance bound. I linked one curse to the other."

Caden definitely didn't like the sound of that. "What does that mean?"

She sat back on her heels. "The curse can't be broken unless you die, which is no solution, or unless we destroy the moon, and Tito's adamant we not try that." She picked at a bright-yellow leaf on the ground. "Sometimes enchantments counter each other. That's why Jasan's enchanted paper clips keep his blood dagger wound from being fatal. Why can't curses counter each other, too?"

She wasn't saying what he thought she was saying, was she? "Have you cursed me again?"

"With resistance." She started speaking faster, more excitedly. "Don't you see? The resistance curse will be coupled to the compliance curse; they'll occur together. And if you're cursed dually with resistance and compliance, they'll cancel each other out." She took a deep breath. "I think."

"You think?" he said.

"I'm almost positive." She leaned forward and took his hand. "You said Ms. Jackson could smell the magic. She'll know. Rath Dunn's tested you enough that he likely knows when, too. This is the only chance to fix it before the half-moon."

Caden pulled away from her. He stood and brushed leaf litter from his jeans. Nothing about being doubly cursed seemed good.

"I think this is the only way," Brynne said. "I really do."

Caden took a calming breath. "If you say so." He crossed his arms and tried to be less irritated and more accepting of his scheming sorceress of an ally. "Do you think it has worked?"

Brynne twisted her hands together. "We won't know until the curses activate."

Well. That didn't seem ominous at all.

After they separated, Caden called Jasan. He was relieved when he answered. "You're all right," Caden said.

"I am," Jasan said. "And we won't let the next part of the spell happen."

"We won't." Quickly, Caden told him about the contact with the Greater Realm. "Bring your Enchanted Whisk of Mixing," he said. "We need to warn them as well."

From the driveway came the sounds of wheels crunching on gravel and of a car engine. Caden ended the call and grabbed his bag. Officer Levine had arrived to take them to school. Rosa stood on the porch to see them away, but she kept shaking her head. "I don't want to send you, but I have to."

"It's in the paperwork," Caden said, and grabbed his school things. "We also have to go."

Tito and Jane burst out the door, Tito pulling his hair back, Jane stuffing papers into her bag. Rosa gazed at them with her brows drawn and a frown. "I don't want to send you somewhere dangerous. You know that."

"We know," Tito said. "But we've survived school every other day; odds are we'll survive today, too."

That didn't seem to make Rosa feel any better. She took a deep breath. "I'll find a way to keep you safe. Be careful today. Text me at lunch to let me know you're all right."

"We will," Jane said.

Officer Levine seemed equally dismayed. He drove them to school in his patrol car—Brynne got the front seat. Apparently losing her hair gave her special rights to the best seat most befitting of royalty. Caden, Tito, and Jane sat in the back. No one kicked her seat like they did when Caden was in front.

"So," Officer Levine said after they were on the road, "are you all really okay?"

Jane leaned her head back and put in her drops. Brynne tugged at her cap. Tito fidgeted. Caden raised a brow. "Not entirely," he said.

"Do you want to talk about it?" Officer Levine said.

Jane glanced at Caden. She seem calm and collected, and she smiled at him kindly. "We try not to ask Caden that question," she said.

It took Caden a moment to realize he'd been insulted. He bristled. "And why not?"

"Because the answer is always yes," Brynne said, and grinned.

It seemed Caden needed to explain himself. "That's

because talking is often necessary." He caught Officer Levine's gaze in the mirror. "Jasan will die if we don't stop this spell."

When they got to the school, brown-suited grounds workers were planting crimson-colored bushes around the school's stone walls. No doubt that was Rath Dunn's doing. He did enjoy spectacle.

His head heavy with thoughts, his gaze on the red-rimmed school, Caden got out of the car. The grass was more brown than green now. There were no clouds overhead, but in the distance he saw a fleet approaching.

Tito, Brynne, and Jane got out of the car, too.

"Call me if you need me," Officer Levine said. Slowly, he pulled away.

Brynne was quiet. She tugged her cap down. "Everyone will notice I don't have hair."

"Probably," Caden said.

Jane squinted at him, then leaned closer as if to see him better. "That's not helping, Caden," she said.

"People will notice," Caden said, then caught Brynne's gaze. "But you're a powerful sorceress of the Greater Realm. What do you care what the students of Asheville think? And Jane, Tito, and I will be with you."

"We got your back," Tito said.

What more could Caden say to ease Brynne's worry? She liked vengeance. Jane, too, for that matter. He suspected that shared trait made them better friends. He straightened his posture. "If anyone says anything cruel to you, flip them over."

"Flip them over?" Jane said.

"With her telekinesis magic." He made a circular motion with his hand. "Knock them over. Like you did downtown with the teachers and the tables. Except don't hurt anyone."

"Oh," Jane said. "I like that idea."

Caden knew she would.

Brynne pursed her lips. "I would feel better knocking over people," she said.

"And since you'd use magic, no one will be able to prove you've done anything wrong."

Tito looked from Jane to Caden to Brynne. "Okay," Tito said. "Haven't you knocked assassins over with your telekinesis magic and killed them? And you set that mountain on fire by accident that time, right?"

"Indeed," Brynne said, and sounded proud.

"Well, let's not magic any bullies. If someone gives you trouble, just ignore it."

"Oh," Brynne said, "I won't ignore it."

Tito seemed exasperated. "Fine, but don't do anything that could accidentally kill someone, okay?"

Brynne's silver eyes glinted. "Even Derek?" she asked.

That seemed to give Tito pause. Derek had teased him. Finally, Tito said, "I've forgiven him. I'm not wasting my time hating him. So no, not even him."

24

THE ASSEMBLY IN RED

𝕴n Caden's first class, Manglor announced, "The tyrant Rath Dunn has called an assembly." He led Caden, Tonya, and Ward to rows in the back left, close to an exit. Instead of sitting on the aisle like teachers typically did, Manglor sat between Ward and Tonya, one giant arm behind each and his knees bunched against the seatback in the row ahead. He gestured Caden to that seat. "Stay close."

Caden pointed to a different seat, one that the knees of Manglor the Conqueror weren't crammed against. "I'd prefer this one."

Manglor narrowed his eyes, but Caden held his gaze. Caden stood in the aisle, unwilling to lose their battle of wills, when someone grabbed his arm. Sharp nails pinched, and his heart beat faster. He twisted back.

Mrs. Belle stood behind him. It seemed it wasn't only Brynne who snuck up on Caden. It was everyone. With one hand, Mrs. Belle held on to his arm, with the other she directed her morning science students to the middle section. Her hair was held into a bun with a yellow Ashevillian pencil. Her red nails looked long and freshly polished.

"You warned me," she said quietly. "So I'll return the favor and help you. Those of us against Mr. Rathis must band together."

"How?"

"I've decided to go with them, to let them lead me to their spell."

That would help no one. "What? No. They'll sacrifice you."

"They've never seen me after dark. I am something to behold." With a wink, she left to sit with her class.

Caden was wondering just what that meant when Jasan hurried down the aisle to him. He wore a brown leather jacket over a fitted blue sweatshirt. No doubt Jasan intended the jacket to hide his wrist, but Caden saw the pink tinge near the sleeve, and it made him queasy. His brother was always bleeding.

Jasan pushed Caden toward the cramped seat before Caden could fully explain that he didn't want Manglor's giant knees against his seatback. "What was that with Mrs. Belle?" Jasan said, and slid into the seat beside him.

The other teachers and classes filed down the aisles.

Mr. Faunt led his morning math class toward the front rows. Brynne, Tito, and Jane normally had their morning honors English course with Mr. Bellows. Of course, Mr. Bellows had been blown away the night before. They entered behind stout Mrs. Grady instead. She appeared to be in charge of Mr. Bellows's class as well as her own.

Brynne caught Caden's gaze. Her hat fit snugly on her head. She smiled, but she looked a bit wobbly as she sat down.

Suddenly, the auditorium lights flashed on and off. The speakers pounded with drumbeats. Then all went dark, all went silent. When the lights turned back on an instant later, the curtains opened and Rath Dunn stood center stage. He'd trimmed his beard to a sharp point. He wore a three-piece red suit and shiny, brown-and-white shoes.

"He deserves to die for this spectacle alone," Jasan grumbled.

Ms. Primrose sat in a chair stage left. She seemed shadowed in blue, and she neither moved nor blinked. Was that Caden's imagination or did she seem less human than usual? Meaner and more shaded in blue? Was that because Rath Dunn stood in front of her and brought out her Blue essence, and was he unafraid of that because he held power over her?

She had said he'd let her rage. That was something Caden hoped never to see.

Mr. Creedly stood hunched over by the edge of the

curtains. His beady eyes followed Rath Dunn as he strode across the stage. The shadows around Mr. Creedly's long limbs seemed to lengthen toward Rath Dunn as if to engulf him, but then they drew back. The hatred on Mr. Creedly's face, however, didn't.

With the air of a dictator, Rath Dunn surveyed the audience. "Welcome." He cocked his head and peered toward the right rows, the rows opposite Caden. "I'm sorry, Brynne," he said suddenly with feigned sympathy. Something cruel flashed in his expression, and he pointed at her. "No hats in the building. No exceptions. You'll need to take that off."

Everyone in the auditorium turned to Brynne.

Caden started to stand, but Jasan reached across him and forced him back. This had to be addressed. Caden opened his mouth to—

"No," Jasan said. "This isn't the place or time."

"But he's harassing Brynne."

"Brynne will be fine," Jasan said. "Don't be distracted by his antics."

Everyone stared at Brynne. Caden felt helpless and stared, too. Her face was ablaze, and for a moment, she sat frozen and red. Then she stood. Caden feared she'd light the stage on fire. But she didn't. She raised her chin, reached up, and yanked her cap off.

"That's a good look," Rath Dunn said with a chortle, and ran a hand over his shiny head. Brynne sat, though she wore a defiant expression. Students began to whisper. Murmurs bounced off the acoustic walls. Caden saw Jane say something to her, and Tito put his arm around Brynne's shoulders.

Onstage, Rath Dunn seemed full of glee. "Now, down to business." He reached out as if to pull the crowd to him. "As you know, Mr. McDonald was tragically lost"—Rath Dunn moved his right hand over his heart—"and sadly Mr. Bellows was lost in yesterday's windstorm. Sucked into the sky no less. We're here to discuss the tragedy and move forward—"

Suddenly, Rath Dunn's feet flew out from under him. He was a red-spinning blur. His face careened toward the stage, and . . . he caught himself like an acrobat, like it was easy.

In one swift move, he jumped back to standing. His eyes glinted and scanned the audience. He paused for an instant and looked at Brynne. Then, with great flourish, Rath Dunn took a deep bow. Applause rang out from the audience.

Jasan let out a sigh. "Your sorceress shouldn't taunt him like that."

"I think she meant to kill him."

"He's not so easy to defeat," Jasan said. He kept his voice low, his words quiet. "He's good at strategy as well as combat. He isn't weak to magic."

So Caden had just seen. Brynne had thrown him, and he'd reacted with ease. Caden frowned at Jasan. "You plan to fight him."

Jasan took off his jacket and set it in his lap, where it covered his wrist and hand. "I'm not so easy to defeat either."

In the front, Rath Dunn held out his palms to quiet the cheers. "Settle down, settle down," he said. "It's time to come together as a group. Move past our differences. Those of us who can will benefit." It seemed like he was addressing the teachers specifically. "Everyone needs a purpose."

Caden studied his brother. His skin was paper white. "You look pale, Jasan."

Manglor leaned forward. "I expect my allies fit for battle, and he is fit."

"Fit and ready," Jasan said, but Caden's stomach twisted.

Onstage, Rath Dunn motioned to Ms. Primrose. "If you have troubles dealing with these losses, feel free to talk to our school's counselor. As you know, Ms. Primrose is in the *small* office near the gym." Now he was taunting her. "She always does her job."

Maybe Ms. Primrose truly had no choice but to help him. Caden wasn't sure, but Ms. Primrose's already-cold expression iced over and she sat sword straight. Of one thing he was certain: no sane person would go to her to talk of their feelings. Fickle old Elderdragons were unsuited for counseling middle school students. For counseling anyone, really.

What *would* happen if her essence was lost? He knew what had happened to Jane when she'd lost her tears and Brynne when she'd lost her hair. His heart ached when he thought of what would happen to Jasan if they failed to stop the third part of the spell tonight. Still, Caden couldn't help but wonder what would losing part of Ms. Primrose's essence make her? Would Rath Dunn still have some degree of control over her? He didn't seem afraid of her, so Caden feared he would.

"As soon as the school day ends," Jasan whispered, "we need to establish contact with the Greater Realm."

"While you do that," Manglor said, his voice low and deep, "I'll see if I can capture Ms. Jackson. Stop the witch before the spell."

"We have to stop the sacrifice tonight," Caden said.

"If Manglor can't catch Ms. Jackson before tonight," Jasan said, "he and I will hide in the woods, catch them unawares, and stop them there. I with my sword and he with his ax."

"And I'll go with you and help," Caden said. "As will Brynne and Sir Tito and Lady Jane—"

His words were interrupted by Rath Dunn bellowing from the stage. "Now get to class." His gaze zoomed to Caden. "Jump up now. That's an order."

Was Rath Dunn testing his curse now? Neither his compliance curse nor his new resistance curse would be active until tomorrow. By then, the four-part spell would be stopped. All would be okay. It would have to be. Caden stayed in his seat.

Rath Dunn watched him for a second more. Then music blared again. The lights flipped on and off. All went silent.

All went dark. When the lights turned back on again, the stage curtains were closed.

Jasan squeezed the arm rail tight enough that Caden swore he heard the seat groan. "You'll stay away and stay safe. Manglor and I won't need help. I won't be a bird nor he a dog tonight."

In the auditorium, Caden saw Mr. Faunt leading his class away. He saw Mrs. Grady and Mr. Wist. He saw many teachers who looked strong: the wraith and the banshee, Mr. Faunt and his razor-sharp nails, lanky Mr. Frye, Mr. Limon with his strange brow, the nurse. Likely, they were all loyal to Rath Dunn and Ms. Jackson. "You might need help anyway," Caden said.

Jasan stood but then leaned down to Caden. "You worry too much." He paused and added, "Little brother." Jasan rarely referred to Caden as his brother, and he almost never directly addressed Caden as such. Did he truly think it would lessen Caden's worry?

"I think I worry just enough," Caden said, and stood up to leave the assembly. If Jasan and Manglor were to battle villains in the woods at midnight, Caden would find a way to fight beside them whether they wanted him there or not.

Rosa was waiting in her pickup when Caden, Brynne, Tito, and Jane were freed from the last class of the day. Jane's eyes were so bloodshot they were completely red. The fake tears the doctor prescribed her only seemed to help so much. Brynne's hair was gone. If they didn't stop this next part of the spell, Jasan's blood would be gone, too.

Caden thought of the five-jeweled emblem, of Landon's emblem. People would die in Asheville and in the Greater Realm if they didn't stop it. He got in the front seat, and no one complained. "Let's hurry home," he said. "I need to contact my family."

Rosa glanced at the three in the back, then at him. "All right."

"My brother is coming over."

She took in a deep breath. "That should be interesting."

"He's a noble Elite Paladin," Caden said. "It should be an honor."

Rosa glanced in the rearview mirror, seemingly watching the school get farther away. She seemed relieved when they turned the curve. "We'll see, Caden," Rosa said. "Elite Paladin or not, he needs to behave in my house."

Jasan was waiting on the porch when they pulled up. He'd gotten to Rosa's house fast, but he got everywhere fast. They wasted no time once home. Brynne spelled Jasan to speak English; and as Rosa and he tried to be civil, Tito, Brynne, and Jane set up the tablet.

Tito plugged his fully charged tablet into the wall, then set it on the coffee table. The cord stretched from wall to table like a tripping trap. He plopped on the floor with his back against the couch.

Brynne prepared the water and pan. She sat on the

floor, too, cross-legged. Caden remained standing. He could see the tablet easily that way. Also, the floor had yet to be swept today. Better he be neat and clean to speak to his father.

Jane gathered her Enchanted Hammer of Smashing and the other items: the Enchanted Whisk of Mixing brought by Jasan, Brynne's Magical Hairpin of Unlocking, and two more shimmery metal items Caden hadn't seen before—an enchanted coin and an enchanted spoon—and kneeled by the table and tablet.

"Those are new," Caden said.

"I made them this morning," Jane said. "Just in case we need more power."

Thus they were enchanted items one hundred and thirty-six and one hundred and thirty-seven: the Enchanted Coin and Enchanted Spoon of Spell Sacrifice. But would a lot of small enchantments add up to the same thing as one big one?

Jasan glanced at the window, likely thinking of the fading day, likely thinking of their brothers and people also in danger a realm away. "We need to hurry." He sat on the green interrogation couch, in the middle, as if he were the highest-ranked person in the room. Which, Caden supposed, he was.

Rosa soon made him move over, though, so she could sit on the couch, too. The house was hers, so Jasan couldn't protest. "How will this work?" Rosa said.

Brynne explained the telepathy magic and made sure they were thusly spelled. Then, to make the contact easier, she also magicked Rosa, Jane, and Tito so they would understand anything they heard spoken. Jane demonstrated how she would smash enchantments, and Tito told Jasan about the tech of his Ashevillian tablet.

Jasan nodded, but Caden didn't think he really understood. Caden was fairly certain Jasan didn't understand much of this odd world. He certainly understood less than Caden.

"We're ready," Brynne said.

25

THE OCTAGONAL ROOM

This needed to work. Caden held his breath. Rosa and Jasan watched from the couch. Both had their arms crossed; both had iron expressions. Brynne sat by the tray of water. Tito cringed as he watched.

Jane raised the Enchanted Hammer of Smashing. She brought it down with a large splash. And missed every item in the pan. Her cheeks went rosy. "I can't see that well," she said, and Caden worried about her eyes. She raised the hammer with renewed vigor.

Pound. Pound. Pound. Pound. Pound.

The four enchanted items turned dull and dented. Silver flowed across the water's surface. Quickly, Brynne grabbed the pan and poured the enchantment-and-life-force-enriched water atop the screen.

Caden leaned closer for a better view. So did the others. Jane got especially near to it. The electricity in the house flickered as if drained by a great power. The strange electrical noises Caden had grown accustomed to went silent. Caden's stomach sank. Had it not worked? He didn't know much about Ashevillian tech, but he did know nothing good came of a blank screen.

The quiet lasted only a moment. Soon the house, the electricity, the sounds and the lights returned to normal. Then the tablet's screen glowed silver, and the silver turned into an image.

An octagonal room came into focus on the screen. Caden knew it at once—the king's strategy room. They viewed it from a round mirror opposite the heavy carved door that served as the only entrance or exit. The mirror allowed the king and whoever else might be in the room constant vigil over the entry point.

Two people stood and faced each other.

One was Caden's father, King Axel.

Caden had not seen his father in many months now. His chest felt tight. His stomach fluttered. His father was alive and well, and Caden would warn him; then he would tell him Jasan had been wrongly convicted of murder and treason.

But what would the king say to Caden? Certainly, he'd be happy Caden was alive. Then again, Caden had gotten stranded in another world. He'd yet to slay a dragon or stop a villain. Would the king's brow also furrow with disappointment?

It didn't matter. The king needed to be warned, and Jasan needed to be vindicated.

King Axel wore his grand robes, those of the finest midnight-blue elvish wool and embellished with gold and silver threads. His sword was strapped across his back. His scepter—both a symbol of the king and a weapon—sat nearby on a small pedestal table. It was strange for him to be doubly armed in the castle and while wearing his finery. Obviously, the king thought these were dangerous days.

The other person in the room wasn't visible immediately. He wore black and blended into the shadows. Small, glinting daggers were attached strategically from his thigh to his ankle, and Caden was certain there were more blades hidden underneath his garments. It was third-born Lucian, gifted in stealth, the only Elite Paladin Caden knew of who also acted as a spy.

Jasan gestured Caden and the others to move back. He leaned close to the screen. "King Axel," he said. He hadn't said "Father," Caden noticed. No response. "Lucian." Again, no response. Jasan glanced up at Brynne.

"It should work, if there's enough magical power," she said, and chewed on her bottom lip. "We used more this time."

"Do they need the telepathy mojo cast on them, too?" Tito said.

Brynne shook her head. "No. Only one side needs the sorcery."

The king's voice rang from the tablet's speaker. "What of Crimsen?"

Crimsen was Rath Dunn's home in the Autumnlands. "They move their mercenary army near our borders, as do the Valley gnomes. They look too few in number for a credible attack, but they seem ready to start one."

"Are you certain?"

"Tomorrow, midday, they wait for a signal."

Caden wondered at that timing—midday. The first part of Rath Dunn and Ms. Jackson's spell had happened at dawn, the second as dusk, the third was to occur tonight at midnight. If Caden was guessing, midday would be the planned time for the fourth part. Was what was happening in Crimsen connected?

The king seemed suspicious. "You know this how?"

Lucian smiled. His cheek was dimpled on the right side, and it made him seem younger than he was. "I took a walk around the gnome captain's planning tent."

The king didn't smile. "You were ordered to stay to the border, Lucian, not venture beyond it."

To break even a small command of the king seemed completely insane. Lucian hadn't done as he was ordered? Caden was taken aback.

Lucian seemed unrepentant. "I did as I thought best, Father."

"You did as you wanted."

"I did."

Now Caden was certain he was hallucinating. No one ever talked to the king like that. Not even first-born Valon. Not even traitorous, second-born Maden. No one.

Caden glanced at Brynne. She blinked at the screen as if confused by what she saw. Jasan, however, sighed. He didn't seem surprised by this at all. Truth be told, neither did the king.

Jasan seemed to notice Caden's shock. "He's often like that," Jasan said. "In private. With family only."

Was not Caden, although younger and with only one shared parent, part of Lucian's family, too? "I've never seen him act like that."

"It's because the king shelters you from his behavior," Jasan said. "He shelters you from a lot of things."

Jasan was honorable and honest. Caden was certain he spoke the truth. He wasn't sure, however, the king sheltering Caden was the only reason. "If you say so."

Caden focused back on the screen. The king paced the room. He cleared his throat. "And the other thing?" Did the king's voice crack? Caden thought it might have. "What have you found?"

Lucian's dimple disappeared, as did his grin. "Landon isn't the only one missing, which isn't a good sign. But Maden's heard rumors he was last seen near the dark woods. He and I will search all night through the snowfall if we must."

No. No. No. The one person third-born Lucian should

not venture into the dark woods with was traitorous, second-born Maden. And he should definitely not go with him on a night when a sacrifice was to be made. Caden looked at Jasan. "Lucian is in danger."

Jasan's face was stone. "Assuming he and Maden aren't accomplices."

Just because Maden was a traitor didn't mean their other brothers were. "Why do you think Maden has an accomplice?" Caden said.

"Why shouldn't I? They all convicted me, and even the powerful need help toppling a king. How could Maden not have allies in the castle?"

Caden wouldn't listen to that type of reasoning. "Maden's accomplice is Rath Dunn." He signaled to the screen. "And it seems the mercenaries of Crimsen and Valley gnomes. Not another of our brothers."

"Maybe," Jasan said.

Caden looked back at the screen, at his father. The king pulled his hand into a fist. "Find Landon," he said. "I lost Chadwin, I lost Caden," the king said. "I won't lose a third son to these dark times."

"Third?" Lucian moved like a midnight panther. Silent and certain. "Not fourth? As we banished Jas—"

The king stopped him with a glower that would give the bravest of panthers pause. "Don't say that name in my presence."

Lucian stepped beyond the king's reach and near the

door to the chamber. "If he were the cause of our troubles, if he betrayed us," Lucian said, "then why have our problems only increased since"—Lucian paused—"Jasan was banished?"

Caden never had seen the king strike one of his brothers, but he feared he was about to. Luckily, he didn't. The king turned away. "I'll deal with you later. Go find Landon. Get out."

Lucian did. Quickly and quietly, and the king was left alone.

"Lucian seems no traitor to me," Caden said.

The green interrogation couch creaked as Jasan stood. His body was tense, his jaw tight. Obviously, Jasan was troubled. Rosa looked like she wanted to pat his back. "I'll be outside," he growled before she could.

"I'll go with you," Caden said.

"I want to be alone. Stay here and figure out how to communicate with them," Jasan said. "I'd prefer to warn them before Lucian, the one brother who seems to have finally considered I'm innocent, is murdered."

Why did Caden feel angry? Well. No matter why. He did. And he needed to say something. Often, he needed to say things. "I never thought you were guilty," Caden said. "So he's not your only brother who has considered that you might be innocent."

Jasan ran his hand through his hair. He closed his eyes and took a deep breath. "I meant," Jasan said, slowly and carefully, "the only brother besides—" If Jasan said half brother, Caden was going to punch him. Jasan didn't. "Besides my little brother."

Brynne, Tito, and Jane watched Caden now instead of the screen. The attention was uncomfortable, and Caden felt his face flush. "That's more accurate," he said. However, while Caden preferred "little brother" to "half brother," neither was ideal. "Younger brother, you mean."

"Don't push it, *little* brother," Jasan said. He grabbed his jacket and pulled it on. In three quick steps, he was gone. The screen door creaked open and slammed shut.

Caden got up to follow him, but Rosa reached out and stopped him. "Let him go, Caden," she said. Then she looked back at the tablet like she didn't know what to think of what she'd seen and heard.

Caden collected his thoughts. Landon was missing. Lucian was about to go out alone with Maden. They needed to speak to the king, to warn him, warn Lucian and the others. He felt his heart begin to race; he felt his breath catch, and he had to calm himself.

"Are you okay, Caden?" Jane said.

Rosa stood up and did pat Caden's back.

"Mostly," Caden said. "But we need to speak, not watch."

Brynne pulled at her cap. "Then we need more enchantment power."

Caden looked down at the screen. The king stood, his

back to them. How could he continue to believe Jasan was a traitor? Truth be told, Caden wasn't completely surprised. If King Axel had been convinced Jasan was traitorous, it would take irrefutable proof to convince him otherwise. Once the king made up his mind, it was hard to change it. The king's gift, resolution, was something to behold.

Tito tapped the screen. "Is it frozen?"

The king was unmoving like a mountain. They watched. Nothing happened.

Brynne sat back on her heels. "No, he's just not doing anything."

Not true, he was standing. "He's deep in thought," Caden said.

Brynne frowned. Jane cocked her head pensively. They needed to find a way to do more than watch the king. They needed to speak to him.

On-screen, the king scratched his rear.

"Huh," Tito said. "I guess even royal butts itch."

Suddenly, Jane stood and faced them. "I've decided," she announced. "I'm going to enchant the tablet. It needs to be done."

"First of all, no," Tito said. "Second of all, how would you even do something like that?"

"Like I do all of them. I hold the item and concentrate on what I want it to do. Like with the hammer. I wanted a hammer to magically smash things. So I held it, concentrated on that, and I pricked my finger. Once the blood hits the item, I feel energy flowing from me to it."

Tito scrunched up his brow. "Life force, you mean."

Jane nodded. "To enchant the tablet, I just need to concentrate on it as a device to contact another world. It's more complex, so it takes more thought, and the metal parts are smaller." She squinted at the screen. The king had left, and the room was empty. "But once I figure out how I want it to work, the rest should be quick."

Quick was good.

Caden had never realized enchantment was such fast magic. No wonder enchanters so easily spent their life spans. An enchanted tablet, however, sounded like no small bit of item magic. "It sounds like a powerful enchantment."

Brynne touched Jane's elbow. "Small enchantments only, remember. That's how you'll live. That's how you'll become an enchantress until old age. The first of your kind."

Rosa held up a hand. "Wait? What do you mean by life force?" She peered at Jane. "And what does it have to do with how long you live."

"Oh, you're not going to like it," Tito said. "Her enchantments take years from her life."

Rosa's frown deepened. "What?"

"I told her to stop," Tito said.

The sound of a heavy door opening came from the tablet. Caden and the others looked at the screen. First-born

Valon entered the octagonal room. His expression was schooled, his jaw tight.

"That's Valon," Caden said. If he and his friends couldn't warn Caden's father, Valon would be the next best thing. "He's first-born and crown prince."

Caden tried to speak to him, but as expected, there was no response.

"I don't have a choice," said Jane. "I have to enchant it. I don't want Ms. Jackson to win."

"None of us do," Caden said.

"And it's not only your brother who's in danger," Jane said. "If the spell is completed, it will drain many lives in Asheville and in the Greater Realm, right? Including your family."

Brynne nodded. "Ritual magic drains life. That's what fuels the spell," she said. "A powerful spell with powerful ingredients will drain the city. The communication spells are small by comparison. The one by the river killed all the grasses and trees. Probably some animals, too. The four-part spell is larger. It requires *four* human sacrifices. It will drain human and plant life alike if completed."

Rosa listened to them, her mouth a tight line, her arms crossed.

"We need to warn the other side," Jane said. She rubbed her finger along the edge of the tablet. On-screen, fourth-born Martin entered the room. "We need to save Lucian. Caden shouldn't lose another brother. I know what it's like.

I lost my mom. I'll enchant the tablet," Jane said. "One last big enchantment."

"That's what you said about the ladle," Tito said.

"No," Rosa said, and her voice was like steel.

Caden tugged his coat tighter around his shoulders. Jane was willing to give up years of her life span, possibly her life, to help him, his people, and his kingdom. "Your life is as important as Lucian's, as everyone's."

"This is my best chance to help," she said. "I want to do it."

"You're not enchanting that tablet, young lady," Rosa said. "And that's final."

An idea was battering around in Caden's mind, an idea he didn't really like and one he didn't want to say out loud. It was a good idea, though. "Watch the tablet. I've a better idea," he said, and turned toward the kitchen. "There is something Jane needs to enchant, but it isn't the tablet, and it isn't complex."

Tito frowned, the right side of his mouth lower than the left. "Then why do you look so upset?"

Rosa turned to him as if to scrutinize his mood. "I'm not upset," Caden said. "I'm finding a solution. Like leaders do."

Brynne and Tito exchanged a pointed look. "Is he our leader?" Tito said.

"Not mine."

Caden ignored them. "I'll be back."

Although Rosa didn't organize the utensils in the exact best way, she did organize them. Caden found the gleaming metal scissors in the bottom drawer. He returned to the living room and placed them in front of Jane. She picked them up and held them close to her face to better look at the silvery blades.

"Enchant those for cutting," Caden said. He turned to Brynne. "That would be a small enchantment, correct? It shouldn't cost too much life force."

Rosa seemed uncomfortable with the entire conversation. "Exactly how much life force are we talking about?"

"It would be tiny," Brynne assured her. "But why would we need enchanted scissors?"

Jane seemed happy with the idea of enchanted scissors. There was no indication of worry at all. Truly, enchanters liked to enchant. It was, as Ms. Primrose would say, in their nature. "Why wouldn't we?" she said.

"Well, prince," Brynne said. "What's your great idea?"

Caden slipped off his coat. "We need more power. To make contact. And sacrificing small enchantments isn't enough."

"It's not." Brynne dropped her gaze to his coat.

He nodded to it.

"Your plan is for us to destroy the coat?" Brynne said.

It was enchanted with warmth and protection. It was a symbol of Razzon. The coat sized to fit whoever owned it. And—very important—it never got dirty. "It has powerful magic. Much more than the stapler or whisk had. And it's been passed from person to person in my family."

"Giving away enchanted items makes them stronger," Jane said knowingly.

"I remember," Caden said.

His father had given the coat to him, and his father to him, and so on. But when it came to the true value of things, it was a coat. An item. A thing. It wasn't important like a person. It wasn't important like Jane or Jasan or Lucian. In battle, there was always sacrifice. Better it be his most precious belonging than one of his more precious friends.

The coat felt warm where it was draped across his arm. It brought comfort. It was his connection to his homeland. To use it to help protect Razzon only showed how powerful that connection was. "I don't think a hammer, even an enchanted one, will destroy enchanted wool. The blood dagger ripped the fabric. An enchanted blade is needed."

"Like scissors," Jane said.

"Indeed," Caden said.

"Are you sure, Caden?" Jane said.

Was magically ripping Caden's coat to shreds worth the chance to speak to his father, his brothers, worth a chance to warn someone? It was, even if it felt like he was losing all he held dear one person, one thing at a time. That he didn't say. Instead, he said, "We need to stop this spell to save countless lives. It's worth it."

"Jane," Rosa said. "I'm not comfortable with you enchanting anything."

But the scissors Jane held were glimmering with enchantment. "It's already done, Rosa," Jane said. Caden deemed them magical item number one hundred and thirty-eight—the Enchanted Scissors of Destroying His Most Precious Possession.

The tablet screen continued to glow on the coffee table. Jane held out the scissors.

The room was quiet. "You sure about this?" Tito said. "I know you love that coat, bro."

True. The coat meant a lot to Caden. But it wasn't because it was warm or never got dirty. Although those were things he really liked about it. It meant a lot because his father had given it to him. It meant a lot, too, because it was a symbol of the best parts of his heritage and people. "Whatever love I feel for my coat, I feel more for my friends and family. You included."

"And there you go," Tito said. "Making it weird."

Jane offered the scissors to him, handle first. "Do you want to do it?"

Caden didn't want to be the one to destroy his coat. He didn't want to touch the scissors either. He shook his head. "You do it." He transferred his Summerlands compass, Landon's charred emblem, and his cell phone from his coat pocket to his jeans. Hopefully, fate's favor would grant them success, and this would work.

He handed the coat to Jane.

Caden didn't want to watch its destruction either. "I'll wait with Jasan outside," he said. Rosa got up to follow him, but he held up his palm. "I want a moment alone with him."

Without his coat, he immediately felt the chill of the autumn evening as he went out to the porch. His ugly turquoise sweater wasn't as warm or as meaningful. It wasn't appropriate finery for an eighth-born prince. Quietly, he shut the screen door behind him. They'd call him once the deed was done.

The clouds looked like a stormy sea, with waves of gray and white and darkest blue. The air continued to grow colder as evening approached. By the woods, Caden noticed Sir Horace. He peeked around a tree and watched. Good. Later Caden would need him to get to Biltmore Forest.

Jasan paced back and forth on the porch, his mouth a tight line, his jaw clenched. He was on his cell phone. He put it away when he saw Caden.

Jasan reached out and touched the collar of Caden's sweater. "Where's your coat?"

"They're shredding it for the communication spell." Caden wrapped his arms around his chest. Truly, it was colder without his coat. "It's the symbol of our people, but I told them to do it." Caden felt like he was confessing a great sin. "Even though Father trusted me to keep it safe."

"It's a coat," Jasan said.

Caden raised a brow. "One you wanted."

"Not anymore."

"It means a lot to me, and to our people," Caden said.

"Its purpose is to protect the royal family and the people of Razzon. Shredding it to warn them serves its purpose. If the king doesn't like it"—Jasan waved a hand as if to dismiss the king as nothing—"so be it."

Caden squared his shoulders. "Maybe *I* don't like it."

Jasan tapped his fingers on the railing. He was waiting for something. Impatience and talk of their father seemed to have made him surlier. "Maybe I don't like you," he mumbled.

"Doubtful," Caden said.

Jasan snorted. "Maybe I don't like anyone."

Caden had to think on that one.

From the mountain road, Caden heard the cars zooming down the hill.

"Listen, Manglor can't track the witch. Even if he could, Rath Dunn likely has a backup strategy. Manglor and I are going to stake out the forest to stop the villains." Jasan pointed to the door. "You and the others warn the Greater Realm. Then stay inside and lock the doors."

"We should help you."

"The best way for you to do that is to remain where I won't worry about you."

It was cold without his coat. And the night would only get colder. Caden wrapped his arms around his chest. "You should trust me and my friends, Jasan."

"I'm trusting you to warn our people and save Lucian. That's quite a lot."

Caden shivered. "I can do more."

Something warm flopped across his shoulders. "Here. You can wear my jacket. Until I want it back."

"It needs to be cleaned," Caden said.

Jasan raised a brow. "Then give it back to me."

Caden was warmer now. The nonmagical leather offered some comfort. "No. I'll keep it."

"Warn the king." With that, and with a quick turn toward the trees, Jasan was gone.

The leather felt soft and supple. It had the slightest smell of the Ashevillian soap Jasan used. The sleeves were long and the shoulders a bit big, and there was a smidge of blood on the right-sleeve cuff.

No matter what Jasan ordered, Caden would go to Biltmore Forest tonight. He would be there to help Jasan. His curse hadn't been activated yet. He didn't have to follow anyone's orders, not even his brother's.

Rosa met Caden on the porch not a minute later. She nodded toward the woods. "Was that your brother running off?"

Caden nodded. "He runs into battle."

She frowned, and her brow creased. Then she looked at Caden and ran a finger over the collar of Jasan's jacket. She knew Caden only wore his enchanted coat. "Jane says they're ready," Rosa said. "Come back inside."

Caden hadn't been prepared for the carnage in the living room. Midnight-blue fabric soaked in the pan of water.

A piece of the embroidered Winterbird's wing floated, damp and dull, above the other pieces. Tito and Brynne held what remained of a sleeve while Jane held the scissors. Stray threads lay on the green couch and the carpet.

The threads bothered Caden. He pointed to the threads. "Use all of it," he said.

Tito tossed the loose threads into the pan. The water with the scraps of once-enchanted wool shimmered gold. Caden watched. He waited. They would make contact this time. They had to.

Suddenly, Rosa hugged him tightly. Why she'd hugged him then, he didn't know.

Brynne poured the shimmery gold water over the tablet. When the glow faded, the octagonal room remained in view. It seemed the connection had kept to the circular mirror in the king's strategy room.

Caden hoped to see his father, but King Axel hadn't returned to the room. First-born Valon was still there. So was fourth-born Martin. They were silent. Likely, they waited for the king.

Caden's coat lay in tatters. Landon was missing. Chadwin was dead. Jasan would bleed out if the third part of the spell was completed. Too much was lost already. This had to work. They had to be able to warn them. And Caden couldn't risk waiting for his father to return to the room. What if the screen went black again?

Brynne gestured to the screen and nodded.

Jane and Tito watched. Rosa leaned over and waited.

Caden opened his mouth to speak, but a large man passed by the mirror. He was so tall his head was higher than it and so broad the view of the room was completely blocked as he walked by it. Maden.

For an odd moment, Caden lost his words.

"Prince," Brynne whispered. "This is our only chance."

On the tablet's screen, Valon, Maden, and Martin froze. Had they heard Brynne? Valon made a subtle motion to the others to move apart.

"Whoa," Tito said.

His brothers spun toward the mirror. Valon pulled his long blade, Martin his bow. Maden heaved his heavy broadsword into the air.

It was Caden's only chance. He needed to speak quickly. He needed to warn Valon and Martin. And the one he needed to warn them against had a broadsword raised and at the ready. He needed to say the right thing. Despite his gift of speech, he'd discovered it was a hard thing to do.

26

THE BATTLE IN THE MIRROR

Caden's first-, second-, and fourth-born brothers stared at the mirror, their faces twisted in various stages of surprise and confusion. Valon stepped forward. He was first-born, gifted in leadership and heir to the crown. Martin and Maden stayed behind him. That was always the way. Valon in front, the others falling into line according to relative birth order.

Martin, ever accurate, got to the point. He glanced at Maden, then peered at them, and it was obvious he could see Caden in the mirror. The two-way connection was finally working because he said, "Caden?" Like Lucian, he also had a dimple, and it showed as he smiled. "You're alive?" He seemed happy. Maybe not as happy as he would have been if Caden were Chadwin back from the dead, but happy nonetheless.

Caden leaned close to the tablet. He wondered if his face looked huge. "Alive and well. As you can see."

"All I see is a strange room. Where are you?" Martin said.

Suddenly, Brynne crammed in beside Caden. "Prince Martin, tell my parents I'm alive. Please."

Martin's dimple appeared again. "The girl is there, too, then."

Valon raised his hand to silence him. "I'll ask the questions," he said, taking charge.

Fourth-born Martin released a silent sigh but seemed content enough in his place or, at least, accustomed to it. Second-born Maden, however, cut his gaze to Valon. His expression darkened.

Had Caden's brothers always acted in these subtle ways? Had he failed to notice? Maden was gifted in strength—powerful and larger than life. Was it hard for him to stand in Valon's smaller shadow?

Valon never let any of them forget he was first-born. Caden had never thought about it, and since Caden was eighth-born, he was so far from the crown that he never worried about being king. It simply was the way things were. But maybe Maden had resented it? Looking at Valon now, Caden could understand how Maden might.

Valon neither looked happy to see Caden nor unhappy. He studied Caden like a piece of information in a greater puzzle, like he was something Valon needed to understand to lead properly. The few times Valon paid Caden attention, it was always of this kind.

"Tell us where you are, Caden," Valon said. "How did you get there? What's happened?"

Rosa, Tito, and Jane watched and listened.

This was the most Valon had ever directly talked to Caden. Certainly, Caden had been at dinners and practices aplenty with him. But Valon and he never interacted unless it was through others. He was distant, a bit like the king, but less interested. At least Maden used to listen to Caden speak about the animals of the castle when they passed in the Great Hall. Leadership was about more than control. Just like strength was about more than power.

Without thinking, Caden's gaze flicked to Maden. Caden needed to choose meaningful, succinct words. Maden knew that Caden knew he was a traitor. He'd asked Rath Dunn to bring Caden to their side last spring. But if Caden named him as such, Maden would attack, and Valon's back was turned to him.

Valon spoke softer. "Caden, Father will want to know where you and the girl are so we can retrieve you." A wry smile tugged his lips. "Her parents haven't been easy to handle."

"We're in the Land of Shadow." Maybe if Caden kept talking, he'd have more time. Maybe someone else would come into the octagonal room.

The cozy room behind Caden probably wasn't what

Valon expected. He furrowed his brow. "The Land of Shadow?"

Behind Valon, Maden inched back. From where Maden stood, he could attack Martin and Valon, strike them down while their backs were turned. But Martin noticed. Martin and Maden exchanged a knowing look. Martin put his hand back on his bow. He returned his gaze to Valon's back.

What was happening? Caden's heart began to race. His thoughts felt fast and tangled. No, that wasn't right. He felt unsure, confused, and betrayed. But there was nothing tangled in his understanding. Lucian had been shadowing Martin. Landon was nowhere to be seen, and Jasan said Maden likely had accomplices in the castle.

But how could Maden—and Martin—betray the king, betray Jasan and Chadwin? Just for power? For the crown? Because they resented Valon? Did they resent the king, too? Did they not care that Chadwin was dead and Jasan banished. Then again, their father had doted on Chadwin. Jasan looked like the first queen, and the king sometimes had favored him, too. Valon was first-born; their father treated him like a future king.

Maden and Martin seemed at ease with each other. They stood side by side behind Valon, their hands on or near their weapons. Their gaze on their first-born brother's back. Caden wasn't sure what to do.

Swift, succinct, blurting seemed the best strategy.

"Maden killed Chadwin; Jasan's innocent; Rath Dunn is here."

Caden expected swords to be drawn and a battle to begin. It didn't. Though Maden and Martin kept their hands on their weapons.

"I wouldn't kill Chadwin," Maden obviously lied.

How could he lie so easily? People in the Greater Realm told the truth. Except for Manglor. But what power did untruth hold over others? A great deal, Caden realized. If anyone should know the strength in words, it was Caden. That was why he always used them with honor.

"I don't lie," Caden said. Good leaders liked reason, so it was with reason that he made his case to Valon. "The night Chadwin died it was only you, Jasan, and Valon there. Valon knows he didn't betray Chadwin. And if Jasan were to lose his temper and kill someone, he wouldn't attack them from the back."

Martin seemed more surprised now. He glanced again at Maden. "Jasan is alive, too?"

Maden gestured to Martin as if to say "It's nothing to worry about."

"Jasan tries to save the king."

"Valon," Martin said. "Do you really think our hot-tempered little brother would try to save us after we banished him?"

That was right. Jasan was younger than all of them but Caden. Sometimes Caden forgot that. He always thought of all his brothers as simply "older."

Valon turned from the mirror to them. "Maybe," he said—his hand remained close to his weapon—"if he were innocent."

"No one's innocent," Maden said, and closed his hand around his sword's hilt.

"Did you betray us?"

"Father's too stubborn to lead, and you're too arrogant. What the kingdom needs is strength. We have enemies everywhere."

"And Rath Dunn isn't an enemy?"

Maden shrugged, and his broad shoulders rippled with muscles. "Well, he is strong. And he keeps his promises." Then he chuckled. "Unlike me."

"Then it seems, brother, you are our enemy."

Valon, Martin, and Maden stared at one another for a moment. A fight was imminent. There wasn't time for thoughtful words. Instead, Caden began to yell out everything he knew as fast as he could, about Rath Dunn, about the spell, about the sacrifices. Brynne did as well.

Maden rammed forward into Valon. Valon dodged, veered into the pedestal table, but caught himself. Martin pulled out his bow and aimed at Valon. An arrow whizzed by the mirror. Valon held up the table as a shield; the arrow punctured the tabletop and stopped halfway through.

Though not as fast as Jasan, Maden was always much faster than expected. His size wasn't a hindrance. It gave him reach; it gave him long strides. He drew his sword and swung it in a large, quick circle. Martin ducked, reloading his bow. He and Maden moved like a team, like his brothers always did when fighting an enemy.

Valon blocked Maden's swing with his long sword. They faced each other.

"I always knew it would come to this," Maden said.

He heaved Valon away. Valon hit against the mirror, partially blocking the view. The tablet made a strange beeping noise. In what view was left, Caden saw Maden raise his mighty broadsword and throw it.

The sword spun hilt over blade, and Valon darted from its path. The sword slammed into the mirror. Like splintered ice, the mirror cracked. The screen of Tito's tablet fractured, too, and the tablet started to spark.

The image blinked. Another arrow whizzed past, its path jarred by the cracks in the screen. Valon charged Martin, grabbed his wrist, and tossed him against the wall. Martin's bow flew from his hands, and he cradled his arm to his chest.

"Stop it," Valon said.

"We've long tired of your orders," Martin said.

Maden stood near Martin and pulled him to his feet. For a fleeting moment, something akin to remorse flashed in his expression. "It's far too late to stop," Maden said. "It can't be undone."

While Martin cradled his left arm, his right reached for something: a dagger, Caden suspected. Valon wouldn't see it. His view was blocked by Maden.

"He has a dagger!" Caden yelled.

The tablet started to smoke and sizzle. The screen went black. Sounds of battle, of clanking metals and whistling arrows came from the tablet's speaker. Then Caden heard, "It is too late"—that was Maden's deep voice—"for you. For your orders. And it's too late to find Landon," before the scene went silent.

27

ESCAPE FROM THE ATTIC

Wait? What? What did he mean it was too late to find Landon? The charred emblem flashed in his mind. Maybe Caden did know what he meant, but he couldn't think about it now. The screen was black. There was no sound. What happened to the connection?

The tablet was still plugged into the wall. But the screen looked fractured, busted. It looked as if the broadsword had hit it from the other side, where it should have hit the mirror in the octagonal room.

Jane peered down at the tablet. "The screen shattered."

Caden had too many thoughts racing through his mind to respond. That was a rare thing. Brynne sat back on her knees. She was a bit pale, likely drained from casting powerful telepathy spells on them all. "The sword broke it."

Tito's tablet was broken, and so was Caden's family.

"Why did it break?" Tito said.

Brynne waited as if she expected Caden to speak. When he didn't, she did. Brynne motioned to the sizzling device. "Since the connection was strong, the mirror and tablet were acting almost as one combined device . . . I think . . . so when the mirror broke, so did your tablet."

Jane pushed at the tablet with one finger. It popped, and a large gold spark lit up the room.

"Huh," Tito said. "I better unplug it."

Landon's charred emblem was in Caden's jeans pocket. He brought it out and looked at it, traced the five star sapphires across the broken wing. How could this happen?

Rosa spoke slowly and evenly. "Explain exactly what's happening."

At moments like these, she reminded Caden of the Elite Guard: calm and capable even in periods of turmoil. A future Elite Paladin also should behave that way. Caden must concentrate on the matter at hand. Time for grief could come after the city was saved.

Then Caden and Sir Horace could ride out to where the rigging dagger was buried and bury Landon's emblem beside it. For now, he put it in the pocket of the leather jacket. He told himself that Valon, Martin, and Maden hadn't killed one another.

Caden spoke to Rosa. "My brothers are fighting. Maden and Martin have betrayed the others." With Rosa, he felt it best to be direct, factual. "Just as there is a spell here, there is a connecting spell there. We must stop it here and trust that Valon survives and stops it there."

Rosa wore an odd, unsure expression.

"Jasan fights for his life against villains in the woods. I must go help him."

Rosa straightened and put her arm around Caden's shoulders. "Whatever is happening with your family, I'm here, and I'll look after you."

Just as she finished speaking, there was a soft knock on the front door. The deadbolt turned, the door opened, and Officer Levine walked into the room. He had a key in one hand, groceries in the other.

His jacket was wet from the spotty rain, and a pine needle was plastered to his sleeve. He hung his coat on a small hook by the door. When he saw the broken, drenched tablet, and Rosa with her arm around Caden's shoulders, he said, "What's happened?"

"My brothers are killing one another," Caden said. "While Jasan fights to stop them, to stop the spell, and to save himself and both realms. I have to go help him."

Officer Levine raised his brow in concern. Rosa squeezed Caden tighter. "You're safe," she said.

That didn't matter now. "We need to get to Biltmore Forest," Caden said. "Jasan is fighting the villains. He's in danger."

Officer Levine nodded. "I'll call it in."

"Fine," Caden said. "But he needs my help. He could bleed to death, and the local medics know nothing of magical wounds. I need to go to him."

"I don't want you getting hurt or put in danger," Rosa said. "Let the police handle it."

They finally both believed him and now wanted him to stay home? Caden wouldn't do it; he needed to get to the forest. He jerked away from Rosa. Neither she nor Officer Levine acted as if they'd let him go. "I'm going to my room," he said, and from his room, he'd escape and get to the forest.

As he rushed to the stairs, he heard Tito say, "I'll go up with him."

Caden flew to the attic room. It wouldn't take long for Rosa and Officer Levine to figure out he planned to sneak away. While he couldn't scale down the side of the house like Jasan, he had a perfectly good escape rope tucked under his bed beside his box of Ashevillian tech. His horse was outside. He would get to Biltmore Forest.

How many allies did Rath Dunn have? The wraith and the banshee and Mr. Faunt made three. How many others? What did Mrs. Belle mean, they'd see her true self tonight?

Jasan and Manglor were strong, trained, and formidable. But they were only two people. They would be outnumbered in the dark Ashevillian forest, and from what Caden had seen, most of the banished were dangerous and formidable, too.

Then there was Ms. Jackson. She would be there. She was old and powerful, and Brynne's strong magic hadn't moved her during the windstorm. She'd been less affected than even Rath Dunn. Ms. Jackson alone was a powerful foe.

When Tito got to the attic room, he started rummaging through his messy side of the taped line and stuffing random items into his backpack, but Caden paid him little attention. Instead, he checked his phone. Maybe Jasan had called. He hadn't.

Caden's steps made the planks beneath the carpet moan as he went to the window. He heard the *tink, tink, tink* of raindrops against the glass. Outside, clouds rushed across the sky. The moon disappeared behind them only to reappear a moment later like it couldn't decide whether to shine or hide. It was about half-full. When morning came, he'd be cursed. Twice. Better to save them all before that happened. "I'm going to go help Jasan and Manglor."

"Yeah, dude," Tito said. "Why do you think I'm packing a bag? I'm coming with you."

Tito was indeed a good and brave friend. Truth be told, Caden wasn't even surprised. "You are a brother in the best sense then."

"Yeah, I don't hate you either," Tito said. "I'll text Jane and Brynne. If we're going to fight murderous teachers in the woods, we'd better sneak out now. The thing about Rosa and Officer Levine believing you? They'll lock us in the house before they'll let us fight monsters in the woods. We gotta get out of here quick."

Like she knew what they were thinking, Rosa called up to them. "Caden? Tito?" she said. "Are you all right?"

Fast as an Autumnlands firefox, Caden grabbed the escape rope, opened the window, and let it down. He hesitated when he looked back at Tito. "If you come with me, Rosa will definitely—" What was it Tito always said? "Blow her top. She'll be angry and disappointed." Disappointing Rosa was Tito's greatest fear.

Tito blanched. "Well, she hasn't gotten rid of you, and she thought you were completely nuts." He swallowed. "Just because she won't adopt me doesn't mean she won't keep me. Even if she is mad."

Caden swung his leg over the window ledge. "If I tried, I could convince her to adopt you. She just needs to believe the rest of us would be okay with it. And we are."

Tito couldn't hide his hopeful expression, but then he shook his head. "I don't think that's the type of thing someone other than me should talk to her about."

"Caden?" Rosa called again. He heard her walking up the stairs. She seemed to be getting faster with each step. "Tito?"

Tito swung his backpack across his shoulders. "First let's survive tonight. Then we can deal with my issues."

They were in the yard a moment later and running for the woods. Caden heard Rosa calling for them from the open window. Then she heard her yelling, "Harold! The kids are gone!"

Brynne and Jane were waiting for them on the hillside where the yard gave way to trees. Brynne held Jane's hand as if she'd led her, and Caden feared Jane's eyesight had worsened further. Truly, this spell must be stopped for all their sakes and for the sake of the city. "You escaped as well?" Caden said.

"Brynne set the curtain on fire," Jane said. "We ran out while Rosa went upstairs and Officer Levine put it out."

"You set Rosa's house on fire?" Tito said.

"Just the curtain, I've learned to do a small burn," she said, and beamed. "You're not fighting villains without us."

One thing was certain: if they survived, they would suffer Ashevillian grounding punishment for the rest of their days. Of this, Caden didn't doubt.

The night was cold and smelled of rain and the smoke of Ashevillian chimneys. Caden's boots squelched in the mud. Clouds, backlit by the partial moon, zoomed across the sky, keeping the moonlight scattered and the drizzle inconsistent. All in all, it was a miserable night to fight a tyrant.

"Sir Horace will take us to Biltmore Forest," Caden said.

"Sir Horace isn't here," Brynne said.

Sir Horace was near. Caden had seen him at the edge of the forest at dusk, and he often stayed within hearing distance this time of night. Caden ignored Brynne and whistled. As soon as he did, the pounding of hoofbeats echoed from uphill.

"He's always here when I need him," Caden said.

Tito shielded his phone from the rain and mapped out directions to Biltmore Forest. Jane clutched her Enchanted Hammer of Smashing.

Caden asked about the hammer.

"For enchantment smashing," she said. "And also villain smashing."

It seemed Jane was ready to fight.

Sir Horace thundered from the woods a moment later and fell in line beside Caden. Caden patted Sir Horace, and his steed's hair was slick, cold, and flat. "This is a bad night for a battle," he said.

"Are there good nights for battle?" Tito asked.

The wind howled above them. "There are better ones than this one," Caden said.

Brynne shielded her face from the stinging drizzle. "Can Sir Horace carry all four of us?"

Sir Horace was a Galvanian snow stallion. If any horse could hold them all, it was him. And although strong, Jane was small. She wouldn't be much extra to carry. Caden signaled Sir Horace to kneel. "He can carry us, but you must all hold on tightly."

From the edge of the trees, flashlight beams danced in the woods. "Tito! Jane!" Rosa seemed frantic. She called out into the rain. "Brynne! Caden!"

But Caden would have to wait until later to feel guilty for disobeying her. He had to help Jasan. Sometimes even the correct choice had consequences.

Tito looked back like he wanted to run to her, and Caden grabbed his hand. "You can text her from the forest. But we have to go now."

"Yeah," Tito said, and snatched his hand away. "I know, bro."

Caden climbed onto Sir Horace's mighty back. Tito and Jane squeezed on after him. Brynne got on last and in the back. With a swift command, Sir Horace stood. There was no indication the weight was too much. Inwardly, Caden felt a wave of relief. He asked much of Sir Horace, and Sir Horace never complained.

Caden commanded Sir Horace to run, and Sir Horace galloped through the woods and carried the four of them like he enjoyed the challenge.

It wasn't long before they entered Biltmore Forest. The woods seemed darker, damper, and more alive. The wind whipped between tree trunks. Caden slowed Sir Horace to a trot.

Tito pointed over Caden's shoulder. "Listen."

From the direction Tito pointed, voices carried. Lots of them. Beams of light that Caden recognized as flashlights waved about. The villains were also traveling through the woods.

"They must be going to the location now."

"We should move on foot from here," he whispered. "So as to go unnoticed."

Sir Horace knelt, and they got off. Tito took Jane's hand to help her navigate the night-bound woods. Brynne gestured to the lights and noises ahead of them. She spoke softly.

"Caden and I will follow the group," she said. "Jane, you and Tito should cut uphill and across. We'll stay in contact using our phones."

"Good idea," Caden said. "If we have to fight, it might be to our advantage to approach from multiple sides."

"And you think we're going to have to fight?" Tito said.

Jasan and Manglor were outnumbered. If Caden wasn't certain before, the noise and ruckus of the group moving downhill had convinced him. Caden tried calling Jasan; he tried Manglor. They weren't picking up, but if they were staking out the villains, they might have turned off their phones so as not to give themselves away.

"Yes."

"Great," Tito said. He set his backpack on the ground and pulled out a flashlight. He also held a stick. "For fighting," he said. "Which one do you want?"

Caden considered the two items. Neither was a sword. "The stick."

Tito held the flashlight at the ready. "I guess all those mornings running the mountain are about to pay off, huh?"

"I think so," Jane said.

"See ya, Your Highness," Tito said, and they dashed up the hill and into the dark. Caden felt a surge of pride. Jane and Tito were indeed fast. They'd trained well.

"We should hurry, too," Brynne said.

Caden and Brynne chased after the lights and noises. Sir Horace kept his head down and his eyes toward the front. He walked in measured steps. Galvanian warhorses were trained to be quiet when needed. After several minutes, they got close enough to see.

There was a large group marching through the forest. Ms. Jackson glided in the middle of it. She looked like a beautiful and dangerous phantom. But her beauty disappeared when the moonlight passed over her. Her cheeks became sunken in, her hair and nails yellowed.

The large school nurse tromped behind her. The ground sank and squelched where the nurse trudged. She carried someone over her shoulder. The person was draped in a dark fabric, but when light hit her hands, he could see meticulously polished red nails. It was Mrs. Belle.

After her words at the assembly, Caden had hoped she would put up more of a fight.

The trees moaned and swayed around them. Wet leaves sailed through the woods. One slapped against Caden's cheek.

Brynne's phone flickered. She looked at it, then spoke to Caden. Her voice was as quiet as the flap of a whisper moth's wings. "Tito and Jane are behind a small rock, just uphill of the crowd," Brynne said. "They count fourteen villains."

He motioned to Brynne, and they snuck closer.

The villains in view were a monstrous group. Under the darkness and the scattered moonlight, the teachers didn't look like their normal human selves. The new music teacher, the banshee, opened his mouth as if to scream. His jaw stretched wide, and Caden saw rows and rows of spiraling teeth. Ms. Levers, the blood wraith, had eyes that were red and glowing in the dark.

Then there were Mr. Faunt and Mrs. Grady, the math teachers. Stout Mrs. Grady carried a bone club almost as large as she. When a small tree got in her way, she clobbered it, and the trunk snapped in two. Mr. Faunt slashed the underbrush with long, tapered fingernails that cut like blades. Mr. Frye followed, floating as if made of mist. As did Mr. Limon; in the moonlight, his prominent brow had massive and curled horns.

The villains trudged together in a monstrous midnight parade.

"I don't see Rath Dunn," Brynne said.

Caden considered his arm. He hadn't thought about it, but the blood dagger wound had started to ache dully after they'd dismounted from Sir Horace. It was still faint but it was there. "Be careful. He's here somewhere."

"I don't see Jasan or Manglor either." She checked her

phone. "Neither do Jane and Tito."

"They'll stay hidden until they think it's most advantageous to attack."

Brynne checked the time. "It's almost midnight. Something will happen soon."

And then something did.

Skittering noises came from behind and zoomed toward them. Caden and Brynne whipped around. Something bumped against Caden's boots. He grabbed his cell phone from his jacket pocket and used it to light the ground. Small, dark forms funneled across the forest ground. Mice. Rats. Rodents of varying sizes.

Brynne stood still. They raced over her shoes and past her. "A swarm."

Caden knew of only one individual who could control swarming mice. Mr. Creedly.

The only light close to them was from their phones, but Caden saw Brynne's face and knew that she was thinking the same thing. In the entire school, Mr. Creedly only liked two people: Ms. Primrose and Mrs. Belle. He considered Rath Dunn an enemy; he considered Ms. Jackson an enemy. If Mr. Creedly was here, it wasn't to help the other villains; it was to attack them.

Back toward the villains, a horrible, shrill cry pierced the woods. It echoed off the trees and the ground. Caden covered his ears. Brynne, too. The banshee was screaming. Suddenly, another, deeper battle cry filled the air. It sounded like Manglor. And if he'd made a move, no doubt Jasan had, too.

Screaming, yelling, and cursing erupted from the teachers ahead of them. Caden heard weapons clank. There was no reason for him and Brynne to stay hidden now. They darted downhill toward the fray.

So it was, the third spell battle began.

28

THE FIGHT IN THE FOREST

The trees towered. With the fight underway, villains swung flashlights as weapons. Some dropped them into the leaf litter. The moving light beams illuminated runes and sigils on the trees' massive trunks and roots.

Caden spotted Manglor. He charged at the teachers on the far side. In the waving flashlight beams, Caden saw the part-giant-looking school nurse block Manglor's large flat-bladed battle-ax with her forearm.

Mr. Faunt snuck up suddenly behind Manglor. His nails looked long and razor sharp. Manglor swung the ax around and hit him blunt side, in the stomach. Mr. Faunt fell, robbed of breath. With a sneer, he crawled away from Manglor. The nurse kept fighting and knocked Manglor with her large fist. He staggered back, only to charge her again a moment later.

Mr. Creedly's rodent swarm descended from all

directions. Mr. Limon, with horns curling at his temples, fled uphill.

Mr. Limon jumped a log but slipped on the wet bark, falling onto his stomach. The swarm overtook him. Biting and snarling, they covered him like a black wave.

Where was Jasan? Where was Ms. Jackson? Caden scanned the fighting. There!

On the left flank, surrounded by five teachers, was his brother. Jasan fought his way toward the middle of the fray. Using his sword—Caden's sword—he cut down those in his path. He knocked them away quickly. One. Two. Then three, four, and five. Two more villains jumped in his way—one was the banshee, the other the blood wraith. She had a long, pointed spear—one of metal and glass that she'd obviously created with local materials. Jasan charged the wraith and knocked her back.

When the banshee screamed, shrill and loud and painful, the rats scattered. But they gathered again quickly. The banshee stood behind Jasan. He stretched his jaw and showed his teeth. If he bit Jasan, he'd poison him.

"Ms. Jackson has the vial!" Brynne said.

In the center of the mayhem, Ms. Jackson stood atop a stump, overseeing all. She held the vial above her head, and it glowed red in the night—Jasan's blood, the blood of son.

Jasan's life was in her hands. With no time to think, Caden hoisted himself up on Sir Horace. Brynne swung up behind him. "Run, Sir Horace! To the witch."

Sir Horace plowed through the rats and battling villains. With a mighty whinny, he galloped at Ms. Jackson, but he tripped on a large rat and Caden and Brynne tumbled from his back. On the ground, the rats swarmed them from all sides. Caden and Brynne didn't seem to be the target, but they'd be overcome if in the way.

Caden reached for the stick he'd dropped. He did a sweeping attack and sent rats flying. Brynne pushed them away with magic. Sir Horace bucked and stomped, knocking away the rodents that tried to climb up his mighty legs.

They had to get to Ms. Jackson before it was too late. Caden dashed in her direction.

Brynne did, too, but the lanky sixth-grade English teacher, Mr. Frye, stepped in her way, brandishing a rune-covered flashlight. She dodged his swipe and countered, but he became transparent at the last moment, and her fist passed through him. At the sight of Brynne in trouble, Sir Horace charged Mr. Frye. Again, he seemed to turn to mist. Sir Horace thundered through him. As Mr. Frye became solid again, he kept his body turned to Sir Horace. Brynne took advantage of the distraction and knocked Mr. Frye into a tall oak. He didn't get up.

Caden was so busy worrying over them, he didn't see Mr. Faunt lunging for him until the last moment. Quickly, Caden flipped him with his sparring stick. Mr. Faunt landed on his feet. Jane charged in from the opposite direction, brandishing her hammer like a club. Mr. Faunt jumped back.

Ms. Jackson started to speak. "Earth quake, ground break!" she screamed into the wind. Oh no. The incantation and spell. "With the blood of the seventh royal son," Ms. Jackson yelled, "may the barrier that separates the lands be further undone."

Caden got up. "Jasan! Jasan! Ms. Jackson has the vial!"

Jasan looked up, too focused on his fight with the wraith and the banshee to be surprised Caden was there. Or maybe he just wasn't surprised. Then he saw Ms. Jackson and ran, leaving his opponents stunned and far behind.

He was the farthest away, but he was also the fastest. He tackled her, they crashed to the ground, and the vial flew from her hands and rolled across the ground, the contents unspilled, the ingredient intact.

Jasan sliced at Ms. Jackson with the sword, and she blocked him with her cursed ladle. Blow for blow, punch for punch, she matched his skill and his speed. How was that possible? Even if she was as well trained as Jasan, she couldn't be as fast.

Then a beam of a flashlight hit her skin. Runes appeared on every visible piece of flesh. She had painted her whole body with them. When Jasan attacked, they glowed. Did the runes make it so she was able to mimic his skill?

Before Mr. Wist, the banshee, could follow Jasan, Tito engaged him. Tito swung the flashlight like a Razzonian sword. Mr. Wist ducked and moved easily.

Caden heard Brynne yell, "Don't get bit!" and he saw

Brynne and Sir Horace charge Tito's way to help. Manglor finally felled the nurse, and he lunged toward them as well.

Caden ran to retrieve the vial. The blood wraith blocked Caden's path. Her hair was serpentlike, her eyes completely black. Her expression was frenzy and euphoria. She swung her long, pointed spear over her head. With a bloody battle cry, she jabbed it at Caden.

He dodged, then countered with his stick, but his weapon wasn't a match for hers. It splintered as they clashed. Part of the stick tumbled into the darkness. Caden dropped the remaining stick piece as he jumped out of the way of her next attack. Then he darted back toward her. With a rolling motion, he grabbed her and slammed her to the ground.

But she laughed. She reached out and grabbed at something. The red vial glowed in her hand. "Is this what you want?" she said. Before Caden could respond or grab it from her, she crushed it to sharp, jagged glass pieces and dripping red blood. The red glowing ingredient spilled out and sank into the earth.

The ground began to shake.

Caden fell back. Frantically, he scanned for Jasan. He caught a glimpse of golden hair near the stump, and caught Jasan's gaze just as his brother fell to his knees. It had taken time for Jane's eyes to dry out. Caden only hoped it would be the same for Jasan's blood. Brynne's hair had flown off right away, but she'd also been in a windstorm. It wasn't too late, was it? No one had been sacrificed yet. There was still hope for Jasan. He could still be saved, right?

The forest began to moan. Branches splintered, and trees crashed to the ground. The rats scattered. He glanced back. In the waving beams of the flashlights, he saw large trees topple down. They fell one after another as if pushed over by a stampeding beast.

Jasan remained where he'd fallen, on his knees and breathing hard. Ms. Jackson stood over him, ladle raised, as if ready to beat him with it. Caden needed to get to him.

The forest floor started to shift, to move apart. The giant pine to Caden's left tilted toward the ground, and he scurried away as it began to fall. Air and earth and leaves blew against his back as the tree hit the ground behind him. The crack traveled toward Manglor, Tito, Brynne, and Sir Horace, who were still engaged with the banshee. It would swallow them if they didn't move.

"Run!" he yelled toward his friends. "The ground splits!" Manglor grabbed Tito and leaped away. The banshee jumped back. The waving lights passed over Brynne's face. She turned his way, and her eyes widened as she noticed the toppling trees and the chasm traveling toward her. In a swift movement, she swung up onto Sir Horace's back. They charged ahead. The ground pulled apart in front of them. With a great leap, Sir Horace jumped across it and landed soundly on the other side.

The chasm split the forest, deep and black. How deep,

Caden didn't know, but it looked bottomless. If anyone fell into the pit—Mrs. Belle or otherwise—the spell would be complete. He climbed over a large branch. A large, skittering form dashed past Caden. Its many long, spidery legs scurried over the fallen tree trunks. It walked on the sides of the chasm that had formed. When light shone on it, green eyes glowed in the dark.

It looked terrifying and familiar.

Like all villains, Mr. Creedly's true form could only be seen at night. He was spindly and insect-like, ants and vermin and fur twisted into limbs, teeth, and shadow. He scurried toward the center of the spell, and Caden dashed in the same direction.

Near the crevice, Mrs. Grady dragged Mrs. Belle by the arms toward the gaping hole in the ground. The trees above tilted and leaned on one another like the roof of an unhallowed shrine; the fissure on the ground opened like a black mouth.

To stop the sacrifice, he had to save Mrs. Belle. But Jasan was fallen in front of Ms. Jackson. He needed to save him, too, lest he be pushed into the pit. He started to run toward his brother, but then Jane rushed from the other side, hammer raised, abandoning her battle with Mr. Faunt. Instead, she swung at Ms. Jackson. Mr. Faunt didn't follow her. He ran to help his evil math comrade, Mrs. Grady.

Ms. Jackson blocked with her ladle, but her moves were slower than before, less practiced. The runes again glowed.

As with Jasan, she seemed to mimic her opponent. They were evenly matched. But while Ms. Jackson fought with a cursed ladle, Jane fought with an enchanted hammer.

Through the scattered moonlight, Jane caught Caden's eyes. She blocked a blow from Ms. Jackson. "I'll protect him. Stop the others!"

An Elite Paladin trusted his friends; he believed in his allies. Although it was hard not to run for Jasan, Caden ran for Mrs. Belle. He needed to save her, and he needed not to fall into the crevice either.

Mr. Creedly scurried toward Mrs. Belle. Caden was almost there, too. Just before Caden reached them, Mrs. Grady and Mr. Faunt heaved and dumped Mrs. Belle into the pit. Her veil flew away in the wind.

Oh no.

Ms. Jackson and Jane broke apart; they watched Mrs. Belle fall. Caden darted to the edge of the chasm. He grasped for Mrs. Belle's hand, her ankle, anything to hold onto. Mr. Creedly made a sound like an unearthly screech. His shadowy arms elongated and reached for the falling science teacher, too. And then—something reached out of the darkness to meet him. A long, red-tipped limb, like a spider's leg.

Then another red-tipped leg became visible. Soon an eight-legged creature with ruby red feet and a humanlike face skittered up into the forest. When the moonlight shone, the face was familiar. The creature laughed, high-pitched and fast, and that sounded familiar, too. It was Mrs. Belle, and she looked monstrous.

He doubted she was human enough to fulfill the sacrifice. And she'd hid her true form better than Mr. Creedly. It seemed even the villains hadn't realized what she was.

Mr. Creedly hissed at Mrs. Grady and Mr. Faunt. Mrs. Grady ran. Like a laughing spider with bloodred tips on the ends of her eight legs, Mrs. Belle took chase. Mr. Faunt tried to dash away in the opposite direction, but Mr. Creedly reached out one of his long limbs and grabbed him. In his anger, he hurled him toward the pit.

Quickly, Mr. Faunt used his nails to latch onto a fallen oak. He stopped himself half a stride from the pit.

"Rath Dunn!" Manglor bellowed from uphill, where he and Tito had just defeated the banshee.

"He's there!" Tito shouted.

Near the chasm, a figure dressed in red stepped from the shadows. It was Rath Dunn. He reached out as if to help Mr. Faunt, but instead tossed him into the black chasm.

Caden froze. He waited for Mr. Faunt to crawl out somehow like Mrs. Belle had but he didn't. Was Mr. Faunt human? He looked it more than some of the others. Would he satisfy the spell? Somewhere in the darkness the banshee screamed.

Ms. Jackson started to cackle, loud and mean and cruel, and Jane tackled her.

Jasan lay unmoving. The open ground rumbled shut

until only a small crack remained. Red, sticky rain began to fall, and it blocked the scattered moonlight.

Caden stood there in shock. He heard sirens from somewhere close. He thought he heard Rosa and Officer Levine calling them.

Jane held Ms. Jackson down. Manglor pushed aside a tree, and he and Tito bounded toward the stump, Tito with his flashlight lit. Brynne and Sir Horace galloped to Jasan's side. Manglor crouched beside him and threw Jasan over his shoulder. "We must get him to the hospital."

"Is he alive?" Brynne said. She sounded panicked.

Manglor didn't answer her.

Vaguely, Caden noticed his own blood dagger wound start to bleed. But he was too stunned to understand what it meant or to feel how much it hurt. Manglor should answer that question. Caden needed to know; he stepped toward them.

They surrounded Jasan. All their attention was on him. It didn't register right away that his blood dagger wound began to ache then the way it did when the blade was very close.

WHACK. Caden heard something crack. It might have been his skull. Pain erupted on the side of his head. Something had hit him. He collapsed to the ground, felt the mud squish under him. He saw a pair of red boots. Then everything went black. Everything went silent.

29

THE DRAGON BY THE DOOR

Caden's head throbbed. He was sluggish and cold.

As he gained more awareness, he felt the tingle in his limbs that signified the curse. It felt even stronger than before. Slowly, he blinked.

His cheek was stuck to polished tiles. He heard thunder, and it made the floor rumble. The walls around him were painted red. There was a window that looked out onto an outcropping of rock. Frost collected on the inside, but outside it was sunny. It seemed he'd been asleep awhile.

"You're awake. It's almost midday." That was Rath Dunn's voice. And Caden was in his office. "I was beginning to worry I'd hit you too hard."

Head injuries were nothing trivial. "You did hit me too hard," Caden managed.

"You're alive. That's all that's required." He flip-flapped

his hand. "Since last night, you've been in and out of sleep. But I'm glad you'll be awake for what is to come."

Caden wasn't so sure about any of that.

On the desk, the phone rang. Rath Dunn looked at it but made no move to answer. "Everyone is looking for you," he said.

Did that mean Caden had gone missing again? He'd told Rosa and Jasan he wouldn't do that. And that he'd call. Memories of the night surged back. His chest felt tight. His heart beat loudly. Jasan had fallen. Was he alive?

Rath Dunn walked in front of Caden, leaving Caden to stare at the man's red boots. "Too bad they won't find you. They might suspect you're here with me. But trust me when I say, the guard I have inside the office door is one no one will get past."

Rath Dunn brought out a file from his desk drawer. It was stuffed with papers and purple slips. "Now. We have business. Mediocre grades. Constant detentions. Skipping. It's time I expel you, don't you think?"

Caden's head felt heavy, but his mind was working well enough. "If I'm no longer a student, you can use me as the last sacrifice."

"Well, if you insist. You are from the Greater Realm," Rath Dunn said. "You're lucky, son of Axel."

"How's that?" Caden said. He really needed to get his cheek off the floor. At least, the floor was clean and cool. Fate be thanked for small mercies.

"Ms. Jackson said you'd be docile," Rath Dunn said. "She's a fine creature." He threw the file on the desk and took out a notebook. "A strategist. A planner. A detailed note taker." He turned the notebook toward Caden. "Directions. One can never be too careful."

"For the spell."

"Indeed." Rath Dunn stroked the notebook lovingly. "She even gave me lessons. I wanted to share this triumph with her."

Caden hadn't seen Ms. Jackson fall. "Where is she?"

Rath Dunn snorted. "Arrested. By your Officer Levine. Ah well. They'll all be dead soon enough. And if you want things finished the right way, you should do them yourself. Don't you think?"

"After she did all the hard work."

Rath Dunn guffawed. "Well, yes. But to see a master at her craft. . . ." He put his hand over his heart. "She is brilliant. She does the impossible and makes ritual magic classy." His mouth twisted into a cruel line. "If I didn't need you mostly in one piece, I'd make you suffer before you die for getting in the way."

The bump on Caden's head hurt, as did his blood dagger wound. That meant Rath Dunn had his weapon. Not that Caden was a match for him in combat with or without it. But Caden wouldn't be sacrificed willingly. Be it hopeless or not, future Elite Paladins fought.

"That's quite a determined expression you have," Rath

Dunn said. "Makes me think of Axel."

Caden was prepared to attack as soon as he could lift his head.

A slow, wolfish smile spread across Rath Dunn's face. "Stay down. Don't speak."

Orders.

Had Brynne's curse-curse worked? Would the second curse negate the first? Resist or comply. Resist or comply. Caden felt the two urges fight inside him. At this rate, he would explode before he was even sacrificed. The curse-curse was going to kill him. Then . . .

He sneezed. The tiles weren't so clean now.

Resist or comply. Resist or comply. The curses continued to rage within him. Meanwhile, he did nothing. And the longer it went on, Caden realized something. He had a choice. He could do *either.* Maybe there was hope then. He still had a choice, and Rath Dunn believed Caden didn't. Caden would fight. Somehow . . .

Like his plan to fool Rath Dunn at the beginning of the school year, Caden chose to comply. It was better if Rath Dunn believed Caden had no choice. He stayed down. He was quiet.

"So you have to do what you're told now," Rath Dunn said, his evil smile spreading. "I've been keeping track, you know. Ms. Jackson has been sniffing you, too. A curse like that could be really amusing for me. It's a shame I need to feed you to a spell. But it makes things easier if you're compliant."

Rath Dunn strode back and forth around the room. He prepared spell ingredients. Twice he stepped over Caden. The third time he stepped on him. "You're in the way. Sit against the wall."

Caden sneezed again. That was odd; Caden never sneezed. His royal immune system and training regimen kept him healthy most times.

He dragged himself to a sitting position as he'd been ordered. The red walls looked like blood. The shelves where Ms. Primrose had displayed her many cheap and tacky treasures instead contained books with pictures of food. There was a garment bag next to the mirror. The room felt like a Razzonian ice cave: cold, frozen, and cramped.

That's when he noticed someone else in the room. Ms. Primrose. She stood in the back corner near the door. Her human form was small enough that he'd missed her until now, yet her presence seemed to fill that part of the office. Her pale-blue eyes were more reptilian than he'd ever seen them, and her overly small pupils stretched to long slits. Her skin looked like scales—most of them blue. He saw but one silver speck among them. Even her hair had taken on a blue hue. The thunder he'd felt was her stomach rumbling.

Caden pulled Jasan's jacket more snugly around his shoulders. He hadn't realized how cold the world could be without his enchanted coat. He saw the blood on the sleeve again. Jasan's blood. Now all gone. He felt too stunned to do more than stare at it.

Rath Dunn pulled the garment bag down from a hook

and unzipped it. Inside there was a new outfit. He switched his burgundy sweater and deep-red pants and red boots for a fitted crimson-colored three-piece suit with polished red loafers. The vest beneath the red jacket was citrine brown with shining red stripes. He checked his reflection. "I want to look good for my return." He spun as if to show off his suit. "What do you think?"

Caden felt rage like he never felt before. "I hate you."

Rath Dunn knelt down. "No need for that. None of this is personal," he said. He traced the scar on his face. "Oh wait, it is. Maden, Martin, and I will topple your father. And I'll use you to finish the spell. Poetic, really. Using his sons to destroy him."

"My father will fight you."

"At least two of his sons are dead, and two more have turned against him." He stood and grinned. "That's the price of being relentless. If he truly loved you and your brothers, he'd do what was best for them and give up."

"My father never gives up."

Rath Dunn reconsidered. "You may be right. He is resolute if nothing else. Then I'll feed him to my vice principal."

Caden's father had no contract with the school or with Ms. Primrose. "On what grounds?"

"Do I need any?" He adjusted his tie. "They've no pact with her. Isn't that right, Ms. Primrose? I shall give you all the royals you can eat."

Ms. Primrose looked pudgy, not hungry. "My Blue side

does enjoy indulgences. And kings and queens are tasty."

Caden pointed to Rath Dunn. "So are red-dressed despots."

"He and I do have a pact. As I do with you. I won't eat you either even when you exasperate me. Even when my Blue self so wants to."

Caden was beyond frustrated. If the school was destroyed, if Asheville was leveled by the barrier between worlds being torn apart, what rules would apply? He turned to Rath Dunn. "I don't understand. How have you not broken any rules?"

"I'm careful. Deliberate." He chortled. "And I'm principal. Doesn't that uniquely qualify me? I'm allowed to leave the town. I'm allowed to give others the same permission. Nothing specifies whether leaving means Hendersonville for vegetables or the Greater Realm for domination. Of course, I'll need my vice principal"—his tone turned savage—"to rule Razzon."

"The school and city will be gone. Then what will become of your contract with her?"

"It can be rebuilt, and Ms. Primrose can stay my employee. Here and there." Rath Dunn examined himself in the wall mirror beside his desk. "Now, boy, tell me I look the part of a returning conqueror."

An order. Caden tingled all over. *"Achoo!"*

Rath Dunn moved back. "Don't get my suit dirty."

Another order. Another sneeze.

Rath Dunn waited.

Best Caden pretend he still had no choice but to follow orders. He complied. With both. "You look the part," he said. And as unprincely as it was, he wiped his nose with his sleeve. "I won't get your suit dirty."

"I know," Rath Dunn said. "Because I ordered you not to."

Ms. Primrose cocked her head. "Oh my," she said. There was a trace of amusement in her tone. She peered at Caden like she could see through him. He was certain she knew he could choose to resist as easily as comply, that he had control. Maybe she could smell the curses like Ms. Jackson could? Or maybe Elderdragons just knew magic. Ms. Primrose stared at him, and a silver scale glimmered above her brow. "It's more gentlemanly to use a handkerchief, dear."

It wasn't an order, and she didn't give away Caden's one advantage—that Brynne had mostly fixed him. Maybe Ms. Primrose was impressed by Brynne's curse-curse cure? On Ms. Primrose's arm he saw another flash of silver. Her essence wasn't taken yet; she was angry and ready to feast, but she was still both Silver and Blue Elderdragon. She still had a choice, too.

Rath Dunn yanked his pocket square out. It was red and embroidered with an image of the Bloodwolf, the protector of the Autumnlands. "Use that. Wipe your nose. Have some dignity in your final minutes."

More sneezes. Caden complied.

Then the alarm on Rath Dunn's phone started to beep. "It's time."

The wall behind Caden felt strangely warm. There were probably hidden runes painted all over it, all over the office, maybe hidden throughout the school in all the freshly painted halls and rooms.

Rath Dunn cleared his throat. He pulled a vial from his pocket. It was Ms. Primrose's pink-tinted and rose-scented perfume. He spoke in a booming voice. "Lightning crack, thunder quake, with the essence of the Elderkind, may the barrier between the realms finally unwind."

Then he dumped the perfume onto the floor.

Lightning struck the rock face outside. As it flashed, Caden saw that he was right. Every last inch of the office walls were covered in runes. Then lightning struck inside—in the center of the office, but the bolt didn't fade. It rolled into a spiral and hovered, like an electric tornado. From within it, Caden heard faint yelling and the sounds of battle. Someone screamed orders in Royal Razzon.

It was a voice Caden knew.

It was Valon.

Valon, alive and fighting with the Elite Guard on the other side.

And Caden guessed it was Maden and Martin and the mercenaries of Crimsen they fought against.

"When completed, my spell will drain this quaint

town." Rath Dunn reached down and pulled Caden to his feet. "And those armies on the other side are no match for me, my allies, and my Elderdragon." He leaned in and whispered in Caden's ear. "I win."

Rath Dunn pushed Caden to his knees in front of the sizzling portal. It was narrow. And sparking. It would kill him before he ever made it to the other side. "Stay there until I tell you that you can move."

Caden sneezed. He stayed.

Rath Dunn checked his cell phone. "Ten seconds and it'll be ready for you."

The vortex grew bigger.

"Nine . . ."

Inside, dark forms floated between this side of the sizzling portal and the light far on the other side, which Caden guessed connected to his homeland.

"Eight. Get up," Rath Dunn said.

Caden sneezed. He got up.

"Seven . . ."

In the corner, Ms. Primrose watched.

"Six . . . Five . . ."

She seemed curious but not much more.

"Four . . ."

The vortex swirled and crackled. The force blew back Caden's hair. It was growing in power, and it sounded like raging waters, roaring winds, and moving earth. Rath Dunn's face was lit and gleeful as he watched it. He patted

Caden on the shoulder. Then he gestured to the instant death that was the electric vortex. "Three . . . two . . . one," he said. "It's time." He smirked at Caden. "Jump in."

Caden sneezed. That order he was going to resist.

"Hurry it up, boy."

Caden sneezed. He resisted, but he took a step toward it. Better to play along until the last moment. He didn't want Rath Dunn to get wise and throw Caden into it.

Convinced the curse was working, Rath Dunn's gaze skidded back to the portal. He seemed fascinated by it. Well, it was fascinating in a horrible, dangerous way. With Rath Dunn distracted, one good shove would end him. Caden could destroy the man who none of his brothers nor his father could. He could kill the man who splintered his family, who turned brother against brother, who started the events that led to Chadwin's and Landon's deaths. And maybe Jasan's.

Caden clenched his fist.

But neither he nor Rath Dunn could fall into the vortex. Either of them would satisfy the curse. Both he and Rath Dunn were human and from the Greater Realm.

The portal started to spark and draw loose objects into it. Papers. Pens. Caden's school file. There was no more time to stall. Caden darted for the desk. Rath Dunn turned, reached for him, but missed. Caden's training, his relentless running of the mountain, had made him faster.

Caden skidded around the side of the massive object.

He needed to hold on to something heavy. If this was like the whirlwind, it would look for a life to suck into it. He braced himself against the mahogany.

Rath Dunn lurched for him. "I told you to—"

But instead of moving forward, he stumbled back. His arm was pulled toward the vortex. He had no traction. Nothing to hold on to. Like Caden, he reached for the heaviest object in the room: the desk. But Rath Dunn was too far away.

He'd be sucked into his own spell. His own machinations would kill him. A fitting end in Caden's opinion.

And when that happened, the spell would be completed.

As Tito would say: crap.

Rath Dunn fell backward. Caden grabbed the desk with one arm. He grabbed Rath Dunn by his vest with the other. With impressive strength, Rath Dunn yanked his arm free of the sizzling portal. It looked burned and black, but not damaged enough to stop him from digging his fingers into Caden's upper arm. He looked ready to flip Caden into the vortex.

But Caden was the only thing keeping Rath Dunn from being pulled into it. "If I go, so will you," Caden said.

After three failures, Caden finally had saved someone. It just happened to be the person he most wanted dead.

Without its sacrifice, the vortex swirled in on itself, shrinking smaller and smaller, until finally it closed with a spark. The floor was scorched, the tiles charred. Loose papers covered the floor and floated down through the air. The books stood still on their shelves. Ms. Primrose watched from her corner.

Rath Dunn fell panting against the desk. With his spell incomplete, his plan foiled, he would be out for blood. Caden let go of Rath Dunn's vest and wriggled from his grip. He needed to get away from him, and the office wasn't that big.

30
THE FORGOTTEN TONGUE

Rath Dunn struggled to stand up. In the corner, something was off with Ms. Primrose. Something more than usual. As Caden gaped, she grew and shifted into a dragon before his eyes. Not a shadow of a dragon, but a real, scaly, full-sized toothy beast.

The portal had closed, but Ms. Primrose's perfume had been used, and her Silver essence started to dissipate. Without it, the parts of her that were educator, collector, and charmed by man would be gone.

Her skin shimmered with blue scales. Wings—cramped and folded in the confines of the room—grew from her back. Silver scales dropped from her body. The massive jaws he'd often felt near his neck he now saw clearly. She was a dragon, and, for the first time, she completely looked like one.

Caden needed to find a way for her to hold on to her Silver side. He needed to stop Rath Dunn. Even if the portal failed, Rath Dunn still controlled Ms. Primrose. In his anger, he'd feed as many as he could to her. And he'd definitely kill Caden. After all, he'd already expelled him.

There was only one thing Caden could do that would both stop Rath Dunn and stop her. Nothing charmed Ms. Primrose more than speaking in the forgotten tongue. And other than Caden and Ms. Primrose, the words caused nothing but paralyzing agony for those who heard them. Paralyzing agony was the perfect way to stop Rath Dunn this day.

Caden could speak it only because of his gift of speech. But he'd never spoken the ancient and powerful language without Ms. Primrose prompting him first.

In the corner, Ms. Primrose grew larger still. She snapped her massive jaws. Soon she'd crush Caden against the wall. He tried to pull the language into his mind, but it wouldn't come. He had to think. To concentrate. He couldn't panic.

Jane had found a way to survive her need to enchant when they'd accepted that she wouldn't stop.

Brynne had beaten the unbreakable curse when she'd accepted that it couldn't be broken.

Caden couldn't speak the forgotten tongue without prompting. There was no way Ms. Primrose was going to prompt him, not now, not with half of her self, the kinder half, falling from her like silver rain. But there was someone in the room who could prompt Caden.

He darted to the mirror. He was doubly cursed—with resistance and compliance—and he could choose whether to resist or comply. He needed to be prompted with an order, and he needed to comply with it. He peered at himself.

Blood trickled from his temple. He was pale and his face bruised. There was dirt on his jacket collar. He resisted the urge to shake it off and looked into his reflected eyes. "Speak the forgotten tongue."

Resist or comply. Caden felt as if he were going to burst. He expected to sneeze. But with his order, he hiccupped. And again. And again. Comply, he told himself.

Power filled the room.

He turned from the mirror and to the Elderdragon crammed into the office. His tongue felt split and hurt.

"Ms. Primrose," Caden said in the Forgotten Language of Power.

The dragon snapped her gaze to him. She cocked her head. Rath Dunn grabbed his head and fell to his knees.

What could he say? He could try to convince her that Rath Dunn had broken a rule by clubbing Caden in the head. But she'd never cared about a little blood. If she'd never cared that Caden bled from his blood dagger wound, why would she care about his aching head? At most, Rath Dunn would have to file an incident report against himself.

Silver scales showered down from her wings and body.

Bit by bit, she was losing the benevolent part of herself. If it didn't abate, all that would be left of her would be the vicious Blue Elderdragon. Maybe he could use the language to pull the less vicious Silver part of her back? The language was powerful. Caden concentrated on his words. His tongue tasted like blood. "I call to your Silver aspect."

The falling, shimmering scales stopped falling and hovered in the air.

Caden considered what he was saying. It seemed impolite to speak only to part of her. Maybe that was why her Blue form was so vicious. It was feared. It, too, should be treated with respect. He added, "As well as your Blue."

Ms. Primrose leaned toward him. Her snout was long, her teeth sharp, her scales the coldest and most beautiful of blues. The falling silver scales began to hover and twinkle like fairie fire.

"You spoke first," she said, and even with her dragon voice, she sounded pleased. It looked natural and easy for her to form the words. Her tongue, he noted, was forked. There was no trace of the human as whom she sometimes appeared.

"I did," he said. His head felt heavy. He fought to speak and to speak well. His adrenaline was waning. As was his energy, and the powerful words only drained it faster. "And I speak it because of my great respect for you, for the Blue and Silver Elderdragon. And I implore you not to lose your Silver essence."

Beside the desk, Rath Dunn grunted. His hands were over his ears and his red suit was wrinkled.

Ms. Primrose shifted. Her wings were flat to her body; her head knocked against the ceiling. She seemed to be getting bigger. She cocked her head and peered down at Caden. "The spell may not be complete, but some of my aspect cannot be saved. Such deeds have consequences."

Caden thought of Jane's eyes and Brynne's hair. He thought of Jasan's blood.

"Can you not save some of what was lost?" he said. "The spell has been stopped."

"Maybe," she said. "If I wanted." She moved again, and her wings knocked against the shelves. Books crashed to the floor. "But I am content with but one aspect. It will make things easier."

"I see," Caden said. But if she only wanted one aspect, she didn't have to choose the more vicious one. "Then choose the Silver aspect instead and let go of the Blue."

As she was currently a mostly Blue Elderdragon, that statement seemed to anger her. She brought her snout close to him. Her teeth were longer than Caden's confiscated sword and looked just as sharp. "You insult me," she said.

"No," he said. "I respect both aspects of you. It's just that your Silver side is less likely to kill those I care about. It is nothing personal against the Blue part of your being."

His answer seemed to appease her. She pulled back so that she could look down on him. "Pish," she said in her dragon voice. "What you ask me to give up is of great value to me. What will you give me in return? Something equally valuable."

This was a bad turn of events. Caden's enchanted coat was shredded. Even if he could get jewels and such from his homeland, Ms. Primrose seemed to value cheap, tacky treasures more, and he had none of those either. His Ashevillian possessions weren't worth much.

Then again. To give up her Blue aspect was of great value to *her*. Wasn't magic about exchanges, about equivalencies. That's what Brynne had said. Caden needed to offer to give up something of great value to *him* as a trade. What was truly his and his alone that he could offer?

Caden knew exactly what was valuable to him.

Nothing was more important to Caden than slaying a dragon and becoming an Elite Paladin. No, that wasn't exactly right. Nothing was more important to him than one day serving his father and his kingdom as an Elite Paladin. Then he could prove he was brave and loyal. He would make his father and people proud. He would serve together with whatever loyal brothers he had left and bring his family and people back together.

"I'm waiting," Ms. Primrose said. She held up a claw and glanced at it as if she expected to see an Ashevillian timepiece wrapped around her wrist that she could tap. When she didn't, she set her claw back down. "Offer something of equal value or offer nothing and let me turn blue."

This pact wasn't about giving away something of worth, but about the value of what was given up to the giver-upper. Caden sneezed. He hesitated. Would she truly be terrible as only a Blue Elderdragon?

"*Tick. Tock.* Young prince," she said. Even speaking in the forgotten tongue, her eyes were cold, her sneer cruel. She would be the terror of Asheville. Maybe of the entire Carolina of the North in the South. Or worse yet, she'd attack Razzon.

So there was only one choice. "I will give up serving my king and people as an Elite Paladin."

Had she been more Silver that would likely have been enough. But she wasn't. Not at the moment, and she said, "But you could still serve them? I don't think that's enough. And what do I gain from that?"

His sacrifice had to be equal to hers. It wasn't yet, but it was close, right? Caden concentrated. "Instead . . ." How could he sacrifice more than that? And what could he give her? Then he knew what to say, even if he didn't want to say it. "Instead, I'll serve you. I'll give you my favor. My honor."

Even with a dragon's face he could tell she was unimpressed.

But Caden didn't think it mattered if she liked what he offered. It mattered how much it was worth to him. The Forgotten Language of Power would decide if it was worthy. "Nothing is more important to me. It is the most valuable thing I can give."

The power in the room grew heavier, more suffocating. Caden felt as if his soul were being branded. That meant just one thing. "And so I, too, accept," Ms. Primrose said.

The hovering silver scales turned sparkling blue. They dropped to the floor. Immediately, the power let up. The pact was complete, and somehow Caden didn't faint.

Without the language weighing on him, Rath Dunn recovered quickly. He was already to his feet. The large dragon in the room shrunk back to her human form.

With the spell stopped and the language done, Caden became aware of other noises. Someone pounded on the thick oak door. Without the huge dragon blocking it, whoever it was kicked it open.

Rosa rushed into the room. Officer Levine followed Rosa, his weapon drawn. He motioned Rath Dunn to move against the wall.

"Caden?" Rosa demanded.

Rath Dunn flicked his hand in Caden's direction. With a quick motion, he shoved his blood dagger under the desk, hiding it. "He's fine. He's been in my care. I've done nothing against the rules, nothing to warrant that type of tone."

Rosa froze where she was. She looked Caden up and down, and her anger seemed to explode. "Did you hit one of my kids?"

"I pulled him from a dangerous situation in the forest. At night," Rath Dunn said. "Where he was without his guardian."

Oh, Rath Dunn sounded as if his teeth were gritted, his

jaw clenched. His plan had failed, and he was angry. He'd have to start scheming again. If Caden wasn't using all his focus not to fall over, he would have taunted him about that.

Rath Dunn leered at Rosa. "As his foster mother, you should be thanking me."

"Step back. Hands against the wall," Officer Levine said.

Rath Dunn turned and put his palms so they were flat against the red paint. "I'll have your badge if you keep this up."

"Just arrest him, Harold," Rosa said.

Ms. Primrose stepped between them. "Now, now, there's no need for that, dear. We take good care of our students. I'm certain this can all be worked out." She had returned to her old-lady persona. Was she still intent on keeping Rath Dunn as a school employee? Truly, she should know better now. "Mr. Rathis," she said. "Just go downtown with Officer Levine. I'm sure you can work everything out."

"He's coming downtown," Officer Levine said. "Not so sure about the working everything out."

"Chop chop then," Ms. Primrose said. She turned to Rath Dunn. There was a spike of cold in the air. "I'll run things while you get this sorted out."

"It won't take long," Rath Dunn said.

Caden's vision was becoming fuzzy. Ms. Primrose was a silvery blur. Her hair. Her dress. Even her eyes seemed silver speckled. Though no aspects of the Blue Elderdragon were visible, her small frame emanated power. "It will take long enough," Ms. Primrose said.

Caden swayed on his feet. Likely, speaking forgotten tongues wasn't wise for those with head injuries, and whatever battle adrenaline had kept him up was gone. He tried to grab the wall to steady himself, but the wall kept moving away. "Rosa," he said, and his tongue felt clumsy and slow. "I feel . . . unwell." The room and those in it started to turn. Caden felt himself plunge toward the floor. Rosa caught him just as the room faded away.

NEW RULES

hen Caden returned to consciousness, the first thing he noticed was the smell of antiseptic. Which wasn't a bad smell. It was a good, clean smell. He heard Ashevillian machines *beep beep beeping*. He lay in an uncomfortable bed with sheets that weren't soft enough for a prince. He opened his eyes, but he already knew he was in the hospital.

There was a second bed across from him. The beeping machines were grouped on that side of the room. The person in the second bed slept as if dead. Short, golden-colored hair. Long and lean body. Caden blinked. That was Jasan. Caden pushed himself up.

Ugh. How his head ached.

"Rest a bit longer, child," Manglor said. He reclined in a chair beside the bed.

Caden motioned to the other bed. "Is my brother alive?"

"He is."

Caden was too groggy to be much more than confused. When he was properly awake, he'd likely be overcome with joy. For now, he blinked and said, "How?"

"Blood can be transfused. He already had some done. I believe that the transfused blood kept him alive when his blood was lost. He's been given more now. I donated mine."

Caden only understood the final part of that, but that was the important part. "Thank you."

"He's my neighbor. We protected my home. No need to thank me, child."

While Caden liked Manglor well enough, he wasn't who Caden expected to see. "Where's Rosa?" he said. He was surprised she wasn't there. For that matter—"Where are Tito and Brynne and Jane?"

"The other children are at home with Officer Levine," Manglor said. "Rosa is talking to your doctor."

"How long have I been here?" Caden asked.

"A day." Manglor replied.

That meant Caden was still bound by his curses. "Why are you here?"

"If I leave, the nurses will remove your brother's paper clips, and all the blood I and others gave him will leak out when his hand falls off."

"Then it's good you stay," Caden said.

"Hmmm, it is," Manglor agreed.

Caden cut his gaze to his brother. "Is he really okay?"

Like Jasan heard him, he turned his head. Then he opened his eyes. "I've been better."

Caden felt a rush of relief.

Jasan's voice was weak, but he still managed to sound surly. "I told you to stay safe," he said. "Not come to the forest."

"You needed help."

"Not so much for you to risk your life," Jasan said.

Caden knew Jasan was wrong. He wanted to say so. But he was drifting back to sleep.

The next morning, Friday, they released both royal brothers from the hospital. The doctors wanted Jasan to stay longer, but Jasan refused, and Manglor stood behind him as he did it. Manglor did promise he and his family would keep watch over Jasan as he recovered. And Caden would go home as well. His home in Asheville. With Rosa, in the foster prison.

Later that afternoon, Caden rested on the green couch. The living room curtains were still charred. Outside, an early Ashevillian snow blanketed the mountain. The trees, colorful with red, yellow, and orange leaves, were covered in ice. When they looked like that, Caden could almost pretend the mountainside was a Winterlands hill.

Jane's eyes weren't back to normal, but they were better. Rosa had taken her to the eye doctor. While they were away, Officer Levine stayed with Caden, Brynne, and Tito. He clattered around in the kitchen, cleaning dishes.

Brynne sat beside Caden. She took off her hat. "Feel my head," she said.

An order. After the incident in the office with the dragon and the tyrant and his two nights in the hospital, Caden determined orders made him sneeze, hiccup, or belch. And while he couldn't ignore them, he could choose whether to comply or to resist.

Caden sneezed. Then decided to resist. He wasn't sure why she wanted him to feel her head, but it sounded uncouth. "No, I must respectfully decline."

"Just feel my head, Caden."

He sneezed again. She had a nice round head, but Caden had no desire to feel it. "Why?"

"Rub it and you'll see."

Caden sneezed. "No."

Tito walked into the living room and plopped onto the floor. "I don't want to know what you two are talking about, but I wouldn't let Rosa overhear it."

"Caden is being difficult," Brynne said. She leaned down. "Sir Tito. Feel my head."

Tito shrugged. "Okay." He patted the top of her head. Then he smiled his lopsided grin. "Dude, you've got peach fuzz." Tito glanced at Caden. "That means hair."

"It's growing back," Brynne said.

Caden leaned over and inspected her head. There were

hairs there. Fine white ones. "They're the wrong color."

"So? I can change the color if I desire. The wonderful thing is that my hair is growing." Brynne narrowed her eyes. "It's hair, prince," she said. "So I'm happy."

Jane's eyes were better, but not great. Brynne's hair had started to grow some. Enough of the spell had been cast to affect them. But stopping it also seemed to lead to some recovery. Hopefully, Jasan would also recover some of his own blood, too.

Rosa and Jane showed up soon after. Jane sported a brand-new pair of glasses. The frames were metal, and Caden was certain Jane had picked them so she could enchant them. Officer Levine came out from the kitchen to meet them, drying his hands with a bright-orange dish towel.

Tito grinned at Jane. "You look good in glasses."

"And now I can see clearly again," Jane said.

"That's what's important," Officer Levine said.

Rosa sat next to Caden and put her hand on his forehead. He leaned away. "How are you feeling?"

"Royal heads heal quickly," he said.

For a split second, she looked uncomfortable. "Don't you mean future Elite Paladin heads heal quickly?" she said. It was a kind attempt to make him feel better.

Caden had told no one, not even Brynne, that he'd agreed to serve Ms. Primrose instead of his father and his people, told no one that he would never be an Elite Paladin.

His heart felt heavy. But some burdens needn't be shared. He forced his most charming smile for Rosa. "It is true Elite Paladins also have hard and quick-healing skulls."

Officer Levine examined him as well. "You do look better, son," he said.

Indeed, Caden was feeling better. "I feel better."

Rosa stood back up and surveyed him and the others. Officer Levine set aside the dish towel. He nodded to Rosa.

"Good," she said. "Then we want talk with all of you."

They all scooted over so Jane could sit with them on the green interrogation couch. Brynne stayed on Caden's left, Tito on his right. Jane sat in the space between Tito and the end of the couch. This is what Caden expected. Punishment. They'd willfully disobeyed and run into a forest fight. Brynne had burned the curtains.

"We need to establish some new rules," Rosa said. "First, no deals with dragons."

Caden sneezed. Truly, he wasn't sure he could follow that rule. A deal with a dragon had saved their lives.

"No riding Sir Horace through the hills at night."

Caden sneezed again. He didn't want to follow that one. Sir Horace loved night rides.

"No fighting villains."

Caden sneezed once more. Elite Paladin or not, Caden would always fight villains. It turned out there was a downside to Rosa accepting Caden as sane and from another world. She had a long list of new rules.

The list went on and on. There were new rules for Caden, for Brynne, for Jane. Tito mostly had the same rules as before, but he was local and nonmagical even if he trod on the noble path of the Elite Paladin.

"And Jane," Rosa said. "No enchanting."

Jane was resistant. "Why?"

"Because I said so. No enchanting anything, big or small," Rosa said. "That's final."

Jane reached up and touched her new frames. "Small things should be okay," she said.

Rosa's tone was like the strongest Razzonian steel. "No."

Caden doubted Jane would really stop, but maybe Rosa was enough of a force to keep her enchanting curbed. Truth be told, though, he'd wager those glasses would be enchanted before nightfall.

Rosa turned her attention to Brynne. "No magic at home." She thought about it. "And no magic at school either."

School. So as always, school would go on. "We still must go then?" Caden said, but he wasn't surprised.

Rosa took in a sharp breath. "I can't keep you out. I don't understand why. But it should be safer now."

Some things were beyond even Rosa's control. Caden understood.

"But don't think I won't have rules in place about who talks to you and when and where they interact with you," Rosa said.

"Are there any more rules for us?" Tito said.

Brynne shot Tito a death glare for reminding Rosa.

"A few." Rosa focused back on Brynne. Of all of them, Brynne had the most new rules to follow. "No using magic to steal. No stealing period. No flipping people over. No setting things on fire—not with pyrokinetics or anything else. Got it?"

Brynne arched a brow. She leaned forward, and the couch groaned. "What if I'm attacked?"

Rosa closed her eyes. She seemed to have to think hard on that. "If you're in danger, then defend yourself. By whatever means necessary."

Brynne seemed happy enough with that. "I will."

"Good girl."

Caden grew bored with these new rules. Maybe that was why Brynne feigned sleeping so often when they were lectured. She simply couldn't stay awake.

"Caden," Rosa said gently. "Pay attention."

An order. Inside him the urge to obey and the urge to resist collided. He felt for a moment as if he were going to burst. The power of the curses had to be released. He expected to sneeze or hiccup or belch. Instead, the power was released in a new and terrible way. Gas. A mighty stench descended around the punishment couch.

Caden blushed. Brynne scooted to the edge of the pillow as if offended, which was ridiculous. She'd cursed him twice. Any side effects were completely her fault. He glared at her.

Tito, however, seemed to find it hilarious. "This curse-curse gets better and better."

Jane laughed. As did Officer Levine.

"It's not funny," Caden said. He looked to Rosa. She would understand. "Tell them it's not funny." He pointed at her. "You mustn't give me orders during my time of the month."

"Bro, you've got to stop calling it that," Tito said.

"That's what it is," Caden said.

Rosa covered her mouth with her right hand. The iron in her expression seemed to be splitting away. She looked to the side. Was she laughing? If so, Caden was definitely offended.

32

A MOMENT OF HOME

$\mathbb{I}$t was decided that Caden would spend every other weekend with Jasan to see if the arrangement worked. The rest of the time he'd stay at Rosa's. As for school, it reopened after seven days.

Caden worried about his family and homeland, but they had no more enchantments to sacrifice. They had no way to contact them. The barrier between worlds seemed intact, though. Caden hoped that meant all were safe and the spell had been stopped there as well.

At the school, Ms. Primrose was reinstated as principal. Officer Levine said Rath Dunn had disappeared from his cell. Yet as far as Caden knew, he hadn't returned to school. Point of fact, he hadn't been seen at all. Several teachers and the nurse had also disappeared. No one seemed worried, which made Caden suspect Ms. Primrose did something to them—specifically, ate them. Although, hadn't Rath Dunn claimed he'd yet to break her rules? He frowned at that thought.

Rosa dropped them off at school. The early snows left the lawn white. The ice on the school gave it a silver shimmer. "Call me if you have any problems," she said.

"Of course," Caden said. He and the others trudged inside.

Manglor continued to teach Caden, Ward, and Tonya. In gym, Jasan remained pale. It seemed he would remain anemic and in need of regular blood transfusions. Despite that, Jasan worked the class harder than ever.

Derek raised his hand. "Isn't this a little overboard, Mr. Prince?"

Jasan's lack of blood made him even more irritable. "Start running," he said.

Stout Mrs. Grady had survived the forest, and survived Mrs. Belle too, apparently. Caden kept his promise to her. She taught like normal. Their first day back she gave them a pop quiz. At lunch, she stepped behind the serving line instead of going to sit at the teachers' table. It seemed she had new duties.

Ms. Jackson hadn't disappeared like Rath Dunn. She was a fugitive. There was a video of her escaping from the jail by using her cursed ladle to knock the lock open. There had been sightings of her around town; so as far as Caden knew, Ms. Primrose hadn't eaten her. Truly, she was treacherous. Caden had started to wonder just how old and how powerful she was if she'd managed to avoid a dragon.

Tito returned from the serving line and plopped down a tray with turkey, mashed sweet potatoes, and mushed-looking banana-something he called pudding. Jane placed her tray down and sat beside him. The food didn't appear as sophisticated as Ms. Jackson's or Rath Dunn's menus.

Tito shoved it into his mouth. "I gotta say," he said. "The food isn't as fancy, but it tastes pretty darn good. Evil math people just know how to cook."

With Ms. Jackson gone, Jane also ate from her tray. "It's good," she said. The frames of her glasses shimmered with enchantment, and Jane's vision was outstanding with them on now, but Caden was far from surprised.

Brynne stole bites from both when they weren't looking.

Caden wouldn't eat lunch made by any villain. That didn't mean he didn't have food. When Rosa learned he refused to eat the cafeteria food, she started packing him lunch. He had organic granola, an apple—the apple he'd save for Sir Horace—and vegetable tacos. He arranged it all neatly in front of him. Brynne eyed his broccoli taco, and Caden knew he would need to guard it well.

As Caden arranged the granola next to the taco, Brynne, Tito, and Jane shared furtive glances. Caden expected commentary about his food choices and arrangement, but when they said nothing, he grew suspicious. His friends were good people. But they liked to tease him about his manners.

Maybe Rath Dunn had returned. "What has happened?"

"Nothing bad," Jane said.

Nothing bad was still something. "Tell me," Caden said.

Tito shrugged and looked at the others. "He'll find out soon enough."

From the sound of that, Caden wasn't sure he'd like whatever this "nothing bad" was.

"Don't look so suspicious, prince," Brynne said. "During honors English Ms. Primrose called us to her office." She smiled her dazzling smile. "And gave us each a reward."

"I see," Caden said. He crossed his arms and frowned. "She gave me no reward."

"Yeah," Tito said. "That's why we didn't want to tell you."

They were silent again. It seemed Caden had to ask. "What did she give you?"

"She gave me the blood dagger."

Caden was taken back. "Brynne," he said, "that's an evil blade."

"But one with a strong enchantment that can be smashed and used to contact my parents."

Oh. Then Caden was okay with that. It was a nice reward.

The frames of Jane's glasses twinkled. She smiled. "And she gave me something called a Korvan battle staff."

Another good reward. Korvan battle staffs were good weapons. However, they had a metal core. If such a staff wasn't an enchantment temptation, Caden didn't know what was. He and Brynne exchanged a knowing glance.

Tito still hadn't answered.

"What did she give you, Sir Tito?" Caden said.

He scrunched up his nose. "I don't want you to get upset."

"I won't," Caden said.

Tito stuffed banana mush into his mouth. "A sword," he mumbled.

Wait? What? "A sword?" Caden was feeling a bit outraged. Not that his brave and noble friend didn't deserve a sword. However. "I need a sword."

Tito swallowed his food. "Yeah, that's why I didn't want to tell you."

Brynne seemed amused. "It's a fine elvish weapon with a diamond-encrusted hilt and a blade that shines with sharpness oil."

This was all very unfair.

Tito shrugged. "We can't pick our stuff up until after school, though." He pointed his fork at Caden. "Bro, don't look like that. I mean, I'd rather have a book." Tito flattened his potatoes with his fork. "And I'll let you practice with it."

Caden had given up his dream. He'd made an unbreakable vow in a forgotten tongue not to become the Elite

Paladin he'd always wanted to be. However, just because Caden had to serve a dragon didn't mean he couldn't use a sword. Matter of point, he'd likely need one. Caden couldn't help but feel irritated, a bit empty, and a bit sad.

That's when the speaker in the lunchroom crackled to life. Mr. Creedly's voice hissed out. "Attention, students." He was back to work. Actually, Ms. Primrose had decided to let him be vice principal and secretary. Mrs. Belle was back to teaching science, too. It was hard to look at her nails without imagining her spiderlike form, but Caden was trying. While she wasn't an ally, she wasn't an enemy either. "Caden Prince," Mr. Creedly hissed. "Report to the principal's office."

Ms. Primrose had redecorated her office. She'd painted the walls a silvery gray. Behind her, he noticed a cage, but he couldn't tell what was in it. She'd replaced Rath Dunn's books with bowls filled with her beads and rocks. Although, there weren't as many as Caden expected. He mentioned this to her.

"The rest are at my home."

Caden peered at her. "You mean the town house?"

"You did give it to me, dear."

So it seemed Jasan had yet to get his dragony roommate to leave. "Yes, ma'am. I did." He stood straighter. "I'm staying with Jasan this weekend."

"Well, that's bothersome," she said. "Make sure not to move my things."

Caden knew not to mess with her baubles. "I will treat them with the utmost respect." He nodded to the cage. "What's that?"

She ignored him. Instead, she tutted around her desk, rearranged some buttons so they were lined up in a row. "You ask a lot of questions for one who has vowed to serve me." She huffed like his questions and his service were quite the annoyance. "But that was the pact." She picked up a dented bead and admired it. "And we are both so bound."

Caden was bound to the service of a dragon. Not to the king. Since the pact, he'd felt a strange grief and sadness creep through him. He wouldn't be an Elite Paladin like his brothers and father. It wasn't fair, but he'd chosen his path.

However, as he stood before Ms. Primrose, mighty and powerful Elderdragon, a new worry turned his stomach. He crossed and uncrossed his arms. She was a dragon. He'd seen her in her full form. What if she wanted him to do something against his moral code?

When trying to save the city and stop the villains, it was possible Caden hadn't thought out the ramifications of a pact with her. "I hope," he said, "I can act honorably in my service to you." He cleared his throat. "And you will only give me honorable things to do."

It was possible his words offended her. "Don't I always follow my rules?"

"I won't help you eat anyone. Even if he or she is evil."

"That's not for you to decide, is it?" She tapped her gnarled hand on her desk. "Now stop. You'll make me hungry with all this talk of food." As she finished, a small burp escaped her lips. "And I've eaten enough as of late."

So that's where the missing teachers went. He raised his chin. "As you are now the Silver Elderdragon, I'd hoped you'd stopped eating people."

"I still must eat, dear." She considered him. "So you like me better like this, as only the Silver aspect of myself."

"I respect all your aspects," Caden said. "I'm less afraid of this one, that's all."

"Comments like those are why you charm me."

"Ms. Primrose," Caden said, respectfully, "there is something I've always wondered."

Her hair was silver, her pale-blue eyes had silver specks. She sighed. "What is it, dear?"

"Why is your lair and your school in Asheville?"

She peered at him. "Why do you want to know?"

Truly, Caden had no good reason. "I'm curious."

She tutted and sighed again. Then she seemed to come to a decision. "Well," she said, "I suppose curiosity is in your nature."

"It's a good quality."

"Don't be immodest, dear; it's unbecoming," she said.

Caden waited.

She leaned back in her chair. "If you really want to know, I was brought to this land for the same reason as you."

Caden didn't understand. "You are very old and have been here many, many years." He felt his brow furrow. "I was brought here by mistake but eight months ago, by a mix-up in the words of a spell." The lunch witches had brought Caden to Asheville when they had meant to bring his brother. "I don't see how it is possible that you and I are here for the same reason."

"If you don't understand, it's not my problem."

She ran the school. She made him attend. If he didn't understand, it was her problem. Caden straightened his posture. "As you are an educator," he said, "isn't it your responsibility to help me understand when I'm trying so hard to do so?"

She blinked at him. "You were brought here by imprecise words and magic without thorough thought. The same is true for me."

"I don't understand," Caden said. "Explain."

She raised her brow. Her scales shimmered. For a fleeting moment, Caden thought he saw one lone blue scale among the silver.

"I mean, please explain, ma'am," he said.

After a moment, she spoke. "Long ago, after the other Elderkind went to their various fates, I made an agreement with the Council of the Seasons." Caden had heard of the once-great Council of the Seasons. It was an ancient governing body of the Greater Realm. The Greater Realm Council was patterned after it.

"I agreed to leave them to their own devices. But a dragon still must eat. In return, they agreed to send me the convicted and banished as food and entertainment. I'm generous, though. I don't need to eat all the time. Those who serve me well, who please me, I let live."

"Perhaps you should consider becoming an Ashevillian vegetarian and eat no one?"

"Don't be ridiculous, dear."

She dropped a treat into the cage beside her desk, then turned back to Caden. "Powerful magic often has incantations. They were supposed to say 'To appease the hunger of the Elderdragon, to fulfill our pact, so we don't suffer the fires and go to ashes, villains we send them, to her.'"

"That's not how it sounds in the Common Tongue."

"No, it sounds something like 'to Ashe-villains we send them.'" She waved her hand dismissively. "I had to follow my food. At first, there was nothing here but mountains. I collected my rocks, ate whoever came. I wasn't surprised at all, however, when the city was built up in the valley and was named as it was."

"They sent the villains here before the town was founded?"

"Magic doesn't care much for time," she said. "It got boring, though. So I founded the school." Perhaps Caden looked perplexed, for she added, "I am, at the core, an educator."

"And you were brought here by mistake."

"Many things in all realms, good and bad, lucky and not, start as mistakes."

"Then why make yourself follow your rules? Why not only follow them when you'd like."

"My rules are for balance." She was getting a bit huffy. "They moderate the different aspects of my being."

"But now you're all Silver," Caden said.

"Am I?" Ms. Primrose said. "Are all Jane's tears dry? Does Brynne have no more hair? And Jasan? Does blood still flow in his veins?"

"I see," Caden said.

Something squealed in the cage. Caden's gaze wandered back to it again. She stood and motioned him to look. "The new school mascot."

He moved closer. Inside, he saw a red guinea pig. It had one blue eye, one brown. There was a bald spot atop its head; one leg was charred. Toys and exercise wheels filled the cage. For a guinea pig, it had a nice home. Caden placed his hand on the bars. He slid his gaze to her. "Is that—Ow!" Caden pulled his finger back. The guinea pig bit him.

"It's in his nature to bite," she said, like she was fond of it. "An interesting animal, indeed." And it reminded Caden of how she often viewed Rath Dunn. He peered at it. Was it Rath Dunn?

Ms. Primrose snapped to get his attention. "Enough chitchat. Since you serve me, you'll need to learn when not to talk, too. Now for why I summoned you." She cocked her head. "You gave me back what was lost as you promised. You spoke the forgotten tongue without me prompting you. You've pleased me, and I always reward those who do."

Caden straightened his posture. He sucked in a breath. She was going to give him a reward. Her past rewards had been poor at best. But she'd given Brynne, Tito, and Jane good rewards today. And Caden really wanted a sword. A sword like Tito described would be perfect. Lots of non-Elite Paladins carried swords. But best he flatter her some more so she was in as good a mood as possible. "You are indeed gracious."

"I am," she agreed. "I'm glad you understand."

"I do," Caden said. He knew he shouldn't get his hopes up. But what better reward for him than a fine sword with a sharp blade. "What is it?"

"I'll send you home to your family, to your father. Just until lunch is over. I expect you back for your science class."

Wait? What? "You can just send me home?" He felt his brow crease. "And then bring me back?"

"I'm an Elderdragon, dear." She seemed to be getting irritated with him. "I'm great and powerful. But it's not something I do on a lark. Nor is it easy. Don't expect it again."

"But it's something you can do?"

"If I feel like it." She reached out her gnarled hand and placed her fingertips on his forehead. "This may sting."

"Wait," Caden said. "Jasan should come with me."

She narrowed her eyes. "That's not your choice. Besides, I offered to send him home for good so I wouldn't have to share my town house. He declined. Maybe I'll turn him into a falcon again tonight."

Before Caden could make sense of that, or ask why she couldn't just get her own town house, he felt a pinch. The office faded away. He found himself in the octagonal room. The mirror across from the door was still broken.

There were three other people there. Their backs were turned, but Caden knew them at once. On the left stood first-born Valon. He was bandaged and held a crutch, but he was alive. On the right stood third-born Lucian. His battle daggers were strapped to his leg. The king stood in the middle. They were discussing Crimsen and how to defend the border.

"They will regroup. Maden and Martin will fight with them against us."

Caden stared for a moment. But only a moment. His time was short. Science class would soon start, and he would fade from this room. "Father?" Caden said.

Valon, Lucian, and King Axel turned around. They looked shocked.

"Caden?" King Axel said.

"I can't stay long," Caden said. He needed to explain things fast. "Ms. Primrose, she's an Elderdragon, and—" His voice cracked. It was difficult not to get emotional seeing his brothers Valon and Lucian alive, seeing his father after so many eventful months. He took a deep breath. Best he say what was important while he had some composure. "I've missed you," Caden forced out.

The king's chin trembled. He strode up to him and put his hands on Caden's shoulders. "And you have been missed," the king said. Then, for the third time in Caden's life, his father hugged him.

ACKNOWLEDGMENTS

I truly appreciate all the support my agent, David, and my editor, Jocelyn, gave me as I wrote this book. I'd also like to thank Eric Deschamps for the wonderful artwork. And, of course, I am grateful to HarperCollins for publishing my series!

I also have to thank my friends and family—my mom, Pat; my sister, Sarah; my brother, Orren; my nieces and nephew, Clara, Marie, and Edward; my brother-in-law, Stephen; all the wonderful Balls, especially Sandy and Donny, Jenn and Andrew, and Terri and Donald; Sandra; my friends Kat, Joe, LauraMac, Lorrie, Krista, Christine, Amy, Adrienne, and Janie. They've all supported me even when I was a little bit overwhelmed with everything.

Also, I've met many wonderful people since being published: writers, booksellers, librarians, readers. It's been a great experience. I feel like I've made friends. And I'm very grateful for that.

So to my family, and to my friends old and new, I'd just like to express a heartfelt and warm thank you.